Under the Liberty Oak

PAIGE M. CUMMINGS

Keep Reading

Paige M. Cummings

UNDER THE
LIBERTY OAK

2007

Under the Liberty Oak

For My Father, Dr. Joseph Mercer, Who Told Me Brittan Lee's Stories;
My Husband, Mike Swanson, Who Encouraged Me To Write Brittan Lee's Stories;
My Children, Maggie And Colin, Who Didn't Mind Pizza Again While I Wrote Brittan Lee's Stories; And My HAW Group, Cups Writer's Groups, And The Southern Scribes- Dac Crossley, Peter Wood, Genie Bernstein, Janice Pulliam, Jim Murdoch, Marie Davis, Larry Mcdougald And Donna Mcginty, Who Let Me Read Brittan Lee's Stories To Them Over And Over.

And With Great Thanks And Appreciation To My Friends, Kandy And Ken Duke, Who Love Coastal Georgia As Much As I Do, And Took Hundreds Of Photographs Of The Liberty Oak For Me To Use With This Book

CHAPTER ONE
North Shores, Illinois August, 2005

I was running late for choir practice, almost out the door when the phone rang that Tuesday afternoon. Hesitating at the threshold, I went back inside to answer the call. It could be Beth Ann. I have been waiting almost forty years for Beth Ann to call.

When I was eighteen, I contacted Georgia Bell and got our old phone number reactivated. Any calls went straight to an answering service. Monthly statements advised me of the best long distance plans, low rate mortgages and the rare call looking for my father. When technology progressed, the calls were directed straight to my home here in Illinois. Further technology allowed the calls to be forwarded to my cell phone no matter where I was on concert tour. I wanted to make it easy for Beth Ann to find me.

"Hey, baby sister!"

My oldest brother sounded cheerful. Everybody calls him Four, being as how Marshall Everett Hayworth the Fourth is too much of a mouthful. Four checks up on me on Tuesdays; when my other brother, Jackson Adams Hayworth, calls it's usually on Thursdays. Overprotective is a mild term when it comes to my brothers. They've been this way since Daddy left us.

"Had a spare minute, so I thought I would call. Might be busier later on. Got fifteen minutes till tee-time."

"Where are you?" I asked. I dropped my tote bag filled

with sheet music inside the front door of my townhouse and walked back to the couch.

"Florida. Medical conference, but we're getting in a little golf, too," he said. "Listen, Mama won't tell you this, but she really wants you to stay longer than just Labor Day weekend. She wants you to stay at least a week or two."

I felt the familiar gripping in my chest, the spasm in the middle of my heart that in my childhood I thought was indeed heartbreak, but as an adult discovered was the beginning of a stress panic attack. Liberty. Labor Day weekend. Two weeks away. "I don't know, Four. I've got a lot of things going on here. Classes starting back up. Research for the new recordings. I just don't know."

"Honey, it'll be okay. You'll be okay. All the kids are here, have been for most the summer. You know how much they like to see you. You are the favorite aunt."

"I'm the only aunt," I said, as I thought about it. Jack and Four's ex-wives had sisters and brothers who married, so from a technical standpoint, I wasn't the only aunt. My brothers took every possible effort to schedule the children to visit when I was there and to make me feel like a special aunt. Several of my nieces and nephews toured with me. But it wasn't the same as watching them grow up, as being there.

"They really want to see you. We've had fresh sweet Georgia shrimp every week," he said, teasing me about my second favorite food.

"So what else is new in Liberty in the summer?"

"Well, they've started dredging for the new bridge. There's talk some big Atlanta company is going to drag the Altamaha, Darien and Newport Rivers to reclaim lost pine timbers. Conservationists are up in arms about both of those."

"Think they will find more giant megalo-celado-whatever

teeth?" I asked. "Remember when the scientists from the university came down? When you and Trey and Jack found those other teeth in the pluff mud at the marsh? You even had your pictures in the paper."

"Hey, some of those shark teeth were four inches long! Anyway, I'm not playing in the mud these days. Only when it's rained on the golf course," he said. "Oh, and Mama has a surprise for you."

"What kind of surprise?"

"Now if I told you, it wouldn't be a surprise, would it?"

"I'll think about it," I said. "No promises."

"You'll be fine," he said. "Gotta run! They're calling our tee number." The phone went dead.

I put the phone down on the end -table. The automatic timer clicked and the table lamps turned on. A flash of light reflected off a silver framed photo under the lamp.

Me, Four and Jack. I'm sitting on the ground under the Liberty Oak, slivers of sunlight shining through the heavy branches, filtered by the gray Spanish moss. I was so happy to tag along with my big brothers I had a huge grin on my face. Four and Jack with their blonde crew cuts, trying hard to look cool, their hands on their hips, stood towering over me.

Liberty, Georgia. My home. My heart. My soul.

***

The eBay auction had three minutes to go, and I was winning. The auction was for a first edition of Lydia Parrish's <u>Slave Songs of the Georgia Sea Islands</u>, from 1945. It was only the third copy I had seen for auction, and I had lost the previous two. It would be a great addition to my reference library; I had the Art Rosenbaum recordings in my collection. The laptop balanced on my knees and my hand hovered over the enter key.

I was ready to raise my top bid if needed. When the phone rang, I reached blindly over to the end table, still watching the screen.

"Are you watching TV?" Four asked. "Quick, turn on CNN!"

"Four? What's up?" I could hear voices and laughing in the background.

"Turn on the TV!" he said. "They found something in the river."

I fumbled for the remote, and then flipped through channels until I found CNN.

"What am I looking at?"

The camera panned a crowd of people on a riverbank waving signs, then moved to a view of a several boats in a river- a tug boat, a sheriff's boat, several motor boats. The focus tightened to show an old faded turquoise car pulled up to the pluff mud, surrounded by yellow crime tape. The view tightened to show a pile of leaves, sticks and other silted detritus spilled from the open door of the car. Sodden vegetation lay molded around a small yellowed skull, like a badly fitted doll's wig. I turned up the volume.

...A nineteen fifty-eight Chevy BelAir during the dredge operations digging the new pilings for the Altamaha River Bridge here in Liberty, Georgia. Local law enforcement officials called in to the site have no comments to make on the grisly discovery. More later on the investigation to follow. Right now we'll go over to the Weather Desk for an important weather update. Kurt Havens, here in Liberty, Georgia...

I stared at the closing image of the screen, and then my

stomach erupted. Pushing off the laptop, dropping the phone, I ran to my bathroom and knelt in front of the toilet. Waves of nausea contracted my abdomen and emptied my stomach in heaves. Finally I sat back on my heels. I wiped my face with a hand towel, then stood to rinse out my mouth in the sink. My face was hot, and then cold as the beaded perspiration evaporated. My legs trembled as I walked back out to the living room.

"Brittan Lee? Brittan Lee?" Four's voice bellowed from the phone, now lying on the floor.

"I'm here," I said sitting down on my green magnolia print couch. I picked up my laptop, a disassociated part of me pleased to see that the auction still had eighteen seconds left. "What was that?"

"The contractors found something when they were dredging for the new Altamaha Bridge. Word's already out. Everybody thinks they found Beth Ann."

"What? Don't talk crazy." My fingers froze on my computer's touch pad, and I just stared as the eBay auction ended without my final bid. "It can't be Beth Ann. That... that wasn't Beth Ann." I felt nauseous again. "Besides, didn't everyone say she was buried in the ruins of the fire?"

"Well, everybody but you. The contractors found somebody in a rusted out Chevy at the bottom of the river. Not too many little girls have gone missing in the past fifty years. Whole town's full of federal agents the sheriff called in. Beth Ann's mama has collapsed again. Jack said she asked Mama to please call you. You have to come down for the service. You were Beth Ann's best friend."

I could hear Four talking, but the voices inside my head were louder. Twin voices of grief and guilt normally locked away in the white cardboard box in my head. Sometimes, when

I am tired or stressed, the tendrils curl out from under the lid of the box like kudzu vines poking through an old building's roof and they whisper to me: *"It's your fault. Beth Ann wouldn't be dead if it wasn't for you. Your Daddy wouldn't be dead in that fire if it wasn't for you."*

"It was my fault," I echoed the voices. My lips trembled; I pressed my hand against them to stop the quivering. I struggled to get all the voices back inside the box. I needed to lock them away again.

"Brittan Lee, are you all right? Brittan Lee?" Four boomed in my ear, louder than the inside voices.

I swallowed hard. "I'm here. I'm all right."

Shoulders back, head up! Daddy always said. People expect a Hayworth to be strong, to help others in need. It's our place to be.

"Are you sure? You sounded funny."

Four worried too much.

"Verna Hamilton says she would be beholding to you for coming."

I wanted to sound understanding, tolerant even, but old grievances erupted. "The Hamiltons? Four, are you kidding? Mr. Hamilton knew where Beth Ann was, and Verna Hamilton made my life hell for years. She accused me of killing Beth Ann. She called me a liar. She still sends me a card every year on our birthday. Writes 'thanks to you, I have no daughter.' I've got every card in a box under my bed. Like hell I'll come down."

"Honey, she didn't mean that you personally killed Beth Ann; she just meant..." his voice trailed off as if he realized he was just making matters worse.

I plucked an old well-worn Baptist Hymnal from the stack

of assorted music books on my computer table and opened it to the front. My fingers traced and retraced the delicate raised gilt lettering of the library plate in the front of the hymnal. *Dedicated to the memory of Doctor Marshall Hayworth III, 1920-1964.* "What was she doing in the river? Where's she been all this time?"

"Well, apparently there. For the last forty years. There must have been some kind of accident. Whoever took her crashed. Wasn't it raining or something that night? A bad storm? There's not much left except some bones, after the crabs and currents got to her. The medical examiner's an old guy, needs to retire; he went to school with Bruce Wensley at the Medical College. He told Bruce that from the skeletal remains recovered, it appears to be white female about seven to ten. But everybody knows its Beth Ann. Anyway, Mama's going to call you later."

"It was a hurricane, Hurricane Dora. Remember? The biggest to hit the coast since 1893. Four...I told them she wasn't in that building. I told them." I put the hymnal down then picked it up again.

"Honey, yes, you did. But you didn't really know where Beth Ann was. Honey, it's been forty years. You need to come home to Liberty and stay here. We all love you and want you home with us. You want me to talk to your therapist? Have her put you on some Xanax? I'll send you some myself, or just tell me your pharmacist and I'll call in a prescription. You've done really good now; when you come down, don't let this throw you. Nobody still blames you for any of that, least of all Verna Hamilton. You know Verna never let them have a funeral before. She was sure Beth Ann would come back."

"Yes, they do. Or they did. None of my other friends

would play with me. People talked. Said I was ill-behaved, disrespectful. That if I behaved like a proper child, Beth Ann and I would have been in church and not out getting kidnapped. That Daddy wouldn't be dead if I had been in church where I belonged." That familiar pain in my chest ached as I thought about that summer.

"Brittan Lee, nobody really thought that, and you have to know they don't think it now. Everybody loves you," Four said. "Please think about coming down."

I promised to consider the idea, and we said our good byes.

I closed out eBay, turned off the computer and went to the bedroom. In my bed, bundled under a quilt made by my great-grandmother Hayworth, I closed my eyes, but the voices pushed and strained against pink ribbons on the box.

You led her astray; she was such a sweet girl.
Children like that end up in Milledgeville, mark my words.
It's all your fault...

"No!" I sat up in bed, clutching the quilt. My heart was pounding, trying to force itself out through my chest. My chest tightened with that chest-full of quivering worms feeling that I knew was the beginnings of a full blown panic attack. The waves of nausea rolling through my body would be next.

I thought about the two bottles of pills in the bathroom cabinet- a little bottle of oblong white sleeping pills and a taller bottle of yellow capsules for stress.

"Take one if the anxiety become disabling again," my therapist said when she prescribed them. "It will stop the dreams."

"But they weren't dreams," I told her. "It really happened. I saw it and heard it. They just tried to tell me it was a bad dream. I didn't make it up."

"I understand that. But now, they are recurring bad

dreams. So I'm prescribing you something to calm your mind. Take one if you feel the anxiety is creating problems with your music, if you can't concentrate or become agitated. First, try to put yourself in the good place. The place where you feel safe. When you are in the good place, you can put the voices in the box. You will be in control."

I hadn't taken any of the pills for over a year. I didn't plan to take one now. I was big into control; Daddy would want me to be in control. I curled up in the bed and pulled the covers back into place. My eyes closed against the faint glow of my stained glass nightlight. I forced my breathing to be slow and regular. I prayed for the soul of the body that had been recovered; I prayed for the people of Liberty, Georgia of 1964 and of today; I prayed for the strength to handle what might happen. Then I went to my safe place, Liberty, Georgia, the summer of 1964. Before Hurricane Dora.

CHAPTER TWO
Liberty, Georgia

First Baptist Church of Liberty. It started there, and it was coming back full circle.

We left Liberty when I was ten. Mama married Mr. Walden and took me with her to Chicago. I was scared, lonely and angry. Angry at Mama for not grieving for Daddy as long as I did. Scared that I would forget about him if we left Liberty. Lonely without Trulee, Tansie, Jack or Four.

Four and Jack stayed in Georgia. Jack was a first year law student at the University. Four was a second year student at the medical school in Augusta. They returned to Liberty to set up their practices after graduation. Mama moved back to Liberty when Mr. Walden passed away fifteen years ago. Actually, she moved back to Mr. Walden's cottage on Sea Island, but she made the forty-five minute drive to Liberty several times a week. My visits home to Liberty had been short and limited to Mama's birthday, a few days at Christmas, a week or two during the summer. My classmates had fled Liberty for larger cities after high school or college. Our friendships, based on the first eight years of life and a few haphazard letters, had faded. Tansie was the only one I had kept up a correspondence with. Other than Mama, my brothers, and my assorted nieces and nephews, there was no reason to linger and every reason not to.

Forty years ago, when I was growing up in Liberty, Georgia, everyone went to church. There were only three choices for churching though: the Baptists, the Methodists, and for the colored families, the Liberty African Methodist-Episcopal Church. There was, however, a lot of variety within those denominations. There were the foot-washers, the snake-handlers, the Holy Rollers and the tongue-speakers. We were dignified. We were First Baptists.

The First Baptist Church of Liberty was the oldest in the county, standing tall with thick tabby walls and a white steeple and eight sets of stained glass windows telling the life of Jesus Christ. If you looked close enough, you could see the chip in the third window from the back. The deacons tried to repair the damage left when Shaw's 54th Massachusetts came through the town during the Civil War. The colors didn't quite match up, so the halo over baby Jesus' head was destined to be half yellow and half gold forever.

The First Baptist Church had an early service, Sunday School, and a late service which started promptly at eleven and ended just as promptly at twelve. This was important because most of the deacons, ushers, and members of the choir had standing twelve-thirty dinner reservations in the banquet room of Crew's Restaurant down on the Dixie Highway.

My daddy didn't always attend church with us. Doc Marsh was given certain leniency by the congregation. If he wasn't at services, it was understood he was at the hospital either bringing a new life into the world or helping ease an old one into heaven. Mama, however, was expected to be there every Sunday. She had been born and reared a middle Georgia Methodist, and just got dunked when she married Daddy. One didn't rise socially if they were part of the heathen unwashed, Mama said, and Mama desperately wanted to rise. She was in Sunday School and the late service every Sunday, with or without Daddy.

The "attending church" requirement didn't hold for Sunday Evening Training Union or for the Wednesday Supper and Prayer Meeting, as far as Mama cared. Daddy usually took off on Wednesday afternoons, like most the other doctors in town. Daddy used his Wednesdays to work at his farm up on the river. The two doctors who worked with Daddy used their Wednesday afternoons to play golf, like most of the other doctors and lawyers. Daddy said he had enough to do rather than waste time hitting a ball with a stick into a hole in the middle of a cow pasture. But sometimes on Wednesday evenings, he and Mama would join the other doctors and their wives for cocktails, dinner and dancing. "Jukin' and jivin'." That was what Trina, Miss Eugenie's maid that summer, said to the other maids at the park. "Leavin' those chilluns to go make with the devil hisself."

In those days, you had to drive down to Bennie's Red Barn on St Simon's Island to drink and dance, because there wasn't any place in Liberty where drinking was legal. Even the Live Oak Country Club was dry. The members could bring in their own liquor bottles and leave them in the bar, little hand-printed labels identifying who were friends with Jim, Jack or Johnny. Mama bought her Gilbey's Gin at the drive-through liquor store just across the county line in Darien. I don't think Daddy drank much. At least not as much as Mama drank when Daddy had to stay late at the hospital.

Mama and some of the other mothers took turns driving us to Wednesday night meeting, and usually arranged for Mrs. Smith to bring us home. Mrs. Smith played the piano for the choir practice, so she was there every Wednesday. I think Mama and the other ladies slipped her some spare money for her troubles.

I remember the summer Beth Ann went missing. The summer of 1964. Liberty was hit by a hurricane, half of the black community burned down, and I lost my father and my best friend.

*****

Beth Ann and I had turned nine that year. We did most everything together. When my brothers were in town, we would follow them around and talk them into buying us cold Co-colas and wax lips. But in this summer of 1964, Jack and Four were at Granddaddy's farm, the Homeplace. At least that's what Daddy told Mama. Beth Ann and I were on our own for entertainment. Because of our names being next to each other in the alphabet, we were always seated next to each other in school, and we stood next to each other in choir. We were in the Children's Choir and had practice every Wednesday evening after church supper. It was our fourth year in the Children's Choir, and we were getting bored with "Jesus Loves Me" and "This Is My Father's World." We knew we were better singers than the others. We could carry a melody or sing harmony. The other children didn't even know what harmony was. Both of us had taken private piano lessons from Mrs. Smith for going on four years. We were in the John Thompson Third Grade Piano Book. We knew how to read music and count time by the clicking mahogany metronome on top of the black upright Steinway practice piano. I don't think Miss Darton, the new Children's Choir Director, appreciated our suggestions on how to make the choir better. I don't think she liked children at all. She always made a sour face when she saw us.

"That Cheryl Darton is an old maid," Mama said to the Garden Club. Cheryl Darton was younger than Mama, and sort of pretty when she wasn't making sour faces. She wore clothes like in the movies they showed at the Ritz Theatre. Once when I went back into the church kitchen to get some more lemonade, some of ladies in the Guild were looking out the pass-through window at her and talking.

"Well, that's why she's here and not in Atlanta," Mrs. Franklin said. "John Howard's cousin knows people in Fayetteville who know her family in Atlanta. Desperate, that's what she was, throwing herself at him like that. I think the Reverend needs to have a word with her..." They hushed up when Mrs. Franklin turned and saw me, but I heard them.

Miss Darton didn't see me either. Beth Ann and I were in the Baptism tank. I told Beth Ann it would be over our head if it was filled up and she didn't believe me, so we went to find out.

"See," I told her, my voice echoing in the deep, dark well. My nose twitched, and I sneezed from the smell of Clorox. I tapped the tin floor with my foot. "Right here is the holy drain. If we was standing here with Reverend Leeward and it was full, we'd drown. That's why you have to be twelve to get baptized. So you can stand up and not breathe in the holy water."

"No, how tall you are doesn't have anything to do with it," Beth Ann said. "I read one of those little books when I was waiting outside the Reverend's office. It said that children were unreasonable, so Jesus has to forgive our sins. But once we're twelve we have to get reasonable and get baptized otherwise we're going to burn in Hell forever."

I sat down on the steps leading up to the men's changing room to think about that potential outcome to my life. This interpretation of theology did create distinct possibilities of an eternal Hell. I was always being told I was unreasonable just because I was trying to explain how reasonable I was. Sometimes it sure was hard being nine years old.

"What's that door to?" Beth Ann tiptoed to the side of the tank that faced the church. She stretched to reach the sliding door and craned to peek out of the opening. We took turns popping up like jack-in-the-box heads trying to see the Sanctuary. "Oh no, oh no, oh no! It's the ghosts! They're here! We're gonna die just like those little children died!"

At the back of the church, up in the old slave balcony, lights were flashing and moving, reflecting blue and green and red from the stained glass windows. One of the lights was bobbing down the stairs and made a turn at the side aisle.

"It's coming! It's coming! PeeWee was right! Brittan Lee, I'm scared!"

"Beth Ann! Shh! Listen," I grabbed her and held her mouth shut. "Don't bite me. Uuck, don't slobber on me, either." I wiped my hand on my skirt and pointed to the sliding panel that opened into the ladies changing room. We had left it open for a quick escape, just in case Peewee Goodrun was telling the truth about ghosts being in the church. He said that people had seen lights and heard voices late at night, when the church was supposed to be empty. They were the ghosts of the choir members who died when parts of the church were burned back in the War, or maybe the ghosts of the soldiers who died when the main church floor was used as a hospital. Peewee wasn't usually right about anything, but we left the panel cracked just in case he was telling the truth this time. "Something's up there. We've got to close that door."

"We? This was your bright idea," Beth Ann protested. "The ghosts have made it all the way down. They're gonna get everybody. Come on; let's go out the men's side." Her hand shook as she reached for my arm. "We gotta hurry. They're going to turn on the holy water faucet, and we're going to drown!"

"Shh! You know how to dog-paddle! Wait here." I stood up and inched my way down the four steps and then across the bottom of the tank. I felt my way up the steps on the ladies side and listened when I reached the top.

"….aren't in here. Blonde angels, indeed," said a voice. It wasn't a ghost after all, it was Miss Darton. It got louder as she stepped inside the changing room.

"Who?" A man's voice asked. I knew that voice. It wasn't the Reverend, or old Jackson, the janitor. I knew their voices, too, and they were pretty much the only men here on Wednesday nights. I risked getting caught and looked over the top step into the room. All I could see through the green choir robes was the back of his head. His hair was cut real short and it was pale, or maybe that was just his skin coming through. "Who are you looking for? I thought everyone had gone home."

I saw Miss Darton look over her shoulder towards the hallway; the sour look left her face as she turned back to the man. She looked just like one of the movie stars when she reached up to smooth her hair. "Those girls. They think they have people fooled, with those sweet smiles and those precious blonde braids. I see past all that. They're really the Devil's spawn sent to test my calling. They snuck out of practice again. Children like that always end up in the State Mental Hospital at Milledgeville. You mark my words." But whatever else she was going to say was cut off when the man kissed her right on the lips. I saw him reach out and push the door shut, and he didn't even stop kissing her.

I could only see bits and pieces through the robes, but it sure looked like Beth Ann's daddy.

I slid the panel shut up to where it squeaked and hurried back over to Beth Ann. "It's Miss Darton. She was looking for us. Let's get out of here." We slid the panel open going into the men's changing room and felt our way in the dark to the outside door. Beth Ann opened the door just a crack and listened, then peeked through the slit.

"Hey, why's it dark?" The overhead lights were off. The hallway was lit by only the half moons of the night lights reflected on the shiny linoleum. We stepped out, pulled the door closed behind us and started down to the children's choir room, feeling our way along the wall. "We must really be late. I don't hear anybody."

Beth Ann hollered like the Indians were scalping her. She was shaking like the squirrel tail hanging from a bike antenna as she grabbed for my arm.

I screamed as the ghost grabbed my shoulder. Beth Ann and I clutched each other, trying not to fall down.

"Beth Ann Hamilton! Brittan Lee Hayworth! Quiet! Calm down! What on earth? Girls, what is it?" Mrs. Smith gathered us up in a big hug. "Calm down now. It's okay. Shush. Where were you? Everyone's gone home, and I couldn't find you."

"B-b-bathroom..." Beth Ann stammered.

"Lights off," I tried to sound the words. "Ghosts in the church!"

"There are no ghosts in the church." Mrs. Smith stood up and took our hands, yanking our arms right out of their sockets as she marched us outside. "I am going to have to talk to Mrs. Goodrun, PeeWee telling those tales, scaring children. Come on now. We need to get you home."

"But...she...they...he..." I protested as I tried to look back. "Who...?"

CHAPTER THREE
North Shore, Illinois August 2005

*G*lory *to God in the Highest, and to the Son, and to the Holy Ghost.* My cell phone vibrated across the console of the organ, the ring tone that of my favorite hymn. I ignored it as I peered over my half rims at the sheet music on the rack. I hadn't slept well after my phone call from Four; familiar but still terrifying nightmares visited my sleep.

Glory to God in the Highest, and to the Son and to the Holy Ghost, as it was in the beginning, is now and ever shall be. Louder. I glanced at the phone number displayed on caller ID: Mama. She'd call back, or I would call her when I finished practicing. I had a funeral Thursday, a wedding rehearsal Friday, a wedding Saturday and two church services on Sunday. I needed to run through the music for these events at least once more today, or in the case of the funeral, play it for the first time.

Born and bred Southern Baptist from Mississippi, an elderly gentleman, Charles Mayfield, had come to Chicago to spend his last months at the home of his son. The family of the deceased had provided a battered, dog-eared copy of Mr. Mayfield's favorite song. *Death Ain't No Big Deal* isn't part of my repertoire, but I'm not about to deny the deceased or the grieving family their last requests.

I have no doubt that the songwriter ever thought

"Someday when I breathe my final breath,
The doctor takes one look and says you're dead.
The truth is finally going to be revealed
I'm gonna find death ain't no big deal."

would be played on a 30-rank Schantz pipe organ in NorthShores Presbyterian Church, but I hope he would have been pleased with the result. I had found a fresh copy of the sheet music at my favorite Internet site, but it wouldn't be delivered until the next day. In the meantime, I had to try and decipher the actual score from the hand-written comments, erasures and added notes on this battered copy. The vocalist for the funeral service was due at two to rehearse, and the wedding soloist at three-thirty.

Glory to God in the Highest, and to the Son and to the Holy Ghost, as it was in the Beginning, Now and Ever Shall Be, World Without End, Amen, Amen. Loudest.

I snatched the phone from the console.

"Yes, Mama?"

"Do you always answer the phone like that? What if it hadn't been me?" She sounded miffed as she asked the same question she always asked when she called.

"I knew it was you, Mama. I'm trying to rehearse. Can I call you back later?" I pushed the half-rims back up on my nose and leafed through the list of wedding sheet music the bride and her mother had requested. I loved Mama, but there had been a rough period when I hadn't always liked her. It took me a long time to accept that she had done what she had been told was best for me.

"Well, I won't take up much of your time, but I just wanted to catch you up on what's going on. I have a few surprises…"

I interrupted her free flow of words. "Mama, Four already called me yesterday. I know. Beth Ann has been found."

"Well, honey, they don't know for a fact it was Beth Ann," Mama announced. "They just know it was a girl, most likely white, and she was about eight or nine. Those agents, I think they're from the FBI, they took all kinds of samples from the bones and from Verna to try and see if they match."

"So how exactly was this not-yet-identified girl found?" I asked. I reached up and rubbed the back of my neck.

"I thought Four called and told you," she said. "The environmental people are real upset. Everything gets them riled. You can't even put a private dock on your own property without the environmental people making you fill out thirty different request forms. Of course, they do have a point, every hundred feet someone is trying to dig up the marsh, put in more docks, cutting down all the old hardwoods. Don't they realize that people want to move here for those beautiful trees and the marsh views? But we need a bridge, and it's only about fifty yards from the old one. It's not like they're digging up loon nests or swamp salamanders."

"Mama, Beth Ann couldn't drive. We were only nine years old. Who else was in the car? That should tell them who took her." I kept rubbing my neck.

"Nobody," Mama said. "She was the only one in the car."

"Well, now that's plumb crazy. Whose car was it?"

"Well, now why do you think the FBI would tell me anything?"

"Mama, you have more sources than the CIA. Whose car was it?" I pushed my half rims up on my head and rubbed my eyes, tackling my headache from the opposite direction.

"Well, as I understand it from Carla at the beauty salon, who got it from Maurine the manicurist, who got it from the girlfriend of one of those deputies, it was a rental car with Duval County plates. The rental company isn't in business any more, and they're having a terrible time tracking down any records."

I could hear the ice twirling in Mama's tea glass and the crunch as she bit into a teacake.

"It wasn't one of the national chains, just a small local place. The owner was killed in that big hurricane, back in 1964."

"A rental car? That should certainly destroy Liberty's pet theory for all these years. How would a black teenager from Liberty be able to rent a car in Jacksonville? They wouldn't rent a car to a black man in those days."

"Shows how much you know, missy; a 1958 Chevy, that old thing, they'd rent that out. But you're right. Probably not to a teenager. Maybe it was stolen."

"Mama, it happened in 1964. A 1958 car wouldn't have been that old back then." I felt a familiar throbbing start in my temples. I tried rubbing those with one hand and knocked my glasses off the top of my head.

"Back then, as you put it, your Daddy would get a new car every year. A six-year-old car would be used for the maid. And anyway, I spoke to Verna earlier. She's not taking this too well, but that mother of hers—well, she's just aggravating things. Just goes on making Verna's life miserable. Anyway, Verna said the medical examiner promised he would turn the body over to Harrington and Sons by Monday, provided the FBI knows for sure who it is. We all know. I just don't understand why they are dragging this thing on so. She was such a sweet child."

"Mama, why is the FBI involved?" I tried to remember to breathe and loosen my death grip on the phone. My knuckles would hurt for hours and I needed to practice.

"Well, they were here for something else totally separate. Somebody called the FBI and reported that when the fires started during Dora, that it wasn't lightning. Someone set it on purpose to kill that black boy who kidnapped you and Beth Ann."

Mama paused and I heard a funny little catch in her voice.

"That makes it a possible civil rights violation," she continued. "An investigation task force came down, and they're trying to get to the bottom of what was happening that summer. It was just by coincidence, and a strange coincidence it was, that the construction crew found that car. Unless, do you suppose that somebody really knew something? Now, anyway, I talked to Verna and…"

"Mama, I've got people walking in the door to rehearse for a wedding. I've got to go." I hung up, feeling the pain in my temples reach around my head to meet at the back of my neck. I just knew the next words out of her mouth would be "Beth Ann's best friend," and "your Daddy would have wanted you to." I knew I was Beth Ann's best friend. She would always be my best friend. I knew she would come back. I just never thought that this was how she would do it. I dug through my tote bag for some Motrin and took a few gulps from my water bottle.

Glory Be to the Father, and To the Son and to the Holy Ghost… I snatched the phone off the console and scattered music all over the floor.

"What now, Mama? I told you I would call you later." Silence on the phone. I checked the number on caller ID. It wasn't Mama, but it was the same area code. "Hello?"

"Hello? I'd like to speak to Dr. Hayworth, please. This is Special Agent In Charge Benjamin Johnson of the Federal Bureau of Investigation."

"Yes. I mean, this is Dr. Hayworth. How did you get this number?"

"Dr. Hayworth, I'm part of a federal task force currently in Liberty, Georgia. I've been told that you were well acquainted with Beth Ann Hamilton." His voice had a tinge of a familiar cadence, a transplanted Southerner perhaps.

"Yes." I closed my eyes against the throbbing pain and wondered if a migraine was coming on. I don't have migraines, but this would be a good time to start.

"Dr. Hayworth, I need to ask you a few questions regarding the disappearance of Miss Hamilton. Just some basic background information, if you don't mind."

"I told them everything I knew when she first went missing. Can't you check those reports?" I fidgeted with the sheet music.

"We have, and we just need to confirm some information. It would be better if we could do this in person. Will you be returning to Liberty for the funeral services?"

"I thought they didn't know if it was Beth Ann, know for sure, I mean."

"I stand corrected," his deep voice admitted. "If and when the tests confirm the identity of the deceased, will you be returning to Liberty? If not, I can have a local agent in Chicago come by and interview you."

I sighed. "I'm really busy right now. Can we talk about this later?"

"I see. If you will let us know your arrangements, it would be appreciated."

I climbed down from the high organ bench, retrieved my glasses and started gathering the scattered sheet music. The pages were all mixed up and I spread them out on the bench to put them in order. It wouldn't do to start the Wedding Processional for the funeral.

I stretched my back, pulling my arms behind my shoulder and rotating the cuffs. Stress tightens my shoulders, neck and arms and makes playing more difficult. I wandered over to the grand piano, opened the keyboard cover and fingered the keys. Muscle memory moved my fingers to the chorus of one of Beth Ann's favorite. *Some celestial morning, when my life is o'er, I will fly away,* I hummed the words, and then sang them in my low almost husky voice. *I will fly away, O glory, I'll fly away. When I die, Hallelujah, bye and bye, I'll fly away.* In my head, I heard Beth Ann's voice singing harmony, then jumped when I realized someone was singing in the church with me.

"Brendan!" I moved over on the piano bench.

"You have such a beautiful voice," he said as he sat next to me. "Why don't we ever get to hear you sing?" Brendan James has been an associate pastor at NorthShores for ten years, but our friendship predated that by another fifteen. We had even dated for over a year a long time ago. I had ended the relationship when I realized I could never let down certain emotional barriers. I was grateful that we had remained close friends, even after his marriage to a seminary classmate. "Who were you singing with?"

Startled, I searched his face. There was no mocking or teasing in those familiar brown eyes, just the little wrinkles he gets in the corners when he is concerned. "Beth Ann."

"Oh, honey," Brendan put his arm around my shoulders. "You having those nightmares again?"

I fingered the chords again. "Four called. And Mama. They want me to come home to Liberty. Somebody found a little girl's body in the river. They said it could be Beth Ann."

Brendan knew some of my history. "And you don't think it is?"

"I just don't know. What would she be doing in the river? I thought she..."

Brendan reached over and turned me so I had to look at him. "Are you afraid it is or are you afraid it isn't? Won't it help to know for sure?"

I crumpled into his shoulder and felt the tears burning my eyes. My chest heaved as I gasped for breath between sobs.

He patted my back as he would any distraught parishioner, murmuring "There, there," in a low steady voice.

After a few minutes, I regained my composure and sat up. "I'm sorry," I sniffed. "I don't know why...I mean..."

Brendan flourished a snowy handkerchief, always a necessity for a good pastor. "Honey, there are parts to you that you have never let anybody know. I believe that Beth Ann and that summer and your father are all intertwined and locked up inside you. If this is Beth Ann, then maybe you can finally let go of her."

And your father. The phrase remained unsaid between us.

"I know. I mean, I say I know, but I don't really know. I want to know." I blew my nose and tried to give him back his handkerchief. "Part of me doesn't really want to know, because I don't want to have to say good-bye." I tried to simplify forty years of my thought processes.

"Keep it, you might need it again," Brendan waved off my attempts to return his property. "Brittan Lee, you're as hard-headed as they come and you're going to do what you want. But I think you need to go. Closure. That over-used, hackneyed expression. Closure. Maybe you will be able to sing again." He grabbed his pocket, pulled out a vibrating pager and read the LCD screen. "The hospital. Are you going to be all right?"

I nodded. "Go on. I'll be fine." I gave him a quick hug and a smile that was meant to be reassuring. "Go on now."

Glory Be to the Father, and to the Son and to the Holy Ghost. I went back and searched for the phone under the carefully reorganized stacks of sheet music.

"Yes, Mama."

"You don't have to take that tone with me, young lady. I might just forget to tell you about the surprise I have waiting for you. And I forgot to tell you that the FBI might be calling."

"He did."

"Oh. Verna called; she asked when you would be here. For the rehearsals?"

"What rehearsals, Mama?" My voice edged up. I shouldn't get snippy with Mama; she means well.

"Didn't I mention that? Dear me, Verna wants you to play at the funeral. She wants it to be the piano, like you and Beth Ann played, and she wants you to play *His Eye is on the Sparrow.* I told her you would, of course."

It could have been worse from what I remembered about Miss Verna's preference in hymns. Well, her mama's taste anyway.

I ran through my calendar in my head. The summer had been more hot and humid than usual, and the church's decrepit central air conditioning system had failed several times. As a result, several of the pipes had gone out of tune. The reeds were too shrill, and woodwinds were dominating the brasses. The pipe tuner would be working all the next week re-tuning. I had private piano and organ students. There was Tuesday and Wednesday evening choir practice. I volunteered Tuesdays at the battered women's shelter, and held music groups on Thursdays for the low-income children. I chaired three graduate students' dissertation committees. "Mama, I just don't know if I can come down. I have a lot of obligations here."

Mama just ignored me. "If you want to volunteer, then there is no reason you can't volunteer here. Liberty has just as many needs as Chicago and a lot less to help with them. I don't see why you won't move back here. You can fly up to Chicago to teach those seminars, and there are perfectly good recording studios in Atlanta for those CDs you make. Anyway, at the burial, Verna wants you to sing *It is Well With My Soul.*"

"Mama, I don't sing. You know that." I rubbed the back of my neck again.

"Brittan Lee, promise me you will think about this. After what Verna has been through, that poor woman has suffered through all these years. This would be such a comfort to her."

"Don't be so melodramatic with me, Mama. It doesn't work. I'll see about Monday," I said, but as I turned to my music I thought, *What about me? Didn't Liberty put me through enough?*

I flipped through the sheet music for the opening to the Trumpet Voluntary and adjusted the stops. I fingered the opening notes and paused, listening to the echo from the old stone walls. The sound didn't come back to me quite right; more sound had been absorbed than usual for an empty church.

"Hello?" I looked over the console, down the aisles. "Hello? Brendan, are you still there? Is someone there?" I stood and looked down to the narthex, then checked my watch. The soloist wasn't due for another hour, and she knew to come down to the organ box. I shrugged and sat back down on the bench. Old buildings made strange sounds.

CHAPTER FOUR
Liberty, Georgia, August 2005

Small corporate jets still fly into McKinnon Airport on St Simon's Island for the convenience of the millionaires who live or vacation on nearby Sea Island. The public masses fly into the other airport, which was once Glynnco Naval Air Station and is now the regional airport and the Federal Law Enforcement Training Center. The natives always know when new federal agent trainees arrive. The Federals stand out. They are the only ones who believe tropical weight wool can be worn in Liberty during the summer.

At eleven in the morning, the sun was already melting the asphalt into sticky puddles of black goo, ready to capture the high heels of unsuspecting tourists. I climbed down the airliner stairways in my sensible flat summer sandals. I knew better than to look for Mama outside in the heat. She would be sitting inside the small terminal, waiting in the cool. A light traveler, I pulled my rolling tote behind me as I made my way into the waiting area.

"Dr. Hayworth?" I almost walked right into the man. He caught my elbow, steadying my wobble. "Dr. Brittan Lee Hayworth? Let me help you."

"Excuse me," I stiffened and pulled away as I juggled my purse, my satchel and the rolling bag. At five feet eight I'm not short, but I had to strain my neck to even see his face. "Do I know you?"

He stepped back. "I, uh, I'm Special Agent Andrew Zeller, from the Federal Bureau of Investigation. I'm part of the task force. My boss spoke with you on the phone. I can show you my badge if you would like to see it." He reached down for my luggage. "Let me take that for you." He started for the door.

"Wait just a cotton-pickin' minute," I said, grabbing for my bag. "I'm being met by someone." I looked around for Mama or Four or even one of the nephews.

"Yes. Me," he said. "When I called your mother to set up our meeting, she told me your flight number. I told her I would be more than pleased to meet your flight and drive you home. I thought this way we could start going over a few details."

"Mr. Zeller, or Special Agent Zeller, I don't think this is how the FBI is supposed to conduct their investigations. I doubt my mother just volunteered this information. I don't think I know anything that will help you. I told everyone everything I knew forty years ago." I stood rigid in the hallway, but the tall dark-haired agent continued his confident stride toward the door.

"Oh, damn," I hurried to catch up with him. Running didn't help settle the tightness around my heart.

"Now," he said as he pushed open the door. "Are you hungry? Would you like to stop for a cup of coffee? Or how about a glass of sweet tea? I'm learning all about indigenous Southern customs. Your mother has been helping me."

I glanced down at his left hand. No ring. *Sometimes I can't begin to believe my mother. This better not be the surprise she hinted about.* "No, I'm fine for now, thanks. But I would like to see that badge."

He gave me a look that probably melted the hearts of other ladies as he stopped in back of a white Taurus. He fumbled in his pocket for the keys and opened the trunk. The rolling bag fit easily into the empty space, and he tucked my satchel next to it.

"Now," he said. "My identification. Smart of you to ask for it." He removed the leather folder from an inner breast pocket of his blue blazer. He flipped it open, and I looked at the gold badge and the identification card. "My mother doesn't think it does me justice." There was silence. "Little joke. I work for the Department of Just...Okay, very little joke. Actually, I'm retired from the FBI. I come back and help with certain investigations. Civil rights issues. Missing persons. Unidentified found persons. "

He closed his identification case and opened the car door for me. He folded his long legs into the driver's seat, started the car and pulled out on the causeway, heading north on the Dixie Highway.

"So I understand you moved from Liberty when you were nine," he said.

"Ten, actually. I had just had my birthday." I looked out the window at the familiar marshes lining the coastline, the live oak trees dripping with gray Spanish moss. "You're going the wrong way. Mama's house is on the Island. South."

"I thought we should go up to Liberty first. Talk about a few things. You didn't move back when your mother did?" He looked at me. He had a George Clooney cleft in his chin.

"No. Am I under arrest? Aren't you supposed to read me my rights or something?" I smoothed the creases from my linen slacks.

He glanced sideways. Green eyes. With hazel flecks. "If you were under arrest, you would be sitting in the back wearing handcuffs. I just need to ask you a few questions. Now, tell me about your brothers. They both live here?"

"Yes." I don't know why I was answering his questions. Maybe it would make him go away faster.

"Your nieces and nephews."

"Some of them. Most of them." I could feel him looking at me, as I continued to watch the scenery pass by.

"You never wanted to move back here?"

"Special Agent Zeller, do you live in the town where you were born? Does your mother live there? And your brothers and your sisters and your nieces and nephews?" I questioned him in exasperation.

"Yes, as a matter of fact, they do. But I think this is where I'm supposed to say that I get to ask the questions." He had a tiny dimple in his left cheek when he smiled.

I kept looking out the window. The road continued north, passing over several small bridges over the feeder channels on Rice Island, past Two-way Fishing Camp.

"You were what, eight when your Daddy died?"

"Nine. What in the world does Daddy have to do with this?" I half-turned in my seat and looked at the agent. A vague sense of familiarity flickered, and then vanished. "I thought this was all about Beth Ann."

The Taurus slowed as Special Agent Zeller pulled the car into one of the roadside lanes for the fishermen to park and turned off the engine. He got out of the car and walked towards the river. "You never thought there could be some connection?"

"It was an accident. They all said it was an accident, the hurricane. Daddy was looking for me. He thought I was missing, too. I called him, but he didn't hear me." My voice trailed off. "Why did you stop here? Are you going to tell me what is going on?" I followed him out of the car. "Why wasn't this all done back when Beth Ann went missing?"

He had stopped and was observing the men working below, sifting through the mud. A large area was secured off with bright yellow crime area tape. A crowd of on-lookers was watching, some of them drinking something stronger than Coca-cola from the bottles in brown paper bags. Another group stood to the south, waving placards and signs, calling out comments to the workers.

This would be the third bridge spanning the river between Liberty and Darien. Fifty feet taller and four lanes wide, it would replace the old double-span drawbridge built back in the late fifties. Traffic would back up for an hour when the big freighters came through and the center span would be hoisted high above the rest of the bridge to accommodate the tall smokestacks. Stumps of the pilings from the original bridge still stood about seventy-five feet down the river. Pelicans perched on them, resting between fishing dives into the choppy water. Before the first bridge, the settlers used a ferry.

"There didn't seem to be any question when she died. Or I should say when she was thought to have been killed. Things change. Our agency has several ongoing investigations underway in the South. Some people when they get old, or think they may die and go to hell, they want to make amends for things they did or knew about. When they do, we get the call." He gazed across the river to the fishing docks. The main dock, usually lined with shrimp boats, was instead covered with bright tents and fluttering streamers. Even across the river I could see people wandering about and hear the occasional beat of a bass rhythm.

"In the early 60's, the NAACP had several groups located in rural areas. They were training people how to register to vote, pushing to integrate the schools, restaurants," he continued. "It was the basic, ground level core civil rights movement work. One of the camps was about thirty miles north of Liberty. It's still there; it serves a different purpose now, but it's still there," he said as he watched the workers.

"I know. Daddy took me there. Dorchester Academy. Some people got hurt, and Daddy went to take care of them. I used to help him."

"Well, we've been following up on some leads. There are almost no records on this particular coastal area. Technically Dorchester and the activities there are in another county. No complaints, no problems. Until now."

"They're wrong." My voice sounded dead, flat, even to me. "The black community didn't have anything to do with the fire—or with Beth Ann. I told them, but nobody believed me."

"That's pretty much what we want to talk to you about. We received an anonymous tip just before the body was found. Unusual timing. Normally tips come after a discovery."

"I was nine years old. What could I possibly tell you that you don't already know? There are plenty of people around who were here then. Talk to them." I folded my arms over my chest.

"We have. And we will continue to. We plan on talking to your friends."

I kept looking at the work site. "You think my Brownie troop was involved? Maybe the rest of the Children's Choir was jealous that Beth Ann and I sang a duet?"

He ignored my outburst. "One thing keeps coming out. With almost everyone we have interviewed."

"What?"

"That all summer Doctor Marsh's little girl always seemed to be around. That you were an inquisitive, even a nosy child. Some people seem to think you may know something, remember some small detail. My boss thinks you might."

"Remember what?" I wondered if they planned to hypnotize me to get missing details from my subconscious.

Hypnosis didn't work very well with me. It was a control thing.

"He doesn't know. He doesn't know that you know. But somebody seems to think you do. Someone seems to believe that you knew what happened that night."

"I told them what I knew. They didn't believe me then. Why are you asking now?" I rubbed my arms, already turning a mild pink in the sun.

We stood on the bank, watching the men sift the marsh mud through the large screen boxes. Every now and then someone would come over to the screen, photograph a find, and then place it in a bag. Two of the sheriff's dive and rescue boats bobbed in the water just off the construction site, deputies waiting on the dive platforms.

My head bowed, my eyes closed, I offered a prayer to whomever it was that had been buried for so long in the mud and silt. I lifted her up in my thoughts to the love that was waiting. As I felt a sense of peace float over me, my prayers were disturbed by a nudge at my elbow. Ignoring it, I continued to pray that the family and friends of the child would be found and that their long vigil would be ended. Another nudge to my elbow.

"Amen. Do you believe in a Here After, Agent Zeller?" I glared at him.

"Sorry. Didn't realize you were praying. My mother is Catholic. When she prays, her beads are flying faster than her lips. A Here After? I'm not really sure what I believe anymore. It's been a long time since I went to Mass."

The shrimp boats were returning to the docks, gray seagulls trailing behind them, diving for scraps. White caps topped the dark green water; the rough currents rocked the work barge. The early afternoon thunderclouds were starting to pile. Soon we would hear the grumbles of thunder, and the workers would stop until the lightning flashes moved their way north.

"This is it? Where they found her?"

"Um-hmm."

"So is it her, for sure?"

"They're still doing some tests. This isn't CSI:Liberty; we don't really have the entire world population's DNA in a giant database, and we don't have the results back in thirty minutes. Even her mother didn't have anything left to compare DNA evidence against." He sounded apologetic.

"Even her mother? Sounds like you've met Mrs. Hamilton."

"I've interviewed her."

I stared at the car in the marshes. "Beth Ann wouldn't like this. She was afraid of the water."

CHAPTER FIVE
Liberty, Georgia, July 1964

Mama's always said I was a most inquisitive child. Inquisitive. That was her word. Mama liked inquisitive children. Before she married Daddy, Mama was a teacher. She had been the teacher at the Homeplace school for three months when Daddy came home from medical school for the Christmas holidays. She was beautiful with long fluffy blonde hair pulled back and tied with soft chiffon scarves. Daddy always said Mama didn't look any older than her pupils. They fell madly in love during that holiday season. Mama returned to her home to plan the wedding, and Daddy went back to medical school. They were married right after school ended in June. Mama taught until the boys were born, then she became a classroom mother who baked cupcakes with chocolate frosting and went along on field trips to Fort Frederica and the Okeefenokee Swamp.

"Inquisitive children are active participants in the learning process," Mama would say to her friends at Bridge Club as her hands performed magic with a deck of cards. The cards shuffled and bridged and reshuffled into a neat stack, placed in the center of the table for her opponent to tap with her manicured finger to indicate a cut.

"Inquisitive children challenge their limits and reach out for new adventures, because they want to learn. We should encourage that." The other ladies would smile, then laugh and nod their heads.

"That's not what you said when Jack and Matthew tried to set off a model rocket with a cherry bomb engine," Mrs. Smith said. "I believe that episode in adventure turned out the Liberty Fire Department and cost a new ceiling, two windows and a paint job!"

All the ladies were laughing. Trulee came around with the silver tea pot and refilled the ladies' cups. She nodded at me, and I went to the kitchen and picked up the smaller silver tray with lemon slices and the sugar bowl and the creamer. I followed Trulee to each of the ladies and offered them the accessories to the special raspberry blend tea. After a while, I realized that when we came into the room, the ladies just kept talking as if we weren't even there. I would look at Trulee, and she would shake her head. We would make our rounds of the room, and then step back away from the ladies as they sipped from the delicate china cups and nibbled on Trulee's tea cakes.

Auntabelle is Mama's older sister. Four couldn't pronounce Aunt Annabelle when he was little, so Auntabelle became her name. She didn't come to Bridge Club. She had to work at her job at Daddy's medical office. Auntabelle was the office manager, and she wore neat little suits with leather belts and matching pumps. She had to work because Uncle Frank couldn't always hold a job. Daddy said Uncle Frank was always between jobs. Mama said it was such a pity that her sister had to work so hard.

"I said to him, 'Marsh, you have got to find some way to help him.' And Marsh said to me, 'Belle, you can only help a person so far.'" Mama sat back with my second-best Sunday dress, marking the new hem. "Annabelle was the beauty in her class, and so talented with the piano and the violin. We do all we can, for Trey's sake, but…" the words hung in the air.

Trey was my cousin, Frank Littleton, the Third. His daddy was Uncle Frank.

"Belle, Frank has a problem—from the war, you know. Some men never recover from the gassing and the shell-shock. At least Annabelle can help support the family. What is Trey going to do for school?" Miss Roberta asked.

"We wanted him to go to the University in Athens with Four and Jack, but he didn't want to go that far away. Southern offered him a good deal, full tuition with a football scholarship. Marsh told him we would pay for his books and give him a small allowance." Mama looked in her sewing box for thread to match my dress. "Trey works so hard at the marina, trying to save up some extra money. I wish Four and Jack had his ideas on money."

Movement from the doorway caught Mama's eye. Trulee stood in the opening and mimicked holding the telephone. Mama nodded and excused herself.

Virginia Stevens' husband was one of Daddy's medical partners. She watched until Mama was out of the room then announced, "We're setting up a committee. We're going to have to work fast if we're going to have the school ready to open by Labor Day. We are going to use the old Liberty Coast Motel. Twelve parents signed up already. I'm certainly not going to let my daughters…" Her voice trailed off as Mama came back in and sat.

"Southern's got a good program," Miss Roberta said. "My youngest is at Southern. After his brother's behavior at the University, we thought a smaller school might be better for Timmy."

The ladies quieted as they remembered the phone calls from Athens, Miss Roberta and Mr. Edwin's long night drive up to the University and the resulting disgrace as Edwin Junior was suspended for behavior unbecoming a gentleman. Edwin Junior's disgrace was the main topic of conversation whenever Miss Roberta wasn't there.

"Bless his heart, 'cause he's gonna break his mama's," Miss Rudelle always said. "Those ways, she's always praying with that visiting preacher from Ludowisci that Junior will change those ways. So is there any news about Zora Wensley?"

"I'm going up to see her when I go to Atlanta next week," Miss Frances said. "That poor thing, polio is just devastating. I'm so glad they have that vaccine for it now a days. Do you think she'll ever walk again? I remember when she made her curtsy at her debut. She was just the most graceful thing. I hear Bruce is considering moving her to Warm Springs. That private hospital she's in must be costing him a pretty penny. Anyway I want to look for a dress for the Medical Auxiliary Ball. That Lenox Mall has some of the nicest shops. I don't care what people say, I think it is very convenient to have all the stores together like that mall has them. For once, I intend to have the best dress at the dance." She looked over her reading glasses at Mama. Everyone knows that Mama always has the prettiest dresses anywhere. "Anyone need anything while I'm there?"

"Actually, yes, I do," Mama said. "Annabelle says she's lost four white sheets at the laundry. Her birthday is coming up, and I thought I would get her some of those real nice ones, that feel so cool-percale. I want the ones with the floral embroidery around the turn back. You don't have to iron them, and I thought it would make her life a little easier. I saw an ad for them in the Sunday Atlanta Constitution. They're on sale at Rich's. Remind me to give you some money before you leave."

"Bless her heart, Annabelle does deserve some of the nice things in life. She works so hard," Miss Frances said.

***

Inquisitive was Mama's word. *Curious* was Daddy's word.

"That child is into everything. She needs to know what all is happening, who is making it happen and why it's happening. She is just curious about everything. Did either of our boys teach themselves to read at three?"

"Marsh, I think it's because she's an only child," Mama said. I'm not really an only child, but Four and Jack are twelve and ten years older than me, so I was growing up as if I was an only child.

"If I had to do it over again, I would have had one more baby right after Brittan Lee. Only children can grow up to be spoiled and selfish."

"Belle!" Daddy sounded shocked. "Brittan Lee isn't spoiled. She's smart and caring and helpful. Look at her in my office. She greets the patients, Agnes lets her take the temperatures and hold out the band-aids. The patients love it, and they talk to her more than they do me."

"Well, I just get worried that she seems to spend all her time with adults."

Mama was right about that. I was the only child my age in the neighborhood; Beth Ann lived a few miles out in the country. Most of the other children in the neighborhood were five, six, eight years older than I was, and they didn't want me tagging along. I did it anyway until they chased me off. If they weren't watching me, I would follow Four and Jack and Trey to their secret fort out in the marshes behind the old duplexes. They had built a fort out of old boards with a marsh sod roof. Inside, they hung a deer head with antlers, and five shark jawbones with some teeth still attached. I found a box with beer cans hidden under a cot and some magazines with pictures of naked ladies doing funny stuff.

In the summertime, if Beth Ann couldn't come over for the day, I was usually left to my own ways. Sometimes Uncle Frank would stop by, pick me up in his Ford and take me with him on his insurance rounds. He always had papers and things for me to take into the little country stores and diners. I knew all the back roads, farm lanes and alleys in north Liberty County by the end of that summer.

Mama went to the beauty shop every Friday morning, so her hair would look nice for church. If Beth Ann and I weren't playing together, I would beg Mama to take me with her to the salon. Miss Juanita would walk Mama to the shampoo section. The chair would tilt back ways, and Mama's neck would rest in the pink shampoo bowl. Miss Juanita squeezed suds and warm water over Mama's hair, rubbed the sweet smelling shampoo into her scalp and rinsed it out. Sometimes if Miss Juanita wasn't busy, she would free my waist-long braids and gently disentangle my hair. I would lie back in the chair, and feel my scalp being massaged. The roots of my head would tingle, and as the warm water gently rinsed away the fragrant soap, I would fall asleep.

Ladies don't know how loud they talk when their heads are under those dryers, with all the warm air whooshing down. When Mama had to give me "The Talk," I didn't realize that I learned all about Auntie Flow, and birds and bees, and falling off the roof in Miss Juanita's shop.

"Mama," I asked after one excursion, "why is Miss Gloria's daughter going to finish high school with Miss Gloria's sister in

Indiana? Don't she like Oak Academy anymore? Does she get to finish quicker up there because she's fast?"

**

Curious. That was Daddy's word for me.

Spoiled pesky interfering nosy brat. Those were old Mr. Wensley's words. He came running out of the church building just a fussin' and a hollerin' at me. I wasn't being pesky or nosy. I had climbed the big old mimosa tree by the main sanctuary doors. Purple and pink fringed blossoms showered onto the sidewalk. The tassels made my nose itch and I would sneeze. The thick trunk split into three massive branches that split into three more. It was harder to climb than the Liberty Oak, but it wasn't too hard. Daddy had a Deacon's meeting, and he had to bring me. Mama was at a Garden Club meeting, and Trulee was off.

I climbed higher and higher, trying to reach the dried seed pods from the previous season. At the top I could see in the round windows, into a little room above the balcony. I almost fell right out of the tree when I looked in and the room was full of men. I never knew that room was there, and Beth Ann and I had been all over that church.

"Hey Uncle Frank!" I called through the open window.

"Dang and tarnation! What the..." Chair legs scraped on the floor and a door slammed. "You, what the heck you doin' there? Git outta there!" Cranky old Mr. Wensley hung half out of the window, reaching for the tree. "Who's that out there?"

I clung to the tree, frozen, then scrambled down as fast as I could. For an old man, Mr. Wensley was faster. He disappeared into the now-dark room and ran down the two flights of stairs in time to grab me as I fell the last three feet out of the tree.

"You, girl! What were you doin' in that tree?" He shook my arm. "That was a private meeting." I saw him look around the grounds, off past where I saw the other men running, getting into cars and trucks. For a brief moment I wondered why Uncle Frank had not come to see me.

"What'd you see there?"

"Nothing!" I stammered as I struggled to get free. "I didn't see nothing. Let go of me!"

"Hey, there! What's going on?" Reverend Leeward ran out the sanctuary with Daddy and the rest of the deacons. "Salton? What's all this about?"

"Spoiled pesky interfering nosy brat." He shook me again. "Caught her trying to peek into our meeting. Got no right to do that." He spat on the ground. He was as mean as his son, Dr. Bruce, was nice.

"What meeting was that, Salton? I didn't know anything was scheduled today except the Deacons. I'm sure Brittan Lee didn't mean to interrupt you." The Reverend worked Mr. Wensley's fingers off my arm.

I rubbed the marks his rough hands had left. "I wasn't looking at anything. I was just climbing the tree."

"Ah, ah, meeting..." Mr. Wensley looked at the gathered men as if searching for the answer. "Masons. Emergency meeting. You know we can't talk about that in front of outsiders."

From behind, Daddy wrapped his arms around me. "I'm sure Brittan Lee didn't mean any harm. Apologize for disturbing the meeting, honey."

I scowled at the big man. Daddy always said that in an emergency, a child should always look for a man wearing the Masonic pin with the Compass and Square. A Mason would protect a child from danger.

"Sorry," I said. I looked at him again. "Mr. Wensley?"

"What?"

"You lost your Mason pin."

CHAPTER SIX
Liberty, Georgia, August 2005

You need some more tea to wash that stuff down with?"
Special Agent Zeller watched me eat my sandwich
with a strange look on his face.

We were sitting at the luncheonette counter of what used
to be Woolworth's. The counter stools were still covered in
a cracked red vinyl. Ceiling fans rotated with slow, steady
whomps up in the high spaces overhead. I had just finished
my second pimento cheese sandwich and was considering the
very unladylike thought of licking my fingertips to get the last
taste of cheese.

I couldn't believe how easy it was to talk to Agent Zeller.
The thought of having to talk to people churns my insides.
Mama laughs when I say that. She always said that when I was
little, I would talk to anyone about anything. I don't do that
anymore.

"You don't like pimento cheese?"

"It must be an acquired taste." He shifted on his stool and
looked down the length of the counter. "I don't think I ever
saw it on a menu until I came to Liberty."

"They have it other places, but it isn't as good. It takes the
Hellman's."

"The Hellman's?"

"The Hellman's mayonnaise. I don't think I've ever seen
it for sale out of the Southeast. Mama says that Best Foods is

the same thing west of the Mississippi. You just can't make decent pimento cheese without Hellman's. Or deviled eggs." I know I must have sounded like a walking, talking, brainless blonde joke, but I wasn't ready or able to carry on a serious conversation. It was unsettling, seeing where Beth Ann had been hidden for the last forty years. Of all possibilities, this one had never presented itself in my head. I looked at myself in the long mirror behind the counter. My nose was red from the sun and my eyes swollen from the sudden crying jag at the river bank. "Thank you for letting me get a bite to eat. I didn't realize how hungry I was. Do we need to go back to the Courthouse?"

"We'll get there," he said. "Actually, just sitting here is good. I'm learning a lot about Liberty. Background information that helps me understand the people here."

"Mo' tea, Miss Brittan Lee?" The pitcher hovered over my glass.

I smiled my thanks. "Always the best tea in town, Mr. Willis, but don't be telling Trulee I said that. How have you been doing?"

"Hee, hee, oh, I'm just fair to middlin," the elderly counterman laughed as he wiped a minute droplet of tea from the counter. He hadn't changed since I was little, still in a starched white shirt with the sleeves rolled up to the elbow, a red apron protecting it from splatters. His name was embroidered in black thread over the shirt pocket. He was more stooped; his hair had turned white. But he had the same smile, the same kind eyes. "When you was little, you liked my cherry Cokes better. You mama and that Miss Trulee, they not be letting you drink Co-cola at home. You comes here and perches up on that there very same stool. I always makes you cherry Coke and gives you extra cherries." He spoke in the lilting, singsong rhythms of the Sea Islands. Whenever I come home and hear those voices I wonder how I can bear to leave again.

"So how were things here in Liberty in the '60s, Mr. Willis?" Agent Zeller asked.

Silence bounced off of the polished counter top and ricocheted from the mirror. The man washing the dishes froze, his hands still holding a glass and rag. The cook stood motionless, ignoring the burgers sizzling on the grill and the chicken in the fryer. Both of them looked over at Mr. Willis.

The old man's eyes searched the agent's face. "Sometimes, sometimes it's best to not be dwelling on that which is past and over. There was some times that wasn't so good. They always be those who brings their own madness, their own sadness to this here world." He shook his head. "Everybody's got their own troubles, then and now."

It seemed as if everyone let out their pent-up breath at the same time. The cook flipped the hamburger patties and the dishwasher resumed his rinsing.

"Wasn't no troubles in here," Mr. Willis said. "The Doctor Marsh, he tried to make things work, so they wouldn't be no troubles. But Miss Brittan Lee, her be the first one who does it."

Agent Zeller looked between Mr. Willis and me. "Her? I thought you moved when you were nine?"

"I don't…Mr. Willis, what are you talking about?" I was confused.

"Hee, hee, hee," the old man laughed again. "One of them days, it was a powerful hot summer day; Miss Trulee was here for the Doctor. I don't remembers what it was he needed, but he had to have it from heres. She brings Miss Brittan Lee with her, and Miss Brittan Lee wants one of my special cherry Co-colas. She just fussed and fussed. So Miss Trulee gives her what she wants, which is what everybody did with Miss Brittan Lee."

"And?" I was almost embarrassed to ask.

"Well, then, Miss Trulee, she do what colored peoples do in them days, she stands behinds you while you drinks you Co-cola. And you makes such a fuss about Miss Trulee sitting down with you at the Counter to have a cherry Co-cola, too. You say 'Trulee's thirsty too.' You just wouldn't stop until she sat right there and drank her Co-cola. Just to hush you up. After that, nobody ever made a fuss about colored folks at the Counter. Shore and it surprised them northern boys when they came to town." He continued to polish the long counter.

I could feel Agent Zeller tense next to me.

"What northern boys?"

"Oh, just some of them boys they comes in with her big brother, Mr. Jack. They comes around to teach us how to vote. They was part of that group from Dorchester. They comes in, all proud, maybe five, maybe six. Mr. Jack and two other white boys and three colored boys. They walks up to the counter and sits. They looks over the menu, and says 'Are you going to serve us?'" The old man laughed again. "They seemed plumb disappointed when I slid the Blue Plate Specials right in front of them. Right there at the Counter." Mr. Willis wiped down some more of the counter. "I whispers to your brother, Miss Brittan Lee done broke down that wall. I told him, I did. Hee, hee, hee. He just laughed and laughed, and they ate my fried chicken right here. I thinks they be disappointed no police mans come. That Miss Brittan Lee, she always be special to us. "

"I remember. I loved Trulee, and I wanted her to have something special to drink, like I had," I said. "I didn't think it was right, her having to stand up and be thirsty. I think Daddy's phone rang off the hook. People telling him about his uppity daughter."

"Well, now, lots of them peoples is remembering things now," he nodded his head. "That same summer, yes, now, it was that same summer, I remembers it."

"Uh, yeah. I, uh, I may need to come back and speak to you, Mr. Willis. Do you think you could remember the names of the men?"

"Some of 'ems was local boys. Mr. Jack, he was here, but not Mr. Four. Then that boy who what disappeared. And that Bluer Smith, he still here, owns the service station over on the Highway. That other boy, can't quite remembers if he was here that day, but he died in the war, back in, what was it, 1970? That other white boy, don't think I was ever introduced proper." The old man pulled a snowy white handkerchief from his back pocket and wiped his face. "Mr. Jack, he may remember him, they's joined at the hip mos' the summer, I hears."

"I think, uh, I may need to come back and talk to you later, Mr. Willis. Dr. Hayworth, are you ready to head for the Courthouse?"

Agent Zeller looked pale to me as he started to straighten himself from his stool, and then stopped to nod to a shopper.

"Well, Brittan Lee? Home to see your Mama?" The years had been cruel to Virginia Stevens. She was five years younger than Mama but looked ten years older. Her hair was still a glaringly bright blonde pulled up in a French twist with the bouffant top, a style which had flattered her in the sixties. "She's getting older, you know. She needs her daughter to be living here, not a thousand miles away." Mrs. Stevens turned and looked at the younger woman trailing behind her, a spitting image of Dr. Stevens. "I'm sure you remember Cynthia, even though you don't usually call her when you come to town." Cynthia had on a bright Lily Pulitzer tropical dress, which would have been charming had the dress actually fit. I allowed myself that one uncharitable thought.

"Cynthia, nice to see you," I nodded. "You have to excuse us, please. Surely you understand..."

"Oh honey, it must just make you so sad," Cynthia reached over to give me air kisses near each cheek. "To think about poor Beth Ann. Never to experience what we all have, never to marry or have any little children of her own. Oh, I'm so sorry, Brittan Lee, what am I saying? I'm so sorry, you never got married or had any children either, did you?" She tried to hide her little smirk, but I saw it.

"Brittan Lee, where are your manners? I'm Virginia Stevens." Mrs. Stevens reached past me to take Agent Zeller's arm. "How long do you think you'll be here with us?"

"Zeller. Special Agent Andrew Zeller. I'm not sure, we still have several interviews, tests. I'm not really at liberty to discuss it. I'm sure you understand. We don't want to say anything until we have some definitive information." He flashed a smile that included both women. Mrs. Stevens' leathery skin flushed a brighter shade of pink. Cynthia smoothed her skirt over her flat rump. I wondered if he had that affect on all women.

"Now you let me know what I can do to help," Cynthia reached over and took his arm, nudging her mother aside. "Brittan Lee was just a child. I was seventeen when these tragedies occurred; I could probably be much more help than she could. And I can introduce you to all our friends and neighbors. We all used to hang out at the marina during the summer. I even met that black boy there once. He was talking to Trey Littleton." She gave a delicate shudder. "It could have been me he kidnapped." She hung onto his arm and looked up at him, trembling. "It was weeks before I could sleep through the night." Her eyes widened. "Why, Special Agent Zeller, I have a wonderful idea. Why don't you come over for dinner one night? I'll invite the old group over, those who still live here in Liberty, and we can tell you all about that summer."

"That, uh, that would be very helpful," Agent Zeller looked over at me. "Why don't you give me a call over at the Courthouse? They have given us some office space there. There are actually four agents here on the task force."

My stomach churned, and I was once again the small child left on the sidelines as the older children selected teams. I watched Cynthia and tried to think what Mama had told me on one of her weekly phone calls. I couldn't remember if Cynthia was working on her third or her fourth husband.

"Come along, dear, we have a few more things to do," Mrs. Stevens waved to us and departed on a cloud of Estee Lauder Youth Dew. "Brittan Lee, give your mother our love. We'll see her later."

"I need another glass of tea," I slid back onto my stool at the counter.

"Miss Brittan Lee, don't you let that woman get to you," the counterman slid the little dish of lemons across the Formica counter. "Either of thems. They's not worth the air you breathe." His lips disappeared in a tight line. "No goods come of them."

Agent Zeller settled back onto his stool. "So, how do you know Virginia Stevens and her daughter? Er, what is Cynthia's last name? So I can share the invitation with the other agents."

I sipped my tea. "I have no idea. All I can remember are Stevens, Bothwell and Gregory. I think she's had at least one other husband. In high school, she dated most of the high school football team and half of the basketball team. Nowadays I hear she's working her way through the local Medical Association, maybe she'll try for the Bar. Her father was my daddy's partner." My face flushed with embarrassment that I had repeated local gossip and violated Mama's rule about talking bad about other women in front of men. "I'm ready to go now."

"So tell me the truth. What did Cynthia Stevens really do to you? Steal your Barbie? Rip your comic books?" Agent Zeller gestured at Mr. Willis for another Coca-cola.

"If you must know, she stole my very first boyfriend. Well, he wasn't my boyfriend, but he was my first crush. He was a friend of Jack's. Jack brought him home a few times. He was one of the boys helping at the Dorchester School we were talking about. Cynthia met him at the Fourth of July party, and he never even looked at me after that." *He hadn't really looked at me before either.*

"Did he ever look at you before that?" Zeller read my mind. "I mean, you were what? Nine?"

"Chronological age doesn't matter. Southern women bloom early. And she stole him from me." I grinned. I had been heartbroken for at least two or three weeks. "I still feel the pain and never married because of the emotional trauma."

"What was his name?" Agent Zeller looked at me.

"Uh…Tony. He had one of those really long ethnic last names. I don't think I could pronounce it then, and I'm sorry, but I don't remember it now. Jack might remember. All I remember is that he had wavy black hair and green eyes. He talked to me as if I were his own age." I closed my eyes trying to picture him. "He said he had a sister about my age. We talked about school. And snow. I'd never seen snow before, and he thought that was funny."

Agent Zeller stood and looked around. "We've been in here for less than an hour. Almost everyone who has come through that door has started over in this direction, then turned away. You seem to be well known for someone who moved away when she was nine."

"There's no middle ground in a small town, Agent Zeller. People remember you because you are very, very good or very, very bad."

"And which were you?" He seemed serious with the question.

"That's what you're going to have to find out. I imagine it will depend on who you talk to," I said.

Mr. Willis was clearly fascinated by the conversation, his eyes moving back and forth between Zeller and me. He grabbed Agent Zeller's arm as we started to leave. "You be careful with our Miss Brittan Lee," he said. "And don' you be listening to them other folks. She didn't kill her daddy."

CHAPTER SEVEN
Liberty, Georgia, August 2005

The wall of heat slammed against us as Agent Zeller pushed open the glass door of Woolworth's and we stepped out to the pavement. One of the quick-moving summer storms had rained during my lunch, and small puddles reflected the blue sky and afternoon sun.

"Agent Zeller, can you please tell me what this is all about? What does a lunchroom counter semi-protest have to do with Beth Ann's disappearance?"

I had turned right onto Riverside Street and was walking toward the sounds of music. Both sides of the street parking places were full, and I saw a makeshift parking lot at the edge of the docks.

"We'll talk back at the office. I need to make some phone calls. The car's over here." He led the way.

"You have to be nice to Mr. Willis. He was beaten pretty badly and his brother was one of three men lynched back in the thirties. Mr. Willis still limps where his leg was broken and not set properly," I said.

He froze then turned to me. "Why didn't anyone mention this? We've been here interviewing people for five days, and no one has mentioned that men were beaten and lynched. Dr. Hayworth? How in the world do you know about this?"

I stood still while I thought about it. "I think I heard my Daddy getting mad at Uncle Frank about something. Let me remember. Oh, yes. It was one of the days when I went riding with Uncle Frank, dropping off things for his clients. We passed Mr. Willis. He was walking into town, still about three or four miles out. I made Uncle Frank stop and give him a ride. Uncle Frank called him the "N" word, so I told Daddy. Daddy and Uncle Frank had words. Daddy said something about Mr. Willis having had a hard life, and it wouldn't hurt Uncle Frank to give a crippled man a ride into town. Uncle Frank said something about having made his own bed and deserving what he got. Daddy was just furious. I wasn't supposed to be hearing any of this, you know."

Special Agent Zeller stared at me. "Five days and no one mentioned this particular bit of civil rights violence. I've learned more from you in two hours...I'm beginning to understand the nosy part." He took my elbow. "I'm sorry. You must think I'm an absolute idiot. I reviewed the files for this area, and there was nothing about three men being lynched."

"Oh, it wasn't in Liberty. Mr. Willis's family moved to west Georgia over by the Alabama border when he was a little boy," I said. "Daddy told me."

"This way. The car is over here. Hold on, excuse me just a minute." He reached into his blazer pocket and pulled out his cell phone. "Zeller. Uh, uh." He cupped his hand over the opposite ear, and turned away from the wind.

"I'll be right back," I whispered. I wanted to see what was going on over at the pier. It was too late for the Blessing of the Fleet. I hurried toward the music. My music.

"This little light of mine, I'm gonna let it shine. This little light of mine, I'm gonna let it shine. This little light of mine..."

Shrimp boats no longer docked along the city wharf but were moved to a new pier about a quarter mile down river. The activity I had seen from the construction site was not that of the shrimpers and fishermen emptying holds of fresh catch or maids wandering among the stalls of fresh seafood. Colorful flags and streamers fluttered with the wind, replacing the grays, browns and blacks of the old shrimp boats. Craft stands lined both sides of the pier and opened to a central courtyard. Tourists wandered from stall to stall looking at displays of produce, pottery and antiques. Music blasted from overhead speakers. I looked in both directions at the pier, searching for the source of the music.

"Can I help you?" A woman called out from the recesses of a small booth. The counter in front of her held racks of brochures and maps. A giant map of coastal Georgia was tacked up on the side of the booth; little clusters of colored flags identified places of interest for the tourists.

"I was just looking for the singers," I smiled. "Is this a festival of some kind?"

"No, the Liberty Tourism Board is hosting an open air market for the summer: crafts, antiques, as well as local produce. We're trying to encourage more people to swing off of the Interstate and take U.S. Highway 17 down the coast," she said. "Are you visiting Liberty?"

"Yes," I said. "I have family here."

"Well, welcome back," she said. "Here is a schedule of the music. We have a lot of local musicians and groups who come over. Some are from the schools; some popular bands. What you probably just heard was one of our local cultural groups. Yes." She put on half-rim reading glasses and peered at the sheet. "The Liberty Shouters. I know that sounds like a strange name, but a lot of the old gospels and spirituals and work songs were called shouts. We're real proud of the Liberty Shouters. They were the first of the old-time shouters to form as a group and perform. They were invited to sing on Oprah's TV show.

We have several of their CDs for sale." She twirled a rotating rack of tapes and discs and selected one. "These are some of the singers." She held open the inner liner to show me then stared between me and the liner. Her forehead wrinkled as she looked at me again. "This is you. You're Brittan Lee Hayworth. You produced this CD! You played the piano for the singers! Would you autograph some, please? It makes them sell better, and the singers promised a share to the committee for each one sold." She pulled about 25 CD cases out of the racks and provided me with a felt tip pen. I started signing as the woman fluttered about. "This will be so helpful; it makes these so much more desirable. Will you be here very long? Will you come back to sign some more?"

I promised I would and gave her Mama's phone number to reach me when she needed more signed.

I thanked her and turned back to the pier. The first stand held lush produce, big red tomatoes, delicate pods of green okra, early ears of Silver Queen corn. Sunlight filtered in from the open back wall, colored by the jars of jelly and honey.

"Marsh grass honey?" I read the label. "I never knew. How do you get marsh grass honey?"

"We have hives set up near the marsh. The bees pollinate some of the flowers in the marsh grass and that flavors the honey. Homeopaths say that eating local honey is a great way to build up immunity to an area's flower allergies. Would you like to try a sample?" She showed me where there were open jars of the honey and jellies next to a plate of crackers.

"I just had lunch, thank you for asking. Well, maybe just a little taste." I dripped the pale golden honey onto one of the crackers. It was delicious; it tasted as wonderful as the early morning marsh smelled, sweet with an unusual hint of saltiness. I fixed another. "This is absolutely great. How do you manage to keep any on the shelves?"

"Well, this market just started the weekend of the Fourth of July, and it's been good. It's picked up some, with the Labor Day weekend coming up, maybe even more. The Tourism Board set out fliers at the welcome stations at the state lines, and in the hotels in Savannah and St Simons. Excuse me just one minute." She turned to greet new shoppers, a middle-aged, sunburned couple with a small dog.

I had one more tiny sample of the honey. I'm always looking for Christmas presents for my Sunday School class and for the parents of my children's choir. This just might be the perfect thing for this year. I tried to count faces in my head and came up with thirty-six. I mouthed "I'll be back" at the vendor and left to explore other stalls.

Different music, rock and roll, resounded from the speakers. I followed the sounds to the north end of the pier where a small stage had been built, a slight elevation over the original heavy timbers of the dock. A Jimmy Buffett cover band strummed their electric guitars. The group was loud, energetic and encouraged the listeners to head for Margaritaville. Benches provided seating in front of the bandstand, and several small food stands offered drinks and southern specialty snacks. Twenty or thirty people swayed or danced to the music, while at least that many continued shopping.

"Brittan Lee? Brittan Lee?"

Arms encircled my waist and I whirled around. "Tansie! I knew those had to be your children; I was looking for you."

"Girl, don't you look good?" She stepped back and gave me the once-over.

"Oh, honey, don't I wish we were girls?" I hugged her back. "Ohh, nice hair!" I admired the tiny dreads that draped around her oval face. Tiny bits of gold in the hair echoed the glints of gold in her brown eyes.

"No, sirree," she said. "I like being a woman just fine. When did you get in? What do you think about all this? Listen to me just going on. It's just so good to see you."

"You, too. The children sounded wonderful."

"Never thought we'd be directing a children's choir, did you?" she laughed. "And taking them chilluns on tour. Everyone is so excited; I told them you would play for practice. And wait 'til Saturday night and the adult Shouters perform. We've got a version of *Ballin' the Jack* that would make a sailor blush."

"Are you going to make them pull on a rope, too? Remember that picture from Lydia Parrish's photo album? She meant well. At least she started saving the music," I said. "Listen, Jack told me Thomas was running for sheriff in November. Why didn't you tell me that!"

"Yes, can you believe it? My husband, the first black sheriff in Liberty since Reconstruction? About time the old ass Ungler retired. My dining room is the temporary campaign headquarters, but Jax is helping set up the new headquarters. Ooh, that boy is good-looking, just like his daddy at the same age. I think he's inherited Jack's sense of responsibility. Listen, I've got to go check on the children; they're having lunch over at the Welcome Center. We'll talk later." She looked over her shoulder. "The FBI is asking questions. Some folks are getting stirred up. Be careful where you go. Keep one of the nephews around you. I'll call you at your Mama's later." She gave me a quick hug and headed over to the Welcome Center.

I watched her cross the street, then I continued wandering through the market. I stopped in front of a display of watercolor and acrylic paintings. At least half of the painting sites were familiar parts of my childhood: the Liberty Oak, the old fort, the courthouse. Multiple shades of pink and green flooded one water color, a delicate study of antique roses climbing a black wrought iron fence. The lovely watercolor had the entwined DA of the Dorchester Academy in the fence detailing. It had been forty years since I last saw that fence.

"Can I help you?" A woman I assumed was the artist stood up from the rear of the stall. She was dressed for the weather in light, flowing, loose clothes and a big floppy sunhat.

I jumped, startled from my study of the painting. "This is beautiful. They all are. Is this up at Sunbury?"

"Yes." The woman seemed pleased that I could identify the location. "There is an old school there."

"I remember. Are these all yours?" I moved to look at an acrylic of a tabby chapel. I thought it was the one on St Simons Island.

"Yes. I stopped in Liberty last year to sketch and never left. The coast just seems to cast a spell. Are you driving through or do you live around here?"

"I'm visiting family," I answered, as I moved to examine another watercolor. Delicate tans and greens portrayed the marshes leading over to Sapelo Island. One of my treasured childhood photographs was taken from the same viewpoint. "Are you having a good turn out?"

"Hmm, some days are better than others. There are more people out today than in the past week. I think it could be from all the excitement across the river." She gestured at the scene on the opposite side. The sheriff's boats and divers had stopped operations, but the dredge was still pulling buckets of mud from the riverbanks. "They found an old car at the bottom of the river. It had a body in it and the whole town is turned upside down over it. Some old story about a kidnapped child and a fire. I think the ghoul factor has people stopping by. I heard it made the Atlanta and Jacksonville papers and even the local part of CNN."

"Oh, my!" I said. "It must be exciting."

"Well, any publicity is better than no publicity. So if people come to see the construction site, and then maybe stay and buy one of my paintings or Sandra's herbal lotions or Joanie's glass things, it's all for the better."

"Do you all live in the area, or are you just here for the summer?" I asked. Liberty had never been a destination for anyone since the steamboats stopped running. Liberty had no major industry, no shopping malls—just the downtown—and was far enough away to be too long a commute to Savannah. Mama said Liberty hadn't grown since the old witch was hung in 1780, and she was about right.

"Liberty is turning into an artists' colony," she said. "It's laid back, friendly, and cheap. If this Market works out well, then Liberty will be profitable, too."

"It would be good for Liberty to get some of the tourism dollars. Do you live here?" I asked.

"Not in Liberty," she said. "A friend has a big place on a river just to the north of Liberty. He's renting the guest quarters to us really cheap. Even let Joanie bring a small kiln for her glass work and let me convert a room for a studio."

"I knew I recognized that marsh view. Isn't that leading over the Knox River to Sapelo Island? That was painted from the dock at the Sapelo Sound, wasn't it?"

She stared at me for a minute or two. "That's private property. You know your landmarks! Or are you psychic? Who are you?"

"Brittan Lee Hayworth." I held out my hand.

Her back straightened and she stared at my hand for a few

seconds before she took it. "Mary Frances Tilton. I've, uh, heard about you for the past few months. I hope you don't mind us staying at Sapelo Sound. We're generally clean and neat, well, as clean and neat as artists are. We pay our rent in a timely manner, usually."

"Mary Frances, it's okay. If Jack said you could move in, you can move in. Anything that can help Liberty, I certainly support."

"Jack?" She hesitated. "Yes, thank you."

"It was nice meeting you, Mary Frances. I'm going to wander a bit more."

"Okay. The Gullah weavers have some great baskets down two stalls on the other side. The Lewis family has a collection of hand carved walking sticks made by the older brothers. Joanie has beautiful glass work in that front corner. Other than that basic group, every day is a different day at the festival. Listen, we close at six on week nights. If you're still around, find me. We usually all go out to eat. Whoever has the highest bragging rights buys the beer."

"Sounds like fun. I'll try to get back in time. I'm going to go and check out the glass work." I waved good-bye and headed across the pier to the stall flashing with the reflected glory of the stained glass sun-catchers, bowls, fused and melted glass vases and some fused glass earrings.

"How do you make these?" I shouted over the music as I looked at a set of glass window pockets, each done in a different color. Each had a clear glass back and pieces of colored glass making a pocket on the front of the solid piece of the clear glass.

"What?" the artist came closer.

"How do you...oh," my voice echoed in the sudden silence as the band finished their set. "Sorry."

"That happens a lot," the woman said. "We gesture frequently around here. You should be here when the really loud groups play." She laughed as she took one of the window pockets off the wall. "These just take a little practice and a great imagination," she said. "The posy pockets are big hits; you can put in fresh flowers or herb sprays. I just have to guess what color and style the people want. Now the sun catchers—I try to make those with found glass. The old bottles and window glass have such beautiful waves and bubbles. I just smooth the rough edges."

"When do you have time to do this?"

She sat and fanned herself with her hat. "I wish I was twenty years younger so I had enough time to do everything I need to do. Energy is wasted on the young. When I go back home tonight, I'll set up more, fire them, let them cool overnight, and I'm set for the next day."

"Hey ladies!"

"Hey back at you, Mary Frances! What's up?" Joanie pulled one of the stools and wiped her face under the big brimmed hat.

"I came to tell her that some man is looking for her."

"Oh, yeah. Sort of a business thing. We have to go back to his office. Where is he?" I looked around the shopping area.

"Huh," Mary Frances said. "He was right over there; I aimed him this way. Maybe he got sidetracked. Joanie, did you get a chance to meet Brittan Lee Hayworth?"

I'm sure her nod at me had some meaning between the two. It was even more apparent when Joanie tightened her lips and didn't say too much after that. Mary Frances looked down towards the food area. "Well, I wonder where he went. If I see him again, I'll send him this way. Later, then." She went back to her paintings.

"Joanie, what other colors do you have for the window pockets? These would make perfect Christmas presents."

She was slow to respond to my question and wouldn't look me in the eye. "They can be made in any combination you want. There are a lot of them up on the top row," she pointed to the back, where the colored glass plaques hung from a rod. "It's easier to get them from the outside of the booth. Too many shelves to reach over in here. If you don't see the colors you want, let me know. I can fire up any color scheme you want. Just be careful back there. It's just a temporary rope handrail back there. The Tourism Board doesn't want to put too much money into renovating the pier until they know it's going to pay off. I go back there; you should be okay."

I went around the front of the stall and then edged my way between the two stands. The canvas walls billowed with the wind coming off the river; rope tie-downs strummed with the vibrations of the gusts. I picked my way between the ropes to the edge of the pier. From within my canvas alley, I heard Joanie talking to a new customer. A chaos of colors flashed between the gaps where the canvas side walls were tied together and in the two-foot openings between wall and roof.

There was just a thick braided rope serving as a handrail between the concrete edging of the pier and the river. The sun was coming from the west through the stall; the colors of the glass flashed streaks of light blue, dark blue, hunter green, apple green, pink, fuchsia, lavender, and yellow out across the river. Backing up until I felt the rope railing against my rear-end, I watched the sun break into multicolored prisms of light. I hung my purse around my neck, then stretched to my full height. I was able to unhook one of each color. I couldn't hold them all, so I slipped a few in the side pocket of my bag. Clinging to my remaining selections, I edged my way back to the canvas alley.

I had made it a few steps when I felt movement behind me and bumped into something hard. "Sorry," I said.

Something bumped me again, a firm push in the back of my shoulder, causing me to lose my balance and stumble over a coffee can filled with cement, a tie down weight for one of the canvas flaps. I juggled the glass rectangles but wasn't able to catch them all. Dark green glass bounced off the wooden planks and shattered against the cement filled can. "Hey, excuse me. Somebody's out here." I shouted over the music. The canvas wall moved in the wind, blocking the path up to the pier center. "Excuse me! You're blocking the walkway," I shouted while thinking, *Move, Idiot.*

I was semi-wedged backwards between the two tents, my back to the center of the pier, still clutching an armful of glass window pockets. "Hey! Excuse me here!"

Out of the corner of my eye, I saw someone picking their way toward me. A man in a light-blue seersucker suit, a straw hat pulled down over his face.

"Sorry," I said. "I'm kind of stuck here, can't turn around. Can you back out and I'll follow? Then you can look at the glass and the view across the river."

Instead of agreeing or even just backing up, he came forward. I couldn't see his face under the hat. I could see his arm reach out. "Do you want to take these for me?" I asked. "Then I can untangle my feet from these ropes, and you can come take my place."

He just kept coming and with a hard push against the back of my shoulder threw me completely off balance. "Hey, help" I yelled as I felt myself falling. "Help!" My hip hit the rope barrier. Top heavy with my armload of glass, I teetered on the swinging rope. In slow motion, glass went flying and I fell from the edge of the pier. It was thirty feet down into the cold dark water of the Liberty River.

Choking, I forced my way up to the surface, kicking off my sandals, trying to avoid the barnacle laden pilings. "Help, help" I called, coughing. "Joanie!" But the band playing was rock and roll and the music was at full reverb. "Somebody! Help me!" Dog-paddling to keep head above water, I was still clutching my remaining stained glass with one arm. I reached out for one of the pier pilings, but they were covered with years of barnacles. The shells slashed my hands and arms to strips as I held onto the supports. A cabin cruiser motored by in the river causing a wake; the waves bobbled me in the water, pushing me against the pilings. Barnacles scraped against my back, tearing my linen shirt. The raw cuts stung in the dirty water. Panic set in as I tried to stay upright in the water.

"Help, help!" I yelled again. I floated in the water, wondering how I could get out. To get to the shore side of the dock meant navigating through the maze of underwater pilings, cables and heaven knows what other stuff. Another boat motored by; more back wash caused me to bobble and choke on the waves. Something large and solid hit my hip. I froze in the water. Bull sharks had been known to make it this far upriver. A ten-footer had been caught from this very pier. Manatees were a less feared possibility, but it could be the Altamahaha monster. I grew up on stories of the Altamahaha monster, a relative of the Loch Ness monster who followed the ships bringing the Highland Regiment to Fort Darien in the early seventeen hundreds. It swam in the Liberty and Altamaha Rivers.

"Help," I screamed once more, choking as the cold black water filled my mouth. Another solid bump smacked into my back. I spit out water and took another deep breath. "Help!"

One more thump knocked the air out of my lungs, and the cold water filled them. I felt myself sink to the bottom of the river.

CHAPTER EIGHT
Sapelo Sound Dock, August 1964

B eth Ann looked at the hook on her fishing pole and at the bucket of red crawlers and shuddered.

"What's the matter?" I asked. "You want Daddy to bait your hook?"

Daddy laughed at us. "Ya'll wanted to come up here with me to go fishing. I expect fresh fish and hush puppies for supper tonight. Ya'll can bait your own hooks. Brittan Lee, you know how—you show Beth Ann. Put on those two life jackets before you sit down on the edge of the dock. I'm going up to the house to meet with some men. Ring the bell if you need me." He straightened his long legs and stood up.

Beth Ann scrunched up her face, but still reached into the bucket for a fat wiggly worm. Holding her breath, she threaded coils of worm onto the hook and carried the pole to the edge of the dock.

I grabbed my worm and pole and joined her. "Maybe we'll catch the Altamahaha monster! But I don't think Trulee knows how to cook him." I tossed my line in the water and watched the little red and white bobber float on the ripples of the Knox River. Something caught the hook and pulled the bobber under once, twice, three times. "I got a fish!" I jerked on the line and pulled out the bobber and hook, stripped of the bait. "Got away."

The bucket of worms was behind me. I selected a fat one and threaded it on the hook, then wiped worm guts off my fingers.

"I got one, I got one!" Beth Ann yelled. "Oh, it's a big one." She clung to her pole with both hands, trying to raise the tip up, out of the water.

"Pull it up," I said. I grabbed the middle of the bamboo pole and tried to help her raise it out of the water. "It is big. Maybe you did catch the Monster. He does swim up here sometimes from the Altamaha. Keep pulling." Whatever had her bait had pulled the hook and bobber as far out as it could. Despite my help, Beth Ann's pole was being pulled out across the water, too. She scooted up to the very edge of the dock, leaning out, holding her pole.

"Help me, Brittan Lee. Help me, it's getting away." She leaned even further over the edge of the dock.

Just like in the cartoons, the pole jerked real hard. Beth Ann screamed and fell face first in the river, yelling the whole way down.

"Help! Help me! Brittan Lee! Help!" Beth Ann flailed about in the water, her arms waving around, as she went under the water.

"Swim!" I leaned over the edge and yelled. Grabbing the life jacket off its hook, I threw it over the railing. "Hold on to this!"

The preserver eluded Beth Ann's grasp and floated down the river.

"Help me!" She choked and gagged on the river water as her head bobbed up and down.

I ran back to the head of the dock and jerked the rope on the big iron bell. "Daddy, Daddy, help! Beth Ann's a-drownin'!" I yelled over the sound of the tolling bell just before I ran back down the dock and jumped in the river right next to her. I kicked off my Keds and treaded water while I reached for Beth Ann. I put my arm around her neck to hold her up like Four learned how to do when he was a life guard. Beth Ann didn't seem to want to be saved. She grabbed at my arms and tried to pull me down.

"Kick your legs like this." I tried to show her how to tread water, but she kicked me in the stomach. I got behind her and held her, but she kept kicking me and struggling to get away.

"Help, Daddy, help!" I held tight to Beth Ann, but despite me treading water as hard as I could, we kept sinking in the river. "Dear Jesus, we've been good. Please don't let us die. Please help Daddy find us. Please, Amen."

Whenever my head bobbed up in the air, I yelled for Daddy, whenever Beth Ann pulled us under the water I prayed to Jesus. I just knew one of the two would save us. I was getting tired, because Beth Ann was fighting so hard. She was really afraid of the water. I didn't know how much longer I could keep us both from drowning, but I wouldn't let go of my best friend. River water splashed into my face again. Beth Ann's hair slipped out of her braid and twisted around my face. I let go of her to clear off my face and she turned, clutched at me. I could see her eyes get real big, and hear her choking as we started to sink to the bottom again.

"Hold on, Brittan Lee. Hold on baby. Kick, kick."

I heard familiar voices over my head, muffled by the water. Daddy had come to save me.

CHAPTER NINE
Liberty, Georgia, August 2005

L ady! Hey, lady!" The voice was muddled and indistinct. I opened my eyes and tried to peer through the murky green waters. "Beth Ann?" I called out to her, but choked on the water filling my throat. A large gray body floated in front on me, reaching for me. It wasn't Beth Ann. The Altamahaha monster had come to take me to his den at the bottom of the river. I struggled to get away and slammed into one of the rusted iron cables that connected the pilings. Frozen by the pain, I started to sink again into the gray-green murk.

"Hey, lady! You can't swim from the pier. It's too dangerous," the monster's words rose with the bubbles above his head, his one enormous eye staring at me. He reached for my free arm and pulled me away from the cables and pilings. The silt from the disturbed river bottom settled and the water cleared as he pulled me higher and higher. The bright warmth of the sun broke through the swirls of cold choppy waves.

"Over here! Hey, Bobby, need a little help over here!" My monster called out to another one. "Help me get her to the steps!"

I struggled as the two monsters pulled me through a labyrinth of cables, pipes and posts. They made their way from under the main pier to the side of the river. Old cracked concrete steps, poured into the side of the riverbank, had once led from the riverwalk to a boarding spot for smaller boats and were now my safe haven. Deposited on the bottom step, I choked, coughed and spat slimy green froth onto the rough surface. Water dripped from my clothes. Seaweed wrapped in tendrils around my ankles. I sneezed river water from my sinuses, which burned at the intrusion.

"Shit lady, can't you read? *No Swimming from Piers!*" The monster stood over me, hands on his hips. "There's all kinds of dangerous shit down there. Not to mention the sharks and the alligators!"

I slumped on the step, feeling the rough concrete against my cheek. I curled into a fetal ball, coughing and spitting out the dirty water. "Wasn't swimming," I gasped. My stomach contracted and vomited the contents over the step and into the river.

"Hey, lady, relax. Bobby, go get help," my monster ordered as he knelt and removed his head. "Lady, what happened?"

My eyes burned from the river water, and my vision was blurred. I squinted as I looked up at him. He shrank in size as he removed snorkel, fins and dive tanks. "You're not the Altamahaha? You didn't come to save me?"

He scooped water from the river in his mask and rinsed my vomit from the step. "No, lady, I ain't him, but I seen him oncet or twicet when I was diving. I'm Frankie Skelton. I reckon I did save you, but what the hell was you doing under the pier?"

"I, uh…" I struggled to sit up. "I must have fallen in. I was reaching up for…" I looked around and pointed to the glass in my bag. "Those. They were hanging on a high wire, and I was reaching up for them. I must have lost my balance." Violent muscle spasms made me shake, and I fell back over.

Frankie spit into the river. "Dang stupid, having all them people up there before they finished putting up them rails. Surprised more people ain't fallen in. You sure surprised us, falling right on top of Bobby like that. Made him drop his goody bag. Had to go back after it while I started pulling you in." Frankie pointed to the mesh bag on his hip.

"I'm sorry, I didn't mean to land on your friend. Oh, God," I started coughing again and gagged on the green phlegm.

"He got it back, no problem." Frankie squatted and scooped up some more water to rinse the steps. "We go under the pier about oncet a week. Got underwater metal detectors, but they ain't much use there due to all the pipes and cables and shit. You'd still be surprised at all the shit we find; dumb-ass tourists drop stuff all the time."

"Uh huh," I murmured agreement, too tired to move. "Where else do you dive?"

"Oh, all round. Wherever we think we can find sompthin' worth the time. By the beaches and pier at St. Simons is usually pretty good, 'cept for the sharks. Hell, we just do it to get out of the house. We was over there yesterday." He waved across the river at the construction site. "Usually find some good stuff when them contractors start moving old mud. Some big old shark teeth. Some old coins."

I looked across to the workers. "You were there? Diving?"

"Yeah. Look at this. Still works." Frankie held out a Zippo lighter, engraved with initials and a date. It had a small faded medallion attached above the initials. He flicked the flint-wheel and a flame burst from the top. "Cleaned it up. Put in some fluid. Works just fine. Probably could have found a lot more stuff, but the sheriff run us off. Moved the yellow tape further down. Lady, you feeling better? Maybe we should get you up the steps?" He reached down to take my arm. "Shit, lady! I hope you ain't got any of them blood diseases, 'cause you're bleeding like a stuck pig!"

"No diseases," I said. I pulled myself up to my knees and sat for a minute taking inventory of all the cuts and scrapes. My right hand, the backs of both arms, my shoulders all ached. Blood diluted with river water puddled on the steps. I pulled myself up, clinging to the rebar hand-rail. "I'm with a friend. He might be looking for me. Tall, dark hair, some gray. Blue jacket." I froze with a sudden thought. *No one knew I was here except Agent Zeller. Had I checked his credentials close enough?*

"Yeah, well, that might be him with Bobby," Frankie pointed to the top of the steps.

Bobby and Special Agent Zeller bounded down the stairs, two at a time.

"Dr. Hayworth, what happened? Are you all right?" Andrew Zeller landed next to me and helped me sit back down. I wrapped my arms around myself as I started to shiver.

"She fell in," said Frankie. "We pulled her out."

"Thank you," Zeller said. "Dr. Hayworth, are you all right? We need to get you to a doctor." He looked at the blood running down my back and arms. He shrugged off his coat and put it around me.

I winced at the weight across my cut shoulders, but the warmth helped stop my shakes. Through chattering teeth, I said, "F-f-frankie and B-b-bobby are divers. They were across the river yesterday and today."

Zeller's head shot up. "At the crash site?"

The divers noted the pistol in Zeller's hip holster and were backing down the steps.

"Did you find anything?" Zeller asked.

Bobby and Frankie exchanged glances. "Maybe."

"Could you show me?" Zeller asked. "Please?"

They shrugged, unfastened the D rings and pulled the mesh bags off their belts.

"Lookit the size of them teeth," Bobby bragged as he separated out several three-inch long sharks' teeth, still with sharp serrations. "Them other stuff, ain't had much chance to check it out." He sorted out some nails, a few aluminum pull-tabs, coins, some rusted bits of unidentifiable metal, two faded car tags and a length of chain. "Frankie's got the winner. Like them old TV commercials."

Zeller looked at Frankie. "The TV commercials?"

Frankie pulled out the Zippo and flipped the top. "Guaranteed to keep working. Now I got to find me one of them watches that keep on ticking'. I plan to get in that World Book of Records."

I was staring at the flame from the lighter, but I could feel Zeller's green eyes focused on me.

"You gentlemen find all this over across the river?" Zeller asked, keeping his voice casual.

"Yeah," said Bobby. "We just got over to this side when she fell in. Scared the shit out of me. Thought she was a bull shark."

Zeller looked between the two of them. "You know the sheriff's investigating that girl who was found in the old car?"

"Hell," Bobby answered. "Who don't know that? It ain't like it's no big secret."

"Well," Zeller said, "they don't know who was driving the car. That's why the divers are searching. To find any trace of who else could have been there. You may have important evidence here."

Frankie poked Bobby in the side. "Told you."

"Could I ask you gentlemen to consider turning what you found over to the sheriff or the FBI?" Zeller asked.

Bobby frowned at the agent. "We ain't exactly on good terms with the sheriff," he said as he spit into the river. "Seems he don't approve of all our activities."

"I can make sure he won't be upset," Zeller said. "Or you can just turn it directly in to the Special Agent in Charge of the investigation."

Bobby and Frankie exchanged looks and shrugged. "How can we be sure he won't just pick us up?"

Zeller reached over, opened his jacket and pulled a business card from the inside pocket. Taking a pen from another pocket, he wrote "Amnesty" in large block letters and signed it. "Just give this to the Special Agent." He held out the card.

Bobby reached out and plucked the card from Zeller's grasp. Tucking it into a waterproof pocket, he turned, shrugged on his dive tanks and picked up his mask. "We'll think about it." They took two steps backward and disappeared into the murky river.

When I started to shiver again, Zeller put his arm across my shoulders and tucked my head under his chin. "Now, tell me. How did you fall into the river?"

From the pier, a basso profundo rolled out heavy over the water. *Going down to the River Jordan...John the Baptist baptized me...In the waters of the River Jordan...all my sins be set afree..*

When I could control my chattering teeth, I answered him. "I think someone's trying to kill me again.

CHAPTER TEN
Liberty, Georgia, August 2005

B rittan Lee? Are you all right?" Footsteps clattered on
the concrete steps above us. My back and shoulders
were stiffening up. It hurt to turn and look.

"What in the world? I saw you from the pier and came
over," Mary Frances stopped just behind me. I could hear her
catch her breath. "Oh, my god, you're just sopping wet. You
look like a drowned rabbit. What happened?"

"I fell off the pier," I said. "Agent Zeller is going to take
me home."

"Shouldn't you be going to the hospital? That looks like
a lot of blood? Where are the EMTs?" Mary Frances lifted
the back of Zeller's jacket and looked at my back. "That's
going to get infected if you don't get it cleaned and get some
antibiotics."

"I know. My brother is a doctor here. He'll bring me
something." My teeth started to chatter again.

"She's in shock," Mary Frances announced. "I took a first
aid class."

"So did I," Zeller said. "Dr. Hayworth, can you make it up
the steps? Then I can go get the car?"

I tested my legs and was able to stand up. Leaning heavily
on both Mary Frances and Zeller, I stumbled up the steps. At
the top, I sank onto a bench under the oak trees. "I'm okay.
I'm just really tired." I looked at their anxious faces. "Mary
Frances, can you stay while he gets the car?"

Zeller looked back and forth between us. "Don't let her move. I'll be right back with the car." He loped off in the direction of the parking area.

"How did you fall off? Why didn't Joanie hear you?" Mary Frances said as she searched the jacket. "Here, I knew he probably had one. He looked too classy to have Kleenex." She pulled out a snowy white linen handkerchief and dabbed at the bits of seaweed and river dirt on my face. "So how did you meet him?"

"He met me at the airport," I said before I started coughing again. I bent double holding my sides and ribs. "I hope I didn't break anything. Mama's going to kill me. I should have been home hours ago. Yuck." I had to spit out more green phlegm. "Sorry."

"No problem." Mary Frances wiped my mouth. "So where's the other man? The one who was looking for you up on the pier? Do I need to go look for him, too?"

"What other man?" I asked. "I mean, I have two brothers, but I don't know how they would know I was here instead of Mama's. Unless she called them because I didn't get there. This is confusing. They'd call the courthouse, not send out a search team."

"Well, this one is a lot nicer to look at. And a lot younger." Mary Frances continued to dab at my face. "Do you have a comb in your bag?" she asked. "Maybe I could fix your hair a little. It's short enough that I can just sort of fluff it up as it dries."

"I'll be okay. He's taking me straight to Mama's house." I saw the white car turning into the parking lane and started to gather my legs under me to stand. "Here he comes. Mary Frances, I really appreciate this. I'll have to get that drink some other time. Oh, blast!" I counted the window pockets in the side pouch of my bag. "Please tell Joanie I'm sorry. I didn't pay her for these, and I lost most of them in the river."

"If she didn't notice you falling in, I doubt she noticed you taking glass. She did seem a trifle flustered. Too busy with her gentleman friend. Listen, I've got your Mama's phone number in the Market Directory. She's on the Board of Directors. I'll call later and check on you. Most of us were invited to the cocktail party tomorrow night, so I'll see you then for sure." She bent down and picked up the remaining glass, then turned and opened the car door as Zeller drove up. "Oh, this is going to ruin the upholstery for sure. Do you want me to run up and get a towel or something?" she asked Zeller.

"No, I just want to get her out of here." He helped me up, half carried me to the car and buckled me into the car seat. "Which way to the hospital?" he asked.

The arctic blasts from the air-conditioning made me shiver, and I snuggled even deeper into Zeller's jacket. "I don't need a hospital. I'd have to wait for hours just to be told there's nothing broken. I'm sure Mama still keeps plenty of yellow soap. It'll kill anything from the river, and if it doesn't, Four will give me something. Why are we going this way?"

The east side of town was all marshes edging the South River, then more marshes, then the barrier islands and finally the Atlantic Ocean. Seaview Marina still squatted on the marshes like a spider, spreading out long arms to the motor boats and sailboats moored there.

"My cousin Trey always had a ski boat there." I stuck my arm out from the warmth of the coat to gesture at the marina. "Trey was real good with his hands. He would find old wrecked-up boats and rebuild them, fix up the engines, varnish them real pretty and shiny and then sell them. Then he would buy another one. In the summer, Four and Jack would help him. They did it so they could cruise up and down the river and try to pick up the girls on the docks." I adjusted the air-conditioning vent away from me.

"So, that's the marina Cynthia was referring to? Was she one of the girls?" Zeller had a wicked grin.

"So she says now," I said. "But there were lots of teenagers hanging around the marina."

"So, tell me, what did Mr. Willis mean about people being as mean as they want to be? And why did it take so long for this to come out in the first place?" Zeller kept glancing over at me.

"You probably asked the wrong people," I said.

"I'll show you the records in the office tomorrow; let you see who we have interviewed. I did tell you that your name came up a lot? And I do need to spend time more seriously interviewing you. You can start with why you think someone is trying to kill you now and what did you mean by again?"

I adjusted the air-conditioning setting, then rearranged Zeller's jacket. "You do realize that you're driving in the wrong direction. Mama lives south of here." I looked at him. "It happened when I was nine. This is the very deep South. People had strong beliefs, some of them still do. I think that summer was the first time I ever thought about, ever realized that the black community was treated any differently than the white one. The neighborhoods were physically separated. We went to neighborhood schools, so we never questioned why there were no black children in ours. That summer was when I began to realize. You have to understand Liberty and the South. For me it started with Wednesdays at church or rather sneaking out of church on Wednesdays."

***

Liberty, Georgia, June 1964

Miss Cheryl Darton, the new Children's Music Director, didn't like me or Beth Ann. She never let us sing our solos and was always telling us to behave when we weren't doing anything wrong. She didn't seem to fully appreciate our suggestions for the betterment of the choir, so I bet she was really happy that Beth Ann and I didn't come to practice all that summer. Our parents weren't too happy to find out that piece of information, because they had been dropping us off in front of the church every Wednesday at five. After supper, when everyone had gathered in front of the Fellowship Hall, we would all line up class by class. The youngest group of children would lead off down the hall and turned right into the Children's Room. Beth Ann and I would turn left into the janitor's closet and climb out the window back onto Union Street, free for two hours to explore downtown Liberty.

One mile inland from the Atlantic Ocean, guarded by the barrier islands, past the famous 'Bloody Marshes' where the English repelled the Spanish in 1742, across the Doboy and Sapelo Sounds and up the Altamaha and Liberty Rivers was Liberty. Daddy told me that Liberty was laid out by General Oglethorpe, just like Savannah. Liberty was smaller; we only had five parks and squares, surrounded by the old houses, some of them with the big white columns and porches and some with all the curlicue carved railings. One or two had black wrought iron trim-work, like the picture book from New Orleans. I wanted one of those big old houses so bad I could just taste it. Up in Vidalia, my great-aunt Ione had one of those houses. By the front door, she had a petticoat fireplace with a mirror tilted down for ladies to check their petticoats before leaving the house. In the back of closets were little doors that led to passages wandering all through the house inside the walls. They were rumored to be part of the Underground Railroad. Nobody knew I found those passageways, but I heard what everybody was saying, and I kept notes for my stories.

Mama said that those houses took too much to keep up. We lived in a medium sized brick house on the north side of town, where all the new subdivisions were built after World War II. We were near the hospital and Daddy's office and two blocks from the new elementary school. Liberty Elementary School was across the Old Dixie Coast Highway from the Gulf Station and the Howard Johnson's motel and restaurant. Old duplexes sat on the marsh edge, on an old alley paved with crushed oyster shells and shaded with big oaks and some scrub palmettos. Mama and Daddy lived in one of those duplexes when they first moved to Liberty. That was back when Daddy was setting up his practice and Mama was still teaching. Auntabelle and Uncle Frank lived in one, too. Mama got her new house when Jack was born. She liked her house because it was modern and had a picture window in the living room, but my heart yearned for tall white columns, deep porches, old oak trees and secret passages.

Originally the heart of downtown was the boat docks. Liberty was a deepwater port. Seagulls would swirl in the skies before diving at the shrimp boats and the crabbers, looking for an easy meal. Freighters sounded deep horn blasts as they cruised between the red and green harbor lights. The river made an easy access to the town and its pulp mills. Big downtown stores all had their backs to the riverside alley, ignoring the hustle-bustle of the dock hands unloading the big chests of fat white Georgia shrimp and soft-shelled blue crabs. Whenever Mama and Daddy had a cocktail party for the Medical Association, or when Mama hosted the Garden Club, I would come downtown with Trulee, to buy crab and shrimp straight off the dock.

The stores opened to sidewalks on the west end of Union Street and Reynolds Boulevard. I knew summer was ending when Mama would bring me to buy my new school dresses at Alberta's, the skirts all scratchy and stiff with the crinolines. I hated the crinolines, they made my waist itch. At the shoe store I would get new black patent leather school shoes with the little buckles on the straps. There was a big goose who laid eggs filled with prizes. I always picked a green egg. Sometimes Mama would try on a new hat at MiLady's, little tiny wisps of netting with swirls of feathers, big straw sunhats with the stiff brims and the long ribbons that tied under her chin, squatty velvet pillboxes in red or royal blue. Mama and I would walk the four blocks of downtown, both sides of the street, and then I would have a special treat, Mr. Willis's cold Co-cola with cherry syrup and lots of ice at the luncheon counter of Woolworth's.

It was towards downtown and the promise of icy Co-cola on a hot humid Georgia evening that Beth Ann and I headed as we crawled out the little janitor's closet that first Wednesday night. Six in the evening was still fairly bright light in early June. We were confident we could find our way to Woolworth's. Clinging next to the walls, we crept past the main church building, then skittered across the street to hide in the giant hydrangea bushes that lined the sidewalk in front of the old Keister house. We had perfected our skulking undercover technique from watching Barney Fife on television, and not doing what he did. He was always trying to be a detective but didn't do a very good job. Sheriff Taylor had to rescue him every episode.

Big fan leaves hid us as we checked the street for traffic. We moved from bush to bush, skirting the big corner lot.

"I think the coast is clear," Beth Ann whispered. We crawled out from the dark green hideaway, smoothed our skirts, tugging on the itchy crinolines, and sauntered down the sidewalk to meet our destiny.

"Which way now?" Beth Ann asked. We had come out of the bushes opposite the street sign announcing *Court House Square.* At the opposite end of the big grassy lot, at the highest point in the original town of Liberty, stood the Courthouse. Tall and imposing, with a tower even taller than the steeple at church, the courthouse was built of old English brick. A large clock chimed off the hours and half hours, and every evening at eight the carillon would play old classical hymns, bringing the day to a close. Bordering the square were the remains of the historical outer walls. Daddy said the walls fortified the grounds from the Indians and the Spanish. If they attacked, the Courthouse bells would ring and everyone would run for safety to the Square.

Daddy said that the bricks used in building the courthouse were brought over from Ireland and England as ballast in some of the big sailing ships. Those same ships brought rum from the islands and took Sea Island cotton back to Liverpool. He would whisper to me *and the slaves they smuggled from Africa. That was bad business,* he would say and shake his head. "General Oglethorpe didn't allow slavery in Georgia. It was one of the first rules along with no rum and no lawyers. But those rules didn't last very long."

"Is it that way," Beth Ann pointed, "or that way?" She pointed down the other street. Both directions would take us down long, cracked sidewalks. Big, ancient live oaks, draped with Spanish moss, formed a guardian line, protecting the entry to the Square. The biggest, oldest tree in the Square was the Liberty Oak. Huge limbs of the tree reached out, clutched the soil under it for strength and started back up to the skies again. It took eight children holding hands to reach all the way around the worn, cracked, silvery trunk of the tree. Members of the Liberty Garden Club grew saplings from the acorns of the mother tree. Most of the older houses boasted descendants of the Liberty Oak in their own yards. Like many other generations, I had grown up playing in the dense shade of the Liberty Oak, climbing up her wonderful arms to incredible heights, looking down through the canopy of leaves to the people far below. My older brothers, Four and Jack, had shown me the right stubs and rough spots to use to climb all the way to the top, even though girls weren't supposed to climb trees. Under the Liberty Oak was the designated meeting place for teenagers sneaking out for a wild night as well as for the elderly men, sitting at the picnic tables to play checkers and swap stories.

"Every Georgia town has its own version of the Liberty Oak," Daddy said. "Most everyone in Liberty grew up under the Liberty Oak 'til they started building on the north side of town. Now the oak and the Courthouse Square Park are drive-bys, not walk-tos." The name came from the site where General Oglethorpe signed a treaty with Mary Musgrove, giving the land for the new colony.

I liked it when Daddy would stop and read the Georgia Historical Commission sign about the Liberty Oak. We went to Waycross once. Ware County liked to brag they had the oldest oak tree in Georgia, but they were wrong. The minute I saw it I knew it was no Liberty Oak.

Beth Ann tapped her foot and gave me that sour lemon look she always gives me when I tried to further her edification of Liberty County.

"Which way?"

"This way," I announced, and we turned left, heading around the Courthouse Square. "Listen? You hear that?"

Beth Ann stood still and listened, cocking her head in each direction. "I don't hear anything but those kids, playing over there." She looked over at the swing set in the corner of the grassy lawn. "That what you mean?"

"Never mind," I started back down the sidewalk. "I thought I heard somebody calling out or singing. Let's go. I sure am thirsty."

Getting downtown was a lot further than we thought. We hiked down six long blocks of old houses, gradually turning to small businesses before we turned onto Reynolds Boulevard. Blue sky darkened to deep violet streaked with orange and rose. Streetlights began to flicker on, spilling puddles of yellow on the sidewalks. The long frontage of stores—Woolworth's, Alberta's, Montage Books—was dark, blocking the last golden rays of the sun. No lights spilled from the big display windows, no doors propped open to invite us in. The only sounds were the chirping of the tree frogs in harmony with the crickets, occasionally punctuated by a voice from the docks. The streets were empty, with only a car parked along the sidewalks. Every so often an old Chevy or Ford would make a long slow sweep of Reynolds before turning onto Union.

"Brittan Lee, they're all closed! We can't get our Co-cola," Beth Ann pouted. I pout better, but she was right. We were hot, sticky and thirsty. And alone. In the almost dark of that southern June evening.

"We need to go back," I said, reaching for her hand. "Come on, quick. There's some lemonade or some cherry Kool-Aid at the church." I wasn't afraid of the dark. I just didn't think Daddy would want us to be out alone. We hurried back down the same sidewalks we had just come, but now our footsteps sounded loud in our ears. We lifted our feet to avoid scuffing them on the pavement just as we tried to step over the cracks.

"Over here, under the bushes," I yanked Beth Ann just as the headlights of a car skimmed where we had been standing.

"Who is it? Are they looking for us?"

"I don't think so. I don't know, but it makes me nervous. Come on." Crouched over, we stayed under the bushes, picking our way, and avoiding the puddles of light cast by the street lamps. And holding our breath most of the way until we were back at Courthouse Square.

"Whew! What do you think you were doing, dragging me through the bushes like that, Brittan Lee? I must be a sight. Mama's going to kill me." Mrs. Verna Hamilton would, too. She was real strict, a foot-washing fundamental Pentecostal Baptist, who had only strayed from the fold once. That was when she married Mr. Hamilton. He was a Yankee from Chicago. They met when she was on a shopping trip to Atlanta and he was visiting friends. They eloped five days later. I thought that was so romantic. He moved down to Liberty to be with her because Miss Verna would never move to Chicago. Beth Ann said he was a Presbyterian, but since we didn't have a Presbyterian church in Liberty, he attended the First Baptist. He made Miss Verna send Beth Ann there, too. Miss Verna went to the Old Grace River Fundamental Independent Baptist Church with her parents, brothers and sisters. None of them cared too much for Mr. Hamilton, but I thought he was real nice. Sometimes on Sunday afternoons, he would give Beth Ann fifty cents and let her go to the Ritz Theatre with me to see the movies. I heard him tell Miss Verna that we were at a talk being given by missionaries from darkest Africa. Actually, we were watching *Tarzan of the Apes*. I guess it was close to the same thing.

"We'll clean you up good," I promised as I started picking the leaves out of her French braids. "You can tell her we were playing hide and seek in the church yard."

"And you think she'll approve of that? Mama don't like anything that's fun. Sometimes I think she's going to make me stop piano and choir just because I like it." Beth Ann sniffed, and I knew the tears were going to start.

"Now stop that," I scolded. "Your daddy isn't going to let that happen."

"He and Mama have been doing a lot of fussing after I go to bed. I'm real worried about them. She can get real mad, and she gets this funny look on her face and she just hollers at him. He just gets quieter and quieter, and he goes back to his office downtown. I even think he's been sleeping down there when she's on a real tear."

My hand froze as I tried to retie one of the blue bows on Beth Ann's braid. I didn't want to think about choir practice if Beth Ann wasn't going to be there. I looked over my shoulder. "Did you hear that? Quick, up the tree!" Beth Ann reached up for one of the thick branches, and I put my shoulder to her bottom and pushed. When she was up, safe and secure, I climbed up behind her, and we clambered even higher until we were swaying in the river breeze.

"What did you hear?"

"It's a car coming this way. Look down there."

An old red Chevy truck was heading slowly down Church Street, coming right toward us. It pulled over to the side of the road, and the driver got out. A man, a little bit older than Daddy, dressed in rough work clothes walked over to one of the picnic tables under the tree. There was a faint "scratch" sound, and clouds of pungent cigar smoke drifted up into the tree.

"Uh," Beth Ann tried to hold her nose. "Why are we hiding from him?"

"Shh. I don't know why. At least the smoke's good for the mosquitoes."

"Hey, Leroy!" The man seated below us called out as another figure emerged from the dark of the trees.

"Earl," the second man nodded. "How's it going?"

I knew that man. I had delivered papers to him the week before for Uncle Frank. I could see his dirty laundry, white sheets and towels just tossed into the back of the truck, probably going to the Fluff and Fold. He must not be married, or his wife would just kill him for getting those sheets even dirtier.

"Quiet. Ain't seen none of 'em out. They know they better stay offen them streets and down in the Quarters. You seen any?"

"Nah, but I'm ready if I do." He patted his pocket. They sat at the table, smoking those stinky cigars and spitting on the ground. "Hear tell Merle and Bobby-Ray found a couple of 'em the other night. Heh, heh, heh. Them boys ain't gonna go out at night any time soon. They ain't gonna be doing much of anything for a while." The men talked a while longer, but I couldn't hear everything they said, just bits and pieces. Headlights grazed over them as other cars drove past, the horn honking, and an extended arm waving. They would gesture back at the driver. Over the humming of the engines another sound, a faint but a steady drumbeat echoed over the tops of the trees. I listened, trying to pick out the words.

Moses, Moses don't you let King Pharaoh overtake you, Moses, Moses don't you let King Pharaoh overtake you...

"Damn that noise. Like to make my skin crawl," Leroy stood up. "You think they really can talk with those drums?"

"Hell, I dunno. You'd think the telephone be easier. What 'chu hear tell of them coming down from New York, meeting up in Jacksonville? Heard they was going to Brunswick, Waycross, trying to make trouble, talking about rights?" the other man threw down his cigar. "I'll show them 'rights,' right here right now."

"Yeah, I heard about them. Hear we're gonna have another meeting' about all that soon, too. Meantime we just keep on with patrolling. Who you think..." I couldn't hear the rest over the crickets and the tree frogs.

"He better watch hisself, don't matter none if he is white, you just don't do..."

"...later, Leroy. Still got a couple of hours of huntin'..."

High in the tree top, we stayed quiet until we saw both trucks leave.

"What do you think they're hunting?" asked Beth Ann.

My jaws clenched to prevent my teeth from chattering. I clung tight to the rough bark of the trunk as the tree shook and shuddered. Then I realized it wasn't the tree shaking, it was me. Surely somewhere someone was walking across my grave, as Trulee would say.

"Daddy says it ain't legal to hunt in the city."

Across the treetops, the drum beat started again.

Moses, Moses, don't you let King Pharaoh overtake you,...
Moses, Moses, don't you let King Pharaoh overtake you...Moses,
Moses...

***

Liberty, Georgia, August 2005

Zeller looked at me. "Could you identify these men now?"

I pulled his jacket a bit closer and reached out to dial down the air-conditioner. "I'd seen them when I did my driving around with Uncle Frank. Most of them didn't live in Liberty proper. They were from out in the county or west in Long County. Daddy always said the problems came from people who didn't live in Liberty. He said they couldn't protest where they live or their own neighbors would know. " I looked out the window and turned back to Zeller in surprise. "You're still going the wrong way! Mama lives south, on the Island."

"Those aren't the directions I was given," Zeller denied. He pulled a folded sheet of paper from above the sun visor and shook it open. *Main Street to Highway Seventeen. Four miles from downtown. Turn right on Moss Side Drive. Follow the curve to the left. Second house on right.* See, I'm following the directions exactly."

"Sounds more like the directions to Four's house. He lives in Marsh Pointe. You turn on Moss Side to get there. Did Mama tell you to take me to Four's? Oh...oh..achchoo!" I pulled out Zeller's handkerchief and blew my nose. "Sorry, my sinuses are still fighting their soaking. Tell me if this is too much information, but when I was little, I was allergic to everything. I sneezed from the first flowers of spring until the last dead leaves of fall. I went through one of those big size bottles of Novahistine every day. Tasted like sweet liquid ground up pine needles, but it worked. I'm surprised I didn't end up an alcoholic at nine. That stuff was about a thousand proof. Maybe Mama is trying to trick me into staying in Liberty?"

"Why would she need to trick you? Your whole family lives here. Wouldn't it be smarter to stay with them? I know it's a lot more convenient for me." Zeller gave me one of his long, introspective gazes. "Why would you stay on the island with your mother and not here in Liberty?"

"I don't tarry when I visit in Liberty. I stay with Mama on the Island, and I travel in to see Trulee and Tansie and the boys. Back in the eighties I worked with Tansie in formally organizing the Liberty Shouters. I spent a lot of time here when I was in graduate school, doing my fieldwork. But I don't stay in Liberty." I opened my bag and looked for my comb and a lipstick. "If you spent any time with Mama, you know she can be a little manipulative. She's probably going to try her trump card. She wants me to move to Liberty. She assures me it is safe now, but I don't know that she believed me when I was nine. Her plan is working. I am feeling guilty, and moving home would be nice, if I wasn't still scared to live here."

Zeller glanced at his sheet of directions and turned right at the alley where the gas station used to be. He drove to the end of the alley, turned left at the oyster shell lane and parked in front of the second house. "Brittan Lee, why are you scared to live here? Why do you think someone is trying to kill you?"

I pulled his jacket closer and caught a whiff of his aftershave. "Because they tried once before. *They got the wrong damn kid*," I said. The words came out of their own volition, from a place I had sequestered in my mind.

"Say what?" he said, startled.

Repeating the words now created the same feelings of apprehension they always did. My hair prickled at the back of my neck, where my braid used to sit. My stomach tightened in knots. My legs started to tremble. "Uncle Frank said that. He didn't know I saw him. The other men had locked me in the old courthouse jail building with Ebon. It was used as a garden maintenance shed. The man in the red truck said '*You told us the blonde girl with braids. We got the blonde with braids.*' I shivered and swallowed to keep from throwing up again. "I hear his voice at night, when the lights are out and I am all alone. His voice is why I always have a nightlight and why I never sleep in Liberty. Uncle Frank said *'Well, you got the wrong blonde girl with braids. Everybody's looking for Beth Ann Hamilton. Brittan Lee Hayworth is the one you was supposed to get. You got the wrong damn kid.'"*

CHAPTER ELEVEN
Liberty, Georgia, August, 2005

Zeller didn't maintain the studied professional pose of a federal agent. He stared, slack-jawed, then stuttered, "That's not in, I mean, why didn't...What?"

"Really, Agent Zeller," I leaned back against the seat, suddenly too tired to hold myself erect. "You didn't expect them to include the ramblings and accusations of an over-excited, emotional nine-year-old in any official reports, did you? Especially when there were over a dozen adult white men ready to swear I was just crazy with guilt and grief. That my daddy died looking for me. No one believed me. Or I should say no white person admitted they believed me, and no black people were interviewed. Dr. Stevens and Dr. Wensley told Mama that it was the stress, that I must have hidden in the shed to prevent Ebon from attacking me. They told Mama to keep telling me it was just a bad dream. Mama must have believed some of what I said; she never spoke to Uncle Frank again. The first time she spoke to Auntabelle again was at his funeral fifteen years ago." Tears blurred my vision and rolled down my face. I wiped them away and dried my hands on Zeller's jacket. "I waited and waited for Beth Ann. Stood there under the Liberty Oak; it was pouring rain. Probably not the best place to stay when it was lightning, but it kept us a little bit drier. Ebon stayed with me; I couldn't make him leave. Beth Ann didn't come. The men came and they beat up Ebon real bad, and they locked us up in the shed. Uncle Frank thought it was Beth Ann in the shed and that I died in the fire, until I turned up alive."

Zeller didn't move, but I could see the different emotions flicker across his face.

I slumped in my seat. "You don't have to believe me. No one else ever has." I turned away from him and stared out the window. "Can you please just take me home?"

The car didn't move. I stared out the window. This was the alley of the old dingy duplexes. They must have been torn down and replaced with these houses. Even in my current emotional state, I admired the work of the architect; the houses looked as if they had always stood here under the big oaks. I studied them more closely. These were the old duplexes. The classic original lines had been enhanced. New roof lines lifted up an extra half story. Screened half porches were now full terraces with a columned porte-cochere to the side of the house. The landscaping had been done with native plants. Through a side yard I could see back to the marshes.

There were people out on the back terrace. The tinkling of glasses, the sounds of voices drifted around from the back, perhaps a cocktail party or even a shrimp boil. I wouldn't be invited. I didn't have any friends in Liberty, just acquaintances and family. "Zeller," I asked, "Can we please go now?"

With a heavy voice Zeller answered "We're here. These are the directions I was given."

"I don't understand," I wiped my eyes and reached for the paper.

"Peanut!" My car door opened, and I almost fell out. "Holy balls of fire, girl! What in the world happened to you?" My brother Jack caught me as I tilted and helped me climb from the car. "Did you get caught in that big storm?"

Zeller's jacket slipped off my shoulders as I reached up to hug Jack. "Not exactly. I was in the river."

"How in the hell…?" Jack caught Zeller's jacket mid slide. "You're still sopping wet! Mama!" he yelled. "Trulee! Better start running a hot bath now. I think Brittan Lee's turned Baptist again. One dunking wasn't enough. Heck, I could have told Reverend Brown that." He started to laugh until he saw the blood on the lining of the jacket. He looked at the lining, then at me. "Where's the blood from? Come on; let's get you in the house." He looked across the car at Zeller. "Can you bring in her bags please?"

"Blood? What blood? Jack, what's going on?" Mama bustled out to the car. People just kept piling out of the house, knee-deep to the door. Mama must have brought the whole family over to visit. "Oh, my baby! What happened?" She stood on her tiptoes and gave me air kisses on each cheek.

Zeller opened the trunk and unloaded my luggage. "She fell off the pier. I wanted to get her to the hospital, but she wouldn't go."

Everyone gathered in a mass huddle around the car. Various grandchildren had followed Mama out to the car. I felt safe. I was surrounded by family.

"Come along everyone, let's get Brittan Lee inside and into a hot bath," Mama said. "Jax, get the luggage. Leigh, get your aunt some tea. Madison, go ask Trulee for some yellow soap. Quince, call your daddy." Mama, the drill sergeant, slowed down for a minute when she saw Quince was already punching in buttons on his cell phone. "Come on, now. Agent Zeller, thank you for bringing Brittan Lee home, but the next time, can you keep her out of the river?"

Mama broke the tension. Everyone relaxed and headed off to do her tasking. Mama looked more closely at my back and arms. Her eyes filled with tears as she held my scraped hands. "Oh, baby. How in the world?" She exchanged worried glances with Jack.

We had reached the steps to the house. Six steps up from the ground to meet hurricane code. Azaleas filled the border around the house, partially hiding the lattice work between the house and the ground. Mama and Jack helped me up the steps, across the broad porch to the front door. Jack opened the wide screen door and stepped in.

"Mama, who owns this house? I can't just go bathe in some stranger's house. I need to go home or to Jack's or Four's," I said. I was starting to hurt. The initial shock was over, and I could feel the bruises where I had slammed into the posts and the scrapes from rusted cables. I followed Jack into the wide front hallway. In the large sunny living room on the left was a black Steinway grand piano. My piano. "Mama, what?" I turned to her.

"Welcome home, honey! This is our house!" Mama beamed through her worry. "I bought the duplexes. The contractors made each set of them into a single house."

"But Mama, the cottage on Sea Island?" I walked over to the piano. After checking a finger for blood, I sounded a note.

"Had it tuned three days ago, missy," Mama sounded a bit more normal. "I got everything moved over last week. It's part of the renovation of Liberty. This house is more the size I need. The cottage was getting too big. And I'm getting too old to drive forty minutes to see my family and friends."

"Mama, it's beautiful." It was. The old heart pine floors shone. The tall French doors stood open to the breeze off of the marshes. The bead-board wood work and moldings were on display once more, no longer hidden by fake paneling and shag carpet.

Mama beamed. "We're having a party tomorrow night: a house-warming. But come on, let's get you into a hot tub." She led the way to what I assumed was the new master bedroom. At the back of the house, more French doors opened from the bedroom to a large back terrace overlooking the marshes. She went into the bathroom to start running a bath. Jack joined me as I looked over the pale green and tan grasses swaying in the off-ocean breeze.

"Can you figure out where your fort was?" I asked him.

"No. I've looked, but it's been lost to too many storm tides. My kids looked; they finally made their own." Jack put his arms lightly around my shoulders. "What happened?"

"Someone pushed me in. I was behind a booth looking at some things hanging up high. Somebody came back there and pushed me in when I was off balance and had my arms full," I started to shake again. "I couldn't see; the sun was in my eyes. He was tall, had on a hat. Never said anything."

"No way it was an accident?" he asked.

I shook my head. "I don't know. I thought maybe the sun was in his eyes and he just bumped into me, but the sun was in my eyes, not his. If it was an accident, why didn't he call for help?" I still looked out over the marsh as I changed the subject. "Jack, you still haven't ever told anyone?"

I heard him let out a heavy sigh at the change of subject. "No. Never thought I would let a bossy nine-year-old tell me what to do, but you were right. Didn't think it would do any good. By the time I got back into town, they had their minds made up. But if I had, then they wouldn't have stopped until they caught him. That would put a lot a lot of people at risk. I got him up to Dorchester; Gus got him on the Railroad. Took me another day to get back to you. I was scared to hell you were dead."

"I almost was. Don't know why they left me, let me live." The little hard knot in my chest tightened and I stiffened in the doorframe. "I still have nightmares about it. I'm not sure what I really saw and what part my subconscious filled in. My therapist says it isn't important. It's over, and I just have to accept that it wasn't my fault."

"Brittan Lee, I'm sorry. Probably I shouldn't have listened to you, and I should have told everyone." He hesitated. "I was afraid Trey was involved. I was pretty sure Uncle Frank was, I mean, you saw him right in the middle of things. I didn't know about Trey. He was moody all that summer."

"Was he? Involved, I mean?" I asked.

"He never talked about it. Ever. Went off to college, came back, goes to work. Built him a house up at Sapelo Sound. Mama tries to keep him coming to family stuff, but he doesn't usually. Even after Mama and Auntabelle started speaking again, Trey keeps to himself. Barely even stays for Christmas dinner. Never married so Auntabelle doesn't have any grandchildren to dote on like Mama does. In fact, Mama is going to have a great-grandbaby. That's her other surprise. Vickie is pregnant, due around Christmas. Won't that be a wonderful present? They didn't tell anyone until the three months passed because of her history."

My niece-in-law had suffered three miscarriages in two years. "Seems like it was just last week I played at their wedding."

"I know, but it was four years ago. They thought the time was right. Michael's doing good at the firm, and she's still teaching. Plans to take off the winter and spring quarters, then back to teaching. I think I'm too dang young to be a grandfather."

"We'll have to think up some horrible grampy style nickname for you."

I looked at the children gathering on the terrace. It's hard to believe time has moved on with such determination. Jack's oldest, Jackson the Third, Jax for family was almost thirty, his youngest, my namesake Leigh was twenty-three. I had lost so much time from their lives with my self-imposed exile.

"I think we might need to tell now," I said.

He gave my shoulders a squeeze. We stood there and looked at the evening clouds moving over the island, at the family gathering on the terrace. I felt the knot in my chest loosening.

"I'm glad you're back, baby sister. The girls need you, especially Leigh."

"Why?" I started to ask when I heard yelling from the hallway.

"Brittan Lee!"

Four charged into the room. "What in the hell happened? Mama said you fell in the river and hurt yourself. Let me see that back!" He pulled me inside the room and cut the ripped linen shirt off my back with bandage scissors.

"Four!" I tried to cover myself.

"Nothing I haven't seen before. Jack either. We used to change your diaper when you were a baby." He plucked little threads of torn linen from the cuts in my back. "Hold still."

I fidgeted as it stung. "I'm not a baby anymore, and you never changed my diapers. I asked Mama about that the last time you tried to tell that story. What are you doing?"

"Using a magnet to pull out any pieces of metal I can." He finished with his magic wand and started to rub a lotion on my back. "Okay, go get in the tub. Scrub with that yellow soap of Mama's. Have Mama scrub your back good. I put a local anesthetic on your back, so it won't hurt when she scrubs. I've got some antibiotic cream to put on after your bath. I'm going to get you a tetanus shot and some antibiotics. No telling what's in that river water." He pushed me towards the bathroom.

Just before the door closed, I called out, "No penicillin. I'm allergic to penicillin."

"No, you're not," he hollered back.

"Daddy said so. It's all over my medical charts," I said as I settled into the big tub full of magnolia scented bubbles. Daddy was always right.

CHAPTER TWELVE
Liberty, Georgia, August 2005

Ididn't need Mama for my back. She had one of those loofas on a ribbon, so I just flossed the thing up and down. Hurt like fire, too. I couldn't decide whether it hurt more to lie back down in the bubble-bath or try to get out and dry myself.

"Need help?" Leigh startled my internal debate.

"Ahh!" Startled, I slid halfway down the tub, submerged to my nose. "Just trying to catch my breath again. What's everybody doing? What was all that shouting?"

Leigh sat down on Mama's green velvet boudoir bench, her shoulders slumped but rigid at the same time. "That would be Morgan screaming at Jax. She's a little tense, and she left with her new boyfriend. She's on the outs with Uncle Four. Well, not so much Uncle, but his new girlfriend, Desiree. Everybody else is mostly sitting out on the terrace. Daddy's talking to your FBI agent. "

Leigh looked thinner to me.

I pulled the drain in the tub. "He's not my agent, he's an agent. Hand me one of those towels, please. Have I met Desiree?" I asked as Leigh enveloped me in one of Mama's big bath sheets.

"No, it's Des-ser-ay." Leigh said. "Think of it as the tongue sighing over the syllables. That's how she says to say it, anyway. Uncle met her when he was at Disney World last week, when all the doctors were there for a medical conference excuse for a golf tournament. I'm sure glad nobody in Liberty got sick that weekend." Leigh tossed her head back and flipped her hair over her shoulder. "She's a star."

"She's Mickey Mouse?" I asked, confused, trying to follow Leigh's line of reasoning.

"No, she's a star," Leigh repeated the head toss-hair flip maneuver. "She convinced Uncle she was the star in one of those shows in Orlando. Not at Disneyland though. She probably put on a show in her garage, like Mickey Rooney and Shirley Temple."

"I didn't think you knew about those old movies. So why is Morgan upset with her?" In the bedroom someone had put out one of those hostess gown things for me to put on. Leigh helped me slip my arms into the sleeves.

"She thinks Desiree wants to marry Uncle."

"Well, that's a given. Every woman I know wants to marry Four, always have. He's quite a catch. He doesn't have the best track record for marriages, but that hasn't stopped any of them yet." I motioned for Leigh to towel dry my hair. I watched her in the mirror. She had lost too much weight, the bones in her face were pronounced, and her eyes seemed lost in the dark circles.

"Yeah, I bet Uncle was quite the frathlete in college."

"The what? Is there some specific problem with Desiree?"

"Other than her age? She admits to thirty. That's Quince's age. But, she, well, you'll just have to meet her. She reminds me of that woman in the Haley Mills movie about identical twins. What's that word, um?" Leigh ran a comb through my short hair.

"Socialite?" I asked.

"No, that's too nice. Um, gold-digger! No, she is more like that gold-digger's gold-digging mother.It's just something about her that doesn't strike me as quite right. But Uncle's in love," she drew the word out into four syllables. "He thinks she's beautiful. I'll give her pretty—and most of that is the make-up. But he thinks she is so sweet and so lovely and so charming. Gimme a break, she's in show business, she's a star, a diva." Leigh did the head-toss again. "She knows how to act sweet and lovely and charming. The only charms she really has are the ones on that bracelet she's always jingling around. I just feel bad for Morgan and Madison and Quince. I don't know. She claims to be from old Alabama money. I didn't think there was any old Alabama money. She sure doesn't mind letting Uncle Four pay for everything." She ran her fingers through my hair. "Romance is all over the place. Even Uncle Trey has a lady friend. Or at least a lady I've seen him out with a couple of times. I didn't know he could say more than three words at a time. How do you suppose they communicate?"

"The language of love has no boundaries," I said. "Speaking of love, sweetie, how's your young man? Will he be coming down?"

Her fingers tightened on my head and the corners of her mouth twitched. "Oops, sorry. Uh, no, he's sort of busy. Grandmama's calling. Put on some mascara and come on out. Coming, Grandmamma," she said as she left the room.

I hadn't heard Mama calling. I followed the sounds of other voices to the terrace door and stood there for a few minutes listening to my family. This was part of what I missed up in Illinois, just listening to family talk and laugh and just be with each other.

Mama did a good job with her terrace. A swing hung

from a stand that flowed with wisteria. Wisteria and magnolias blossomed on the seat cushions of the wrought iron patio chairs, which made up a seating group. A large table sat at least ten while another table held six. Mosquito pots and citronella Tiki torches kept the flying pests at bay. An outdoor kitchen had been built under one of the old oaks, with a barbecue grill and a big fish pot. I could see the flicker of the gas flame under the pot and smell the spices of a shrimp boil.

Jack had appropriated the swing and was pushing himself back and forth. Mama and Agent Zeller were sitting on either side of a small glass-topped table. Trulee sat beside Mama. The younger generation was watching the shrimp pot boiling over the fire.

Mama looked at Zeller. "When do you think the dredging will be finished? There's a big storm moving over in a few days. Have they actually found anything useful yet?"

Zeller looked up from his conversation with Jack. "Can't speak to what they've found, ma'am. I need to go and check on that myself. Are you and Brittan Lee psychic? She told me the same thing about weather."

"We coastal people learn to read the signs," Mama said. "Whether the seagulls are flying inland. What the air smells like. Where the wind is coming from. Signs like that."

Jack started laughing so hard he had to put down his beer. "Mama, you grew up in Peach County. That is nowhere near the coast." He turned to Agent Zeller. "Mama has a weather radio always on. Her TV is preprogrammed to the Weather Channel, the Food Channel or the Gardening Channel."

"It must run in the family," Zeller muttered before he, too, started laughing. "They both tell tall tales with perfectly straight faces."

Jack sat back. "What kind of tales did Brittan Lee tell you?"

"Well, she told me about getting in trouble at Wednesday night at church. Then there was the one about Mr. Willis, from the Woolworth's. She said his brother was lynched, and he was beaten badly as a young boy. And when we pulled up, she was talking about being blamed for her father's death," said Zeller.

"She, uh," Jack hesitated, then looked at Mama. "She wasn't making that up. Those things did happen. And a lot more."

"Jack!" Mama looked at him.

"Mama, I told Brittan Lee that I would tell Andy everything. I wasn't here that night, but I had, er, contacts. And I was here off and on all summer."

"Well then, old buddy, you and I need to talk about why you didn't tell me any of this." Zeller picked up his glass then realized it was empty and put it back on the table. "No one has told us anything about civil unrest and problems in the community until Brittan Lee did. Everybody said everything was just copasetic and peachy in Liberty, Georgia. Mrs. Walden, tell me a little more about Brittan Lee and Beth Ann. How long were they friends?"

Mama was watching the interplay between the two men. "Well, first thing, you can just call me Miss Belle like everyone else does. The girls had known each other all their lives. Leigh, honey, can you do me a favor and get the pitcher of iced tea from the kitchen. Agent Zeller, please feel free to have a beer or some wine or something stronger if you prefer. It won't bother me a bit. I'm not that strict a Baptist. All my children keep their favorite beverages here." She glanced at Jack. "What's going on with Leigh? That child's been shaking like a leaf since she got here and always looking over her shoulder."

"I don't know, Mama. She isn't talking to me about it. I'm hoping her favorite aunt will spend some time with her." Jack looked over at the terrace door and nodded at me with a raised eyebrow.

"Thanks, but tea is just fine. Technically I'm still on duty," Zeller said. "Tell me a little more about the girls, please. How is it Brittan Lee and Beth Ann were even out at night."

Jack settled into the swing. "Those girls were into everything that summer. Brittan Lee mostly, but Beth Ann joined her whenever she could. I think Daddy knew about it. I heard him talking once to the Deacon at the Liberty AME."

Mama gave Jack a stern glance. "You're going to make Agent Zeller think we were bad parents."

"Oh no," Zeller said. "I would never think that. And please, call me Andrew or Andy."

Trulee spoke for the first time. "The Deacon promised Marsh that he would watch out for the girls. At the time, Marsh thought it would be good for Brittan Lee to see how the colored children were treated. The Deacon was all torn up over what happened. It liked to have killed him, too, the grieving. He raised Ebon after his parents died."

Mama patted Trulee on the hand, then took a sip of her tea. "Marsh would never have blamed the Deacon, no matter what." Her chin trembled just a little. "Well, it all started on the day they were born."

"They were born on the same day?"

"Oh, yes. On the same day. At the same hospital. Minutes apart. Marsh was Verna Hamilton's doctor. Beth Ann was her only baby, and Verna was an older mother. High risk. She was in labor, and Marsh spent the day at the hospital. When he was in the delivery room, I was admitted in labor, too. I stayed home waiting for Marsh, but finally had Trulee drive me to the hospital."

"I thought I just might have to bring that baby into the world myself," Trulee interjected. "It took all the talking I could do to get her to go to the hospital."

Mama laughed. "Marsh delivered Beth Ann, and Bruce Wensley delivered Brittan Lee. Then the mix-up happened." She paused for the dramatic effect. This was one of her favorite stories. "Marsh carried Beth Ann into the nursery. All the nurses thought she was such a pretty baby, all blond hair, blue eyes and long delicate fingers." She paused again. "They thought she was my baby. A few minutes later, Bruce came in with the real Brittan Lee. It must have torn him up, Zora not being able to have any babies and all. Anyway, Brittan Lee had blond hair, blue eyes and long fingers. She and Beth Ann could have been twins." She thought about it and started laughing. "It took the nurses all day before they realized Beth Ann and Brittan Lee had gotten mixed up. It wasn't until the night shift took them out to be fed that the nurses bothered to check their little foot bracelets. I had been holding Beth Ann and Verna Hamilton had been holding Brittan Lee all evening. Those girls kept people confused the rest of their life." Mama shook her head. "They were the same size. They had the same color hair. Their eyes both changed to green from the baby blue. The teachers were always getting them mixed up." She laughed.

Jack added. "That's a true story. Daddy used it as an example of why you should always check a patient's arm band. I heard him tell Four, when Four was fussing about scut work in medical school."

"He did indeed," Four boomed from behind me.

I shrieked and grabbed the door frame. "Blast it, Four! You need to say something when you're standing behind somebody."

"I did say something," he said. He held up a paper bag. "Get yourself something to drink, girl, I've brung the miracle drugs."

"No penicillin!" I said as I walked over to the kitchen.

"Brittan Lee, why do you have to argue with me about this? If I remember correctly, your doctorate ain't the kind that helps people get well," he hollered at me.

When I came out to the terrace, Four had settled into a chair on the other side of the swing. He opened the bag and dumped the pill bottles on the table. "Antibiotics. Tetracycline, take one every six hours on an empty stomach," he looked at me and grinned. "Don't have unprotected sex; tetracycline can have a bad effect on birth control pills," he said in a loud stage whisper.

I felt my face heat up as I turned ten shades of pink. I looked at Mama to see if she heard. She was doing one of those looking-anywhere-but-here things.

"Tetracycline ointment, have Mama or Trulee put it on twice a day. Lortab—pain control. Take one tonight, one tomorrow morning, then one tomorrow night. You're going to be hurting for a while. After that you can take one of these every six hours. Darvocet." Four picked up each bottle and brandished it at me.

"Thank you, Four." I was prissy and determined to change the subject. "So Mama, tell me about this house. How in the world did you do all this?"

"Hey girl, let me see them million dollar hands." Jack interrupted. "Do I need to find the Lloyds of London claim form?"

I held out my hands and flipped them over. "Minor scrapes; nothing broken. You heard the doctor. It'll be uncomfortable, but they're still useable. I can practice, but it might smart a bit. Now, Mama tell me about the house."

"She's on the City Tourism board and the Historical Society. And she helped set up the plans for that City Market on the pier. These houses, hoo-boy, she made a good deal."

"Now, Jack." It was Mama's face that turned pink. "I have several realtor friends. I've been hearing them say what good prices they are getting for waterfront properties and for marsh-front properties. I thought about the old duplexes, and I happened to know who owned them. I went to visit him, but he wasn't interested in selling them. I didn't think anything more about it. I was surely surprised when he up and called and offered them to me. He didn't have any family to leave them to, and I think he knew he was dying."

"Mama, did you flirt with him?" I teased her. I thought about what she said for minute. "Mama? Do you own all four of these duplexes?"

"She owns all four. And the old alley behind the duplexes. She researched the titles and found out the city never owned the alley. And those two big lots across the street," Jack said.

"The Garden Club is going to make those into a little park," Mama said. "I'm going to deed it over to the city. But if they ever decide they don't need a park, it reverts back to me or my heirs."

"So what are you going to do with the other three?" I asked. "I noticed that each of them was styled differently."

"The one next door is going to be mine," said Trulee.

"Oh, Trulee! That's wonderful," I said.

"We all love Trulee," Mama said. "And we all owe her a lot. She's taken care of us for over fifty years. Now we're going to take care of her." She smiled at Trulee. "And I'm thinking about Annabelle for the end one." Mama noticed me tightening up at the mention of my aunt's name. "Honey, I've forgiven her. You need to."

"Mrs. Walden, you must be a very sharp business woman. Liberty's lucky to have you on their side. Where'd you learn all this?"

"Oh, I picked up a great deal from my second husband. I traveled with him, sat in on his board meetings. When he passed away, I had to handle his affairs." Mama paused and dabbed her eyes with her napkin.

"Did you handle Dr. Hayworth's financial affairs, too?" Andrew asked.

Mama, Four and Jack stiffened when he asked that question.

"My sister was the office manager for the practice," Mama said. "She retired fifteen years ago, but she still goes by to make sure her replacement is doing the job right."

"Sounds like Auntabelle," said Jack. "Now if she had just done her job forty years ago."

"Jack!" Mama said. "She...she had her reasons."

"Her reasons cost you," he said. "She lied. She didn't support you at a time you needed her the most."

"Mrs. Walden, what did your sister lie about?" Andrew asked. "Is it at all related to the death of your husband?"

Jack stood and walked into the kitchen. We watched him leave and return with another beer. He twisted off the cap and took a big swallow. "I don't see how it could be related. It didn't seem to have anything to do with money. Daddy didn't leave a big estate. The house was mortgaged, Sapelo Sound was mortgaged. Mama and Daddy had been putting money away for our college funds. Daddy had a lot of patients who couldn't afford to pay their bills. Some of them would bring by produce from their gardens, fresh eggs, meat when they butchered a pig. When Daddy's estate went through probate, there wasn't much money left for Mama and Brittan Lee. Mama went to Daddy's partners to get them to buy out Daddy's share of the medical practice. There was some confusion and bookkeeping issues that clouded the actual value of the practice. It probably was worth a lot more than what Auntabelle's book-keeping figures showed."

I saw Andrew making mental notes.

"Brittan Lee, how was it that you and Beth Ann were out and about on those Wednesdays?" he asked.

"I told you I was an inquisitive child," I said. "And Miss Darton was mean. So we found something else to do."

"Is this another one of those stories I keep hearing about?" Andrew poured another glass of tea.

"It could be," I said.

"Oh, guys, a story," Madison had been eavesdropping. She pulled her stool over to join the group. "I love Brittan Lee stories. Been hearing them all my life. Everybody compares me and Leigh to Aunt B. Especially Leigh, because she looked just like her, right, Gramma?"

Mama nodded. "Little Leigh is the spit of her aunt. But you have a strong resemblance, too. You all four, Morgan too, are beautiful women." She smiled over at Leigh, who didn't seem to notice her.

Mama likes to say that Leigh is the beautiful younger image of me, but that's just because everyone always said I looked just like Mama. In the fading sunlight, Mama could have passed for one of her granddaughters. When Vickie's baby comes, there will be four generations of Hayworth women to liken to each other.

I don't think Leigh had noticed we were talking about her. She and Jax were in an intense conversation of their own. I could see her pointing her finger at Jax. Her face was in the shadows, but her frame was stiff.

"Have you been telling them Brittan Lee stories?" I asked Mama. I was touched that the next generation even cared about my childhood. I only saw them on vacations and in-between concert tours, but I tried to spoil them shamelessly whenever I could. "I thought I was the favorite aunt? The aunt who takes them to Europe on summer vacation? The aunt who lets them drive her classic convertible? The aunt who sang to them when they were babies in the cradle? I can't believe it!" I put my hand to my head in a dramatic gesture.

"Church songs," Madison interrupted. "Or protest songs. But you're still the favorite aunt. But did they always have to be church songs?"

"I never…" I protested to the group. "I don't know what they mean," I said to Andrew.

"We shall not, we shall not be moved," Madison started in a smooth alto.

"We shall not, we shall not be moved," Leigh's voice raised in harmony.

"Just like the tree, planted by the waters, we shall not be moved," Jax and Quince brought in the rest of the four-part harmony.

"See, that isn't church music. It's an Australian union worker's song," I said. "Be glad I gave you some variety in your life."

Laughter echoed off the marshes. "Oh, you know you are our favorite auntie," teased Leigh, her face more relaxed. "Don't pout, Auntie B. Grandmama says you are the best pouter in the family. Go on, now, Auntie B, tell Agent Zeller one of your stories."

"Okay, but first, bring over that big bowl of shrimp you were peeling," I said. "And the hush puppies."

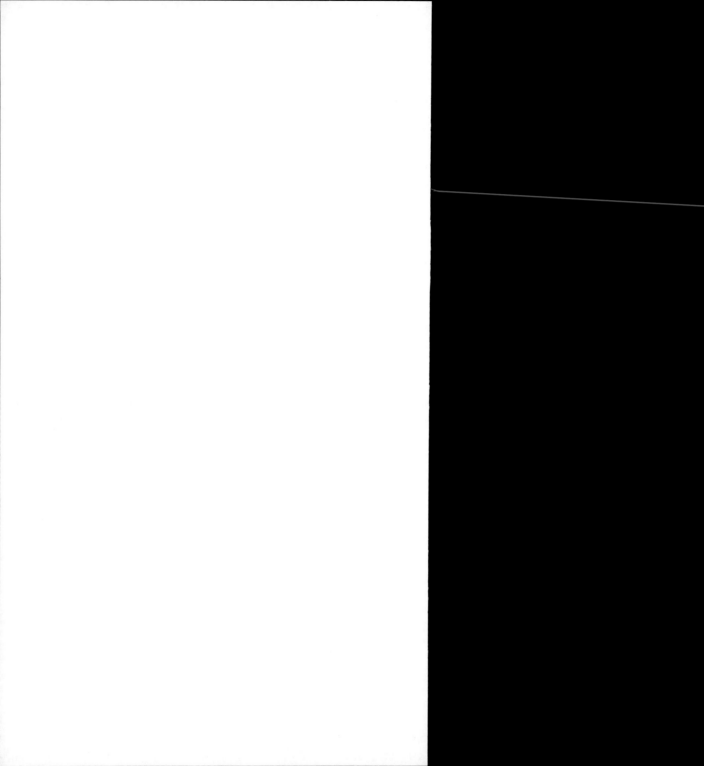

CHAPTER THIRTEEN
Liberty, Georgia, August 1964

On our second Wednesday of freedom that summer, Beth Ann and I made our way again through backyards, alleys and bushes to the Courthouse Square. Beth Ann had heard the Courthouse had a Co-cola machine in the basement, and she had three dimes burning a hole in her pocket. She was aiming for that machine when I heard the same sounds I had heard the week before.

"Beth Ann, someone's singing. Can't you hear them?"

"What I hear is my dime dropping down the slot for that cold Co'cola," she grumbled. "And I've got an extra for you. Would you rather get something to drink or just stand here listening to the Methodists practice?"

"The Methodists are two blocks in the other direction," I pointed. "And this isn't Methodist music. This is different. You can feel this music." I put my hand on my chest where I was sure I could feel the deep bass reverberating in my heart. "I never felt music like this. Come on." I turned in the direction of the music, knowing Beth Ann would come after me. She always did.

We followed the sounds down Mulberry Street, then turned at the corner to see the Liberty African Methodist-Episcopal Church. It was a little bitty church, not much more than one big room, with maybe two little rooms at the back. The plain glass windows were propped open with pieces of stove wood, and the voices poured out the open spaces and filled the night. The First Baptists may have the edge on stained glass windows and gilded pew Bibles, but the AME Choir were the clear leaders in the singing department. Those people sounded like the Spirit was flowing through them as clear as Trey's ham radio. I got the shivers listening to them. I could almost feel the building sway with the beat. This surely was the joyful noise from Psalm 96.

"Boost me up, Beth Ann. I want to see inside. I know that song."

"I don't want to boost you up. Go look in the front door if you're gonna be so nosey." But even as she complained, she leaned against the outside church wall and cupped her hands for me to step on.

I slipped off my black patent leather Mary Janes and stepped into her palms. Even when I balanced against the wall and stretched as far as I could, my head didn't reach the open window. I reached for the window sill and tried to shinny myself the rest of the way up. I managed to get an elbow up on the window sill and braced myself high enough to get a glimpse of the woman playing the piano, just a quick glimpse of her in profile.

"Quit squirming. I'm gonna drop you," whispered Beth Ann. "Quit banging into the wall; they're gonna hear you. Why are they singing so funny?"

I stopped wiggling long enough to listen. The song had changed. The choir was no longer full, no longer raising the rafters about an eternal life beyond the river. A familiar voice instead sang one line, playing chords on an upright piano.

"A Pilgrim was I and a wanderin'," she sang and the choir answered the line in full voice.

"A Pilgrim was I and a wanderin'," she repeated the line, and the conjoined voices repeated, some rising up, some deepening as the harmony grew. The pianist and the congregation continued to repeat the same line.

"Why's she singing like that?" Beth Ann repeated.

"I said I didn't know." I clung by my fingertips to the window as I tried to climb up Beth Ann's shoulder. I wanted to see who that familiar voice belonged to.

"Who's chiles is you?" A shrill voice came out of the darkness by the side of the church.

Beth Ann shrieked and backed up, leaving me hanging on the wall. I lost my death grip on the cracking wood and landed on my backside in the scanty patch of grass. I scrambled to my feet, trying to grasp back some of my dignity.

"Who are you?"

"I axed you fust. What you doing hanging there from the church winder?" A colored girl about our age stood there, glaring at us in the weak light from the window. I don't recall being this close to a colored child before in Liberty, except when Mama or one of the neighbors drove the maids home and we went along for the ride. There were lots of colored children at Granddaddy's, at the Homeplace. My best friend at the Homeplace was a colored child, instead of one of my cousins. But I never really thought about colored children in Liberty.

"I axed you the questun. What was you's doing?" Her hair was braided into about a dozen braids, and the colorful bows at the end of each braid bobbed as she crossed her arms and set her legs firmly on the walkway.

"We were just listening and I wanted to see. Why are they singing like that?"

"Like what?"

"Like that. The lady on the piano sings one line, then everyone sings it."

"They's larning a new song."

"But why are they learning like that? Why don't they just sing it out of the hymnal?" I thought this a very simple question, but the little girl looked at me like she thought I was plumb crazy. Her face got all wrinkled, and she cocked her head to one side.

"What's that? Hymnal?"

Now I looked at her like she was crazy. Or dumb. "It's a book with music in it. That you sing from. It's got hymns in it. You know, church music?"

Her face cleared. "Oh, we got three of them. They's one on the piano, and Sister Jones has one for directin' the choir and Pastor Truckle, he's got one. That's all."

"It sure must take a long time to learn all those songs," I looked around for something to sit on. I couldn't find anything, so I just sat on the concrete and put my shoes back on. I patted the ground next to me. "Sit down. I'm Brittan Lee and this is my friend, Beth Ann."

"I don't want to sit down on the ground. Mama will just wear me out if I get my dress dirty," Beth Ann got her stubborn look on her face. "You know she will."

"I's Tansie Howard and I's nine years old. Why you got two names?" The girl sat down across from me. She looked up at Beth Ann.

"Well, it's really Elizabeth Ann, but it got shorted when I was little."

"My Mama named me after her great-granddaddy and my daddy's great-aunt. I'm only supposed to be called Brittan, but when they're mad at me cause they think I done something wrong, then they use the whole thing. Since I was about four, that's all they do, Brittan Lee this and Brittan Lee that. How'm I supposed to know when I'm in trouble if they always call me Brittan Lee?"

Tansie just stared at me like she didn't understand my explanation.

"Tansie," Beth Ann reached and pulled her arm. "Tell us about those songs."

"Most of them songs don't come outta no book. They're home songs."

"What are home songs?"

"Songs you larn at home. Songs you mama and granny sings to you. Din't your mama ever sing to you? Larn you no songs? My grannie and grampie and all my aunties and uncles, they just sings all the time at home or when hoeing in the gardun. They learnt them songs from they grammies, like *Sing A-Ho That I had the Wings of a Dove*, or *Standing in the Need of Prayer*, or *I'll Hear the Trumpet Call.*"

I scratched my head underneath my braid while I gave these questions some thought. "No, can't recall that she did, not those songs. My daddy did, and we sing together lots, but the rest of the songs I learned from books. I just about have the Baptist Hymnal memorized. I read it so I can sit quiet in church. Mama and Daddy get real mad if I fidget."

Beth Ann interrupted. "Daddy sang *Rock-A-Bye Baby* and *Hush Little Mockingbird.* But Gramma made him stop, so then Mama sang me some hymns."

I clarified for Tansie. "Her Gramma is a real strict church lady. They don't let Beth Ann do much anything fun."

Beth Ann started crying. "And my Daddy's leaving. He's going away because she's so mean, and I won't see him anymore." Big old tears ran down her cheeks, and she tried to sniff them back up, then she had to blow her nose on a piece of Kleenex.

Her eyes big and round, Tansie stared at Beth Ann. "That's turrible. Not having your daddy."

"I know," she said, wiping her face. "I want to go with him."

"You can't," I said. "Who's gonna be my best friend if you leave?"

"Tansie?" A deep voice came from the back doorway of the church. "Who's you friends?"

"Deacon Johnson!" Tansie jumped up and turned to face him.

A very black, elderly man, who once was tall but now stooped and bent with age, came down the three steps to where we had been talking.

I stood and gave him my best curtsey. "I'm Brittan Lee Hayworth, sir, and this is my friend, Beth Ann Hamilton. We just came down to listen to the music." I'd never curtsied to a colored man before, but he was a Deacon and he was old. Even in the Baptist Church, Deacons were important people.

When he spoke, it was with a deep Geechee accent like the people who live near Sapelo Sound. "Well, Miss Brittan Lee, I'm pleased to make your acquaintance. Youh welcome heah anytime. Youh Daddy, he be the one that gived us that pianna."

"That's my piano?" I started for the church.

"You got a new one for Christmas last year," Beth Ann grabbed my arm. "When your Mama redid the dining room. What did you think happened to the old one?" She was right. Mama had replaced her old upright with an ebony Steinway grand piano just like the one in Mrs. Smith's living room. The one the senior music students get to practice on. Mama was real proud of that grand piano. Anytime anyone came over, Mama would play something.

"Doctor Marsh was generous enough to share your old piano with Miss Trulee. She plays for our church services."

In an instant, I knew who that voice belonged to, and I remembered who had sung some of those old songs to me. Trulee. "But it was my piano," I whispered.

"Don't be selfish," Beth Ann whispered as she nudged me. "You gotta share."

"I share all the time. I share my clothes with the little kids at Homeplace and Sapelo Sound. Mama packs them up every season. And I share my toys with the cousins. And I share my books with you. But this was my piano. I learned how to play on that piano. Mama learned how to play on that piano."

"And you didn't even notice it was gone when you saw that new one. You know it has a much nicer tone than the old one. "

"You share your books," Tansie's eyes opened wide as she looked between me and Beth Ann. "I have three books. I can share with you."

"I get three books every week from the Library. I'm in the Summer Reader's Program for the Library Guild. Every week I get three books, and I read them and I have to write about them. When I've done with twenty books, I get a gold star on my certificate. My goal this summer is to get at least two certificates. Are you in the Summer Reader's Program?"

Tansie looked up at Deacon Johnson, then back at me and shook her head. "Colored chilluns can only use the li'brey every other Tuesday afternoon, and we can only read one book at a time."

"Well that don't seem fair. I'd sure get bored with just one book for two whole weeks. I could never get my gold stars. How are you going to get any gold stars?"

"Ebon says it's 'cause white folks are plumb mean and stingy. He says it ain't right to not let colored chilluns be usin' the li'brey. He says it's gonna be changin' soon, all that.

People's is gonna be changing all that, so the colored chilluns can come ev'ry day."

"I'm going to talk to my Daddy about that. He's the mayor, and I bet he can change those rules or something. Daddy believes education and reading to be the most important things." I couldn't wait to tell him what the Library people were doing to the colored children. "Tansie, even if Daddy can't get the library changed this week, I'll still bring you some books each Wednesday. I'll share."

Beth Ann gave me her "Yeah, right," look.

The Deacon didn't seem to be too happy to hear Tansie say all this. His lips got all tight, and he looked at her and nodded over to the doorway. "We are truly grateful for your gift of your piano," he said. "Now ladies, as much as we welcome your visits to our church, it's gettin' late. We need to get you safely back to yours. Tansie, go tell your mama that I shall return shortly."

With that, he took each of our dirty hands into his and with his slow limping step escorted us all the way back to the First Baptist Church. Much later in time, I came to realize what an honorable and courageous act that was.

***

Mama's Terrace, Liberty Georgia, August, 2005

The nieces were quiet for a few minutes. "Is that the piano in the front room?"

"It is," Mama answered them. "That piano was a present for Brittan Lee and me for Christmas in 1963. The old piano, which still had many good years left on it, was donated to the AME Church."

"They still use that piano," added Trulee. "Tansie plays that piano when she has choir practice for the little children.

There is a plaque on the side of the soundboard that says it was a gift from the Hayworth Family. Your mama has that piano tuned twice a year."

"Aunt B, was that when you decided you needed to help people?" Leigh asked.

"Honey, I was only nine!"

"She was always fighting for things to be fair and equal for all." Jack, Trulee and I all spoke at the same time. I spoke the loudest.

"I'm not a civil rights worker. I try to help anyone who needs help. I wanted to play the piano or be a historian. I just thought it wasn't fair the way Tansie and the other children were treated. I thought Daddy could help. And he was trying when…when…when he left us."

All the plates were filled with boiled shrimp and hush puppies. Over the sounds of the family enjoying the food, little tidbits of conversation drifted. The Bulldawgs were opening in ninth place in the Coach's Poll; Four had extra tickets for the first home game, if we, he looked between Andrew and me, were interested in going up and tailgating. Jack needed to get the bush hog and mow down the front fields at Sapelo Sound sometime in the next two weeks. Mama reminded everyone about the cocktail party the following night.

"Um, this is probably as good a time as any to tell Mama that I will be spending a little more time than usual on this trip, and some more time this fall," I said. I heard Mama suck in her breath and felt her lean towards me.

"Really, dear. That will be nice," she tried for a casual note. "Will you stay with me, or should we get your house finished up next."

"I'll stay here with you if that's alright," I said. "The research I was doing for the jacket liner for the CD, the one

Tansie and I are working on with the children, it's turning into a book and possibly another CD of its own. I'm going to be traveling into the smaller Gullah and Geechee communities and getting some more field recordings of the old songs, try to get more history. Then I'm going to Africa to see what songs there are connected by melody or meter or even some of the words."

"Oh, Aunt B, that sounds fascinating! I'm available for the rest of the summer if you need any help," Madison said.

"Summer's over next week. Next Monday is Labor Day. Been forty years since the last big hurricane, and that one was Labor Day week, too." Jack looked out at the water which still reflected the deep red from the setting sun. "There was a red sky this morning, too."

"Brittan Lee, if you are feeling up to it, I need you to come to the office tomorrow morning for some more formal discussion," Andrew said.

Mama looked up startled. "Brittan Lee has to go to Verna Hamilton's to make the plans for the memorial service. I told Verna I would send Brittan Lee out Tuesday morning. Honey, Verna's way out in Cooshea, out west of Sunbury, where her mama lives. She moved back out there after all this happened. They've been holding a vigil ever since they pulled the car out of the river."

"Can I borrow someone's car?" I asked. "I'll go out in the morning, make nice with Mrs. Hamilton, be back here by lunchtime. Andrew, can I come see you after lunch?"

Four stood up and stretched. "Brit, you might not be feeling too much like moving around tomorrow. You're gonna be stiff and sore, so take it easy."

"Hey, Jax," his father called. "What's on your agenda tomorrow?"

By the shrimp pot, Jax and Leigh were again in an intense conversation. Jax was gesturing to her with his beer bottle. Leigh's back was to me, but I could see her shoulders were tense and her back rigid.

He wandered over when his father called again. His grim expression lifted as he approached us. "Got some meetings to set up for Thomas. Got to get his new office ready to move in. Few other things. Why?" He swallowed a slug from his beer.

"Your Aunt B is going to need a chauffeur for a little while. I would prefer she had company whenever she was out of the house," Jack said.

"Jack, these children have better things to do than drive me around," I protested. "I'm sure they all have jobs." I looked at them. "Or beach plans."

Leigh stomped over from the counter. "I'm free for the summer. I'm her namesake, and I will be her chauffeur!"

"What are you carrying these days," teased Jax. "I've got my SigSauer. That little Ladysmith of yours barely knocks a beer can off the post."

"The last time I checked, my scores were higher than yours." Leigh's jaw was clenched.

"Jack, Four! You let these children carry guns? Besides, I can drive myself. I remember where MeMaw Beeker lives," I said.

"Oh, they're just for potting at rabbits up at Sapelo Sound," Jax explained. His dad poked him. "It's not like there is any real crime in Liberty. Now when I go up to Atlanta or even Savannah, lately, that's a different story."

"Do you think that's necessary?" asked Mama. "Brittan Lee can use my car or Trulee's."

Trulee shook her head. "I think you need to listen to Jack. Somebody's trying to start up something."

Jack looked at each of us. "Mama, forty years ago, someone tried to kidnap Brittan Lee. You know it's true, and I know it's true no matter what went on the official paperwork. Brittan Lee has been here six hours and someone pushed her off the side of the pier. I think there's people worried that Brittan Lee may say something about that night that they don't want said. And I don't want any crazy old red necks coming after my sister in their old dirty white robes to finish off what they couldn't finish forty years ago."

Flashbulbs went off in my head like my old Brownie camera. "Sheets. They weren't in white robes. They were just old make-do white sheets with eye holes cut out and a rope around their waists. One of them had little rosebuds near the bottom; they blended in with the spatters of Ebon's blood. I remember thinking how the red and the pink didn't match. But I could see their legs under the sheets. Work boots mostly, some lace-up shoes like Daddy's. I saw Deputy Ungler's uniform pants—that dark blue stripe down the leg. "

There was silence.

I felt myself start to curl up in my chair and rock back and forth. "We were waiting for Beth Ann, Ebon and I. It was raining. The thunder was so loud it vibrated inside me. Beth Ann didn't come and didn't come, and it was getting late. I knew that Mama or Mrs. Smith would be waiting for me at the church, and they would be worried. Deputy Ungler drove by in his patrol car, and I told him Beth Ann was missing. He told me to stay there and he drove off. A few minutes some other cars drove up. Men piled out of the cars like a coven of ghosts. They were all covered in white sheets with little holes cut out for the eyes. The wind flapped those sheets around their legs. They came over. One of them grabbed me and the others went over to Ebon. *Run!* I screamed to Ebon. *Run! You have to get away!* But he wouldn't leave me. They beat him," I shuddered as I remembered the steady thudding of the blows and the blood streaming from Ebon's nose, his mouth. "They had two-by-fours and ropes."

Sobs caught in my throat. "They locked us up in the tabby shed under the Liberty Oak. It was so dark. The only light came with the lightning. I saw Daddy come. I stood on some boxes and looked out the little window. The men took off the white sheets when they saw Daddy drive up. I beat on the door and called for him, but he didn't hear me." I looked at my clenched fists. "I beat on the door until my hands were bloody. I yelled until I couldn't talk. Daddy said he would go get us. He walked away with some other men. I never saw him again."

"As you know, he was caught in the building when lightning struck it. He died in the fire." Jack told Andy. He paused as Mama choked a little bit. "The coroner made determinations based on what he was told by people who had been there."

"Brittan Lee, how did you get out?" Andy asked.

"Jack came back for me," I looked at my brother.

"The doctors told me that it would be better if she thought it was just a bad dream. I didn't know what she had seen or heard. I just knew that Jack found her locked up in that old shed. She would cry all night and shake. Her grades were dropping because she was too tired in classes. Bruce said it would be better to let her think it was all just a bad dream. It wasn't until she went into therapy that the doctors encouraged her to talk about it. Baby, I'm so sorry." Tears reflected off Mama's face. "By then we were living in Chicago."

"So most of Liberty still thinks Brittan Lee was locked up by Ebon, and that Ebon died in the fire?" Andy asked.

Mama nodded. "Either that or she was hiding from him. I didn't see any reason to tell anyone anything different."

"Jack, when you found Brittan Lee, was Ebon in the back room?" Andy asked.

Jack and I both tensed at the same time. "No. No, he wasn't," Jack said.

"So he still could have gone into the building after Daddy?" Four asked.

"No," I said. "I uh, I would have seen him go. There is no back door to that old building."

"So, the real question is what happened to him? And who belongs to the other body from the fire? Who is still around from that night? Who has reason to be worried that Brittan Lee might just remember something?" Andy asked.

Leigh spoke first. "I won't let her out of my sight."

CHAPTER FOURTEEN
Liberty, Georgia, August 2005

Four was right. My entire body was tighter than a just-tuned piano when I woke up; it took me ten minutes to stretch, roll over and drag my aching body out of bed. Trulee had placed my Bible and book of devotionals on the bedside table. I opened my devotionals to the current reading.

Let the words of my mouth and the meditation of my heart be acceptable in thy sight, O Lord, my strength and my redeemer. Psalm 19:14. Fitting, always fitting, but today even more so, since I would be talking to Beth Ann's mama and then to Agent Zeller. I prayed that the words I would say would help and not hurt. There had already been so much pain.

A long hot shower eased the cramped muscles, but played havoc with the various cuts and abrasions that decorated my skin. A contortionist couldn't have gotten Four's ointment on my back this morning.

Mama had completed her move even to the point of having my clothes hanging in the new closet. I fumbled through the clothes hangers and selected a funeral type dress.

"Drat." I attempted and failed to reach the back zipper. Someone downstairs would have to zip me. My damp hair would air dry into soft ringlets. I knew I couldn't hold up a hair blower at the angle needed to dry all of my head. Dabbing on moisturizer and powder did me in. I had to sit down on the vanity stool and catch my breath for a few minutes before continuing with mascara and my contact lenses. After I slipped on a pair of low-heeled sandals, I headed toward the sounds and smells of the kitchen.

"Aunt B! We're twins!" Leigh said as she pointed to her own navy blue tank dress. She was right. With the exception of the cap sleeves on my dress, we were identical down to the sandals. "I wasn't sure what to wear. Thought black would be too hot and floral too gaudy for a funeral."

I looked more closely at Leigh. "Honey, how did you hurt yourself?" I pointed to bruises on the back of her left arm. Fingertip-sized bruises. I had seen bruises like that before.

"Where?" Leigh looked at her upper arm. "Oh, that. I think Jax caught me when I tripped or something. I can be really klutzy sometimes."

"Brittan Lee, honey, what would you like for breakfast? I can whip up about anything. Those boys are in here just about every day." Trulee fussed as she set out a coffee cup and a juice glass on the counter. "Come on now, you need food to keep up your energy. I looked in on you earlier this morning. You were sleeping like your Daddy after an all night session in the hospital. How're your hands doing?"

"I wasn't snoring like Daddy, I hope. Four's pills were miracle drugs. I slept like a log," I said, not mentioning that before I went to bed I double-checked the locks on every door and window in the house, and also not mentioning I caught Leigh in the process of doing the same thing.

The scabs forming on the cuts and scratches on my hands hurt when I grasped my juice glass; I winced as I flexed my fingers. "Let me take those antibiotics while my stomach is still empty, then maybe. What are you eating, Leigh? You aren't dieting, are you?"

"Hush your mouth!" Trulee said as she poured my coffee. "That child doesn't need to diet. She's fine as she is. Men like a little meat on the bones." She watched me try to grip the glass. "I'm going to the root doctor today to get some of her special cream. It'll work a lot better than that stuff of your brothers. Oh, Leigh, your young man called. Told him you were still sleeping."

Something crashed on the counter. I looked over to see Leigh's spilled juice glass.

Leigh looked flustered. "The root doctor? Like voodoo or something?"

"Honey, how do you feel this morning?" Mama paused as she came into the sunny kitchen to zip up my dress. "Did you sleep well? Are you sure you want to do this today? Leigh, what are you eating? " Mama made me tired all over again. "Trulee, what are you doing? You aren't the maid. These girls are big enough to make their own breakfast." Mama went around the counter and gave Trulee a hug and kiss. "But since it's made, I will take a cup of that coffee and a sausage biscuit."

"Oh, I love cooking for hungry children," Trulee smiled as she slid a plate with homemade sausage and scrambled eggs over to me. "Biscuits will be out of the oven in just a minute."

I ate more than I thought I had an appetite for. I miss Trulee's beaten biscuits and Mama's chicory coffee when I am in North Shore. Chicory coffee has its own special fragrance when it is brewing. Mama and Mr. Walden went to New Orleans for their honeymoon, and Mama fell in love with New Orleans coffee. She has it special ordered and sent to her every month from Café DuMonde. I had just started my third cup when Leigh brought me back on task.

"Come on, Auntie B. We don't have all day. Do you have the directions to this place in Cupadooparoopa?" she asked as she searched for her purse and car keys.

"It's Cooshea," I said, "and yes, I think I can still find my way out there. Your daddy never took you to Cooshea?" We kissed Mama and Trulee, and I followed Leigh out to the driveway.

"Hop in," she said as she slid into the driver's seat of a red Porsche convertible. "Fasten your seatbelts 'cause it's going to be a bumpy ride."

"Well, thank you, Bette Davis," I said as I gingerly sat down in the low seat. "Ouch." The motion of reaching back for the shoulder harness pulled on the new scabs on my back. "Good thing I have short hair. When did you get this pea-shooter?"

Leigh looked over her shoulder and with a practiced move shifted gears and pulled out onto the oyster-shell lane. "Hmmm, well, it really isn't mine. It was Quince's last great hurrah before going into his residency program in Massachusetts. He found out it didn't work too well in the snow."

"Isn't it nice that he would loan it to us for a funeral visit?" I looked over at the strangely silent Leigh. "He did loan it to you, didn't he?"

Leigh pulled out onto Highway 17 and gunned the engine. "He's not using it today. He's with Uncle Four."

"Oh, piddle! He doesn't know! We're going to get picked up for grand theft auto!" I clutched the edge of my seat.

Leigh grinned. "He can't drive it anyway. Has too many speeding tickets."

"Better be careful or you'll even up the score," I warned.

Leigh just laughed. "Auntie B, I don't get speeding tickets! I like your FBI agent."

"He's not my agent, thank you," I said. "But thank you. He is rather nice, isn't he?"

"Aunt B, he's totally hot!" Leigh flashed a smile at me. "At least for a man his age. It's too bad about his brother."

"I didn't know he had a brother. Our relationship is strictly professional. How do you know about his brother?"

"Um, he was talking to Daddy, and I was there. They actually met at some kind of conference a few years ago. His older brother was Daddy's age, and he was in college and he went to work with the Freedom Riders. It's so tragic."

"You got all that out with one breath. I'm impressed. So where is his brother?"

"Which one?"

"How many does he have?"

"Three and two sisters."

"Leigh! What is so tragic about the older brother?"

"Oh! He never came home. He disappeared, back in 1964. So whenever the FBI gets one of the older civil rights cases, your agent goes to the scene to see if there are any unidentified men. He's been looking for him for the past twenty years."

"So that's why he's really here," I said.

"Why? It was a little girl not an adult man that was found. Aunt B, was Daddy kidding last night? About your hands? Are they really insured for a million dollars?"

I laughed. "Yes, my hands, Tina Turner's legs and J-Lo's backside." We drove along in companionable silence. Well, Leigh drove. I sat deep in the leather seat, clinging to the sissy bar, until I realized that Leigh was a good driver. Once I had relaxed, I started pointing out my favorite places. About twelve miles north of Liberty, I motioned for Leigh to turn left.

"Is this Cooshea?" she asked over the wind.

"No, this is just a wide spot in the road. We'll go through about five of these before we get to Cooshea," I said. "It used to take almost an hour to get there from Liberty. Of course, we didn't drive quite this fast back then." I gestured for her to turn right.

We drove for a while under the dense canopy of oak trees, sunlight filtered a light green. The road made big sweeping curves, first out to the riverside with the blue herons feeding on the little fiddler crabs, then back inland to a row of fresh produce stands.

"Leigh, can we stop here for a minute?" I asked as we approached the Shell Bluff Diner and Bait Shop.

"Hungry already, Auntie B?" she said as she turned the car into the dusty parking lot. "Is this the fastest way to Cooshea or are you just delaying getting there?"

"Actually, I'm thirsty and I need to use the lady's room," I said as I climbed out of the car. "I've been here before. This is one of the places where my Uncle Frank used to come. I remember the old woman who worked the counter. She was always eating Vienna sausages from a can. She would give me one on a Saltine cracker."

We entered the dim building and nodded to an old man sitting by the window.

When I returned from the restroom, Leigh was sitting at the old counter sipping iced tea and talking to the woman stirring a large stew pot. Her eyes scanned the doorway and the road just outside. She jumped and almost dropped her glass when I laid my hand on her shoulder.

"Auntie B, would you like some tea?" she asked. When I shook my head no, she thanked the woman and we left.

"Just a few miles more," I told her as we climbed back into the car. The convertible roared back into life and we started again on our journey. "So, are you going to tell me what's bothering you?"

"Nothing. Really. Well, just something I've got to think about. I'm thinking about moving to Liberty and teaching school here instead of Columbia. This is just all so beautiful. I wish I had grown up here with Daddy. I can't believe I've never been down some of these roads," she smiled over at me as the wind whipped her hair around her face. "Aunt B, are you going to move back to Liberty?"

"Leigh, who did you hear that from? Oh, last night," I asked. "I have so much I'm doing up in North Shore—all my causes, as your grandmama says. So what brings about your change?"

"Oh, change itself, I guess. Something new, some place different than Columbia," she said. "Trulee said they need good teachers here. And she said there are plenty of problems right around here for you." She paused as she steered into the big curve in the road. "Daddy said that Mrs. Hamilton has been real mean to you. So why are you even going to see her?"

I looked over at her, wondering when my youngest niece had grown up. "Because Beth Ann was my best friend. Because most of my life has been about helping people, and Verna Hamilton is going to need help. Mostly because Mama made me feel guilty enough."

She laughed at that. "Grandmama is good at that," she agreed.

"If I do come back, I already have one good cause," I said.

"What?" she asked. She steered with one hand as she tucked flying hair behind her ear.

"Property rights," I said as I fought the urge to reach over and help her steer. "Up and down the coast, see over there," I gestured to side road to our right. "Just down that road, it used to be all Montgomery property. After the Civil War, the Freedman's Bureau divided up the land among the former slaves. They've lived there for generations, and now families are getting taxed right out of their homes. And it's not just here.

It's happening over on Cathead Creek, and at Blue and Hall landing and Jackson Bluff. Developers have discovered the coast. They buy a couple of acres, build some very expensive homes on spec. It increases the property taxes all over the place, even if the developer hasn't sold the new development. Look at those places," I gestured at old silvery cedar-board cottages with deep porches. "Imagine living there and being forced out because your property taxes went up 400 percent!"

"And that's happening?" Leigh asked.

"It is. Trulee told me. You heard what Mama said last night about her real estate friends. Here, this is it," I told Leigh as we approached the Grace River Freewill of Prophesy Primitive Baptist Church. She steered the car into the unpaved parking lot and parked amidst the trucks, Fords and Chevys filling the lot.

The small church, like so many others in the rural South, stood in the shade of several huge live oaks. Constructed of now-faded white clapboard siding, it boasted a small porch set square in the middle of the front wall. Two tall windows provided light to the rows of rough benches facing the altar. To the right of the sanctuary was the cemetery.

Little stone lambs watched over the final resting places of long dead children. Faded plastic flowers in a Coca-cola bottle were toppled over on one grave, potted plants decorated several others. The headstones were all different sizes, some soaring up to the oaks. A few had the small granite crosses provided by the United Daughters of the Confederacy.

Attached to the church on the left was the Fellowship Hall. A large roofed concrete pavilion stood in the shade next to the Hall. Long rows of planks nailed to upright posts formed tables and benches.

"Wow! Where are the snakes?" Leigh said.

I climbed out of the car and smoothed the creases from my linen skirt. My short hair hadn't suffered from the wind, but I finger-smoothed it to be sure.

"In boxes in the sanctuary," I took a deep breath and nodded to Leigh. "Remember, shoulders back, head up."

CHAPTER FIFTEEN
Grace River, Cooshea, Liberty County, August 2005

The Hall was filled with parishioners, mostly old, mostly women, all white. The room was awash in a sea of pastel polyester pantsuits gathered to support Verna Hamilton in her vigil of mourning for her lost child. People stood in small groups, talking to one another. They parted as Leigh and I entered. I smiled at the first woman and asked about Mrs. Hamilton.

"She's in the back room with the pastor," the woman said. She looked at me, studying my face. "She'll be out in a while. Would you like some tea or punch?" She led the way to a buffet table near the rear of the room. The table was loaded with the baked hams, casseroles and pound cakes of a southern funeral feast. As we followed her, the others in the room fell silent, watching us. I heard the murmured whispering of first one, then another, until the room was buzzing, a hive of angry disturbed bees.

"That one's her. It's her."

"That's Brittan Lee Hayworth. My word, I can't believe she'd show her face here."

"Why's she here? What does she want?"

"Should be ashamed to show her face…"

"She was there, she lied about…tried to blame…"

I smiled and nodded as I passed. I thanked the woman ladling the punch into Dixie cups.

"Shoulders back, head up," Leigh whispered to me.

We stood, smiling, shifting our weight from one foot to the other, aware of the glares and murmurs around us. People moved out of our way, not allowing any possible touch of contamination. They would look up from lowered eyes, then whisper to each other again.

I could feel my face start a slow flush to red; my jaw ached from the forced smiling.

"Auntie B," Leigh said in a low voice. "What soothes the savage beast?" She nodded at the corner of the room where an old upright piano stood between two windows. "Go on."

I stared at her. "I can't just go over and start playing their piano," I said.

"Yes, you can," she said, as she started over to the corner.

I followed her, feeling all the eyes boring holes in my back. I sat on the round piano stool and my hands, by instinct of their own, started into the introduction of the favorite *How Great Thou Art.* By the second verse Leigh was singing softly, and by the third, the elderly congregation had quieted watching us. When the hymn ended, I segued into another.

Shackled by a heavy burden
'Neath a load of guilt and shame,
Then the hand of Jesus touch me,
And now, I am no longer the same

By the time I started to play the chorus, I heard the hesitant voices of those in the room singing with us. We finished the last note, and I moved into the opening chords of the next hymn. The mourners moved closer to the piano, crowding in as I fingered the keys. The piano was not in full tune. Not everyone knew all the words to the music, but for a few minutes we celebrated not the death of a child but the goodness of God.

> *To God, be the glory, great things he had done*
> *So loved He the world that He gave us His Son*
> *Who yielded his life in atonement for sin*
> *And opened the lifegate, that all may come in*
> *Praise the Lord, praise the Lord,*
> *Let the world hear his voice,*
> *Praise the Lord, praise the Lord,*
> *Let the people rejoice*
> *Oh come to the Father, through Jesus the Son,*
> *And give him the glory great things He hast done.*

By now, those gathered in the room were clearly enjoying the music. Several had pulled their folding chairs near the piano. People called out their favorite hymns to me, and I tried to accommodate their requests. I had memorized most of the Broadman Hymnal and the Highway to Heaven by the time I was twelve. At times like these, I thanked God for my ability to remember most of His hymns. An elderly woman gave me her request and I started the introduction.

> *Pass me not, O gentle Savior, Hear my humble cry*
> *Hear my humble cry*
> *While on others Thou are art calling*
> *Do not pass me by.*
> *Savior, Savior, hear my humble cry*
> *While on others Thou are calling*
> *Do not pass me by...*

As the crowd quieted awaiting the next song, I heard a heavy door closing. My fingers danced on the keyboard of their own volition as I looked out the window. A tall well-dressed black man came from around the side of the building and walked to a late model sedan. I watched him as my hands, now tired and aching, placed the opening notes of one last song.

I'm so glad I'm a part of the family of God,
I've been washed in the fountain, cleansed by His blood
Joint heirs with Jesus as we travel this sod
For I'm part of the family, the family of God

The voices in the room silenced one by one until only Leigh and I were singing, my rusty alto and her clear soprano. I could hear the chairs creak as the occupants pushed them back, creating an aisle from the door to the piano. As the sounds of the last chord faded in the room, I heard slow shuffling footsteps approaching the piano. I knew who it was.

"We don't hold with thems that bear false witness," a harsh voice said. "How you kin hold your head up in this holy place, I don't know. You's always been called by the Devil. You caused all this, doing the Devil's work, mixin' with them coloreds. You kin just git out, right now, hussy."

My hands tightened into little balls in my lap. *Just breathe, deep, in and out.* I pushed back the rolling stool, stood up and turned to face Verna Hamilton and her mother, MeMaw Beeker.

"Mrs. Beeker, I'm here because Mrs. Hamilton asked for me," I said.

Forty years of hard grieving showed in Verna Beeker Hamilton's face. When she looked into my eyes, I could see traces still of the pretty girl who had eloped with Warren Hamilton. But when she dropped her eyes, her entire body sagged. The harsh black mourning dress drained what little color remained in her face. MeMaw Beeker just looked like ninety-five years of festering meanness. A short stump of liver spotted skin with stringy gray hair pulled up into a tight topknot. Heavy rolls of flesh obscured the outlines of her body. Her eyes bulged from under drooping eyelids. A black mole still quivered in the corner of her mouth. Even in my childhood, I thought her evil. I felt pity for Verna Hamilton. Forty years of grieving for a lost child, a lost husband and a lost life carried out in the presence of an overbearing and spiteful mother.

Verna looked up at me again. "That was beautiful. That what you played. I liked to think Beth Ann was off somewhere playing the piano. Are you going to play for Beth Ann's funeral? Your mama told me you would. It's her, you know. The FBI man just told me. It's my baby. She's been in that cold river for so long, but now she's coming back to me. Have you thought about my baby since she left us?" Tears ran down her creased face; her voice broke as she tried to continue. She swayed against the man supporting her.

I looked at MeMaw Beeker and then at Verna Hamilton. "Mrs. Hamilton, a day hasn't passed that I don't think about Beth Ann. Every day in my prayers I ask God to look out for her, to let her be safe and happy wherever she is. I never wanted any of this to happen; I didn't plan any of this. The last time I saw Beth Ann, she was happy. Excited. I think about that every day. And I've tried to be happy for her. But I've missed her every day. She was my best friend, and I never had another friend like her. You tell me what you want me to play, and I'll play it."

Verna looked at me and nodded. Still clinging to the man, she turned and walked toward the inner door. MeMaw Beeker followed her, a malignant expression on her face as she turned back to me.

"Al'us was a nosey interferin' brat. This is your doin's," she said.

"Hush, Mama," Verna said. "She was just a child. It weren't her fault. Don't blame her. Don't anybody blame her. There's been enough blaming for forty years. They were just children. Now Beth Ann's been brought home to me." Overcome by her grief, Verna allowed the pastor to help her out of the room. Mrs. Beeker followed them, grumbling under her breath.

I looked at Leigh and nodded towards the outside door. We smiled and made our polite good-byes to the other people in the room. As we reached the door, it swung open. On the stoop was a handsome older gentleman, tall and broad-shouldered, his hair full although snow- white. The woman with him was wearing an expensive navy suit, her ash-blond hair recently styled. Her makeup was movie-star perfect; and like a star, she looked down her nose with what could only be described as disdain.

"Brittan Lee?" His gaze slid over me and focused on Leigh. "Brittan Lee, you've grown up so." His voice cracked as he stared at my niece.

"No, I'm Leigh," she said.

"Not Brittan Lee? I thought," he broke off, pulled a snowy white handkerchief from his breast pocket and wiped his eyes. "I just thought, my baby, all grown up. She would look just like you. They were like twins."

I turned to the woman with him. "Miss Darton?" I stared at her.

"It's Mrs. Hamilton," she said as she reached for Warren Hamilton's arm.

CHAPTER SIXTEEN
Grace River, Georgia, August 2005

L eigh took my arm as we walked back to the car. "Auntie B, I'm sorry it's Beth Ann. I wish I could do something to help."

We walked over to the little church cemetery and looked at the graves. "I just can't see Beth Ann here." I watched a full-tailed red squirrel scamper across several of the graves before he ran up the trunk of an old oak. "I've always wondered where she was and why she didn't call me. I guess I can save myself thirty-nine dollars every month now." I explained the answering service to Leigh.

"Where did you think she was, Aunt B?"

"I thought she left with her daddy. She had been sneaking off to see him on our Wednesdays, because Verna wouldn't let him come back to the house to see her. I thought they had run off together. Then afterward he showed up without her and denied it. Told everyone my imagination was in overdrive. So then I thought she was with my daddy. That way I didn't have to believe Daddy was dead," I explained. "For a long time, I tried to believe maybe they were selling boiled peanuts down on Alligator Alley. Whenever someone else died unexpectedly, I would just put them down there too. Must be crowded with Daddy, Beth Ann, President Kennedy, Marilyn Monroe, and

Dr. Martin Luther King. Did I ever tell you about the time I met Dr. King?" I asked.

"No, is that another Brittan Lee/Beth Ann story?" Leigh sat down on the little brick fence around the cemetery. She dug around in her purse and found me a Kleenex.

I hadn't noticed the tears running down my face. "No, that one is a Daddy and Brittan Lee story, but Jack was there, too. Beth Ann isn't in all the stories. A lot of them—but not all. I managed to get in trouble all by myself without any difficulty." I wiped my eyes and blew my nose. "It was just more fun to have someone to get in trouble with. You know, like when you and Madison do things together."

"I've been told that our antics were close competition to yours, almost but not quite the big cigar!" Leigh said. "But then we didn't have the benefit of growing up together in Liberty, either. Just the summers. Aunt B? Sometimes I think I know how you must have felt. When you had to leave Daddy and Uncle Four and move away. I would cry for days each fall when I had to go home to Columbia and leave everyone here."

I blew my nose again and stood up.

"Aunt B, what was it like? When everything was segregated?" Leigh stood up and brushed off the back of her skirt.

"Well, remember, I was nine. I lived in a white neighborhood; my school was three houses down the street. I didn't know what segregation even was until I met Tansie at her church that first night. I still didn't understand what she meant until one day when I went to the library with Trulee."

***

Liberty, Georgia, August 1964
The grits were bubbling in the pot on the stove, and the

smell of our homemade fresh country sausage filled the kitchen in clouds of fragrant steam every time Trulee raised the lid of the cast iron skillet to turn the patties. Granddaddy made his own sausage from a recipe passed down from his granddaddy. I thought it was delicious until I discovered the main ingredient was the adult off-spring of the droopy-eared Duroc mama pig at the Homeplace. I must not have been very bright; it took two years of the ritual fall hog-killing before I realized where the missing pigs went.

I was in the big pantry, looking for an old box of Quaker Oatmeal. It was an empty box, empty of oatmeal, but filled with my stories. My head was always bursting with stories I want to write about Liberty, and Sapelo Sound and the Homeplace and the people who lived there. Stories I heard when picking up fresh seafood at the docks or when helping Daddy tend to the hurt folks up at the farm.

Mama didn't seem to like my stories. "Brittan Lee, honey, why do you always write so much about the colored people? Here's a nice book for you about General Oglethorpe and Mary Musgrove. Why don't you write about them?" she would say to me. Or, "Brittan Lee, you need to practice your piano lessons. Put away those old stories."

Mama would go through my desk and my bookcases and look for my stories, so I hid them in the piano bench. When she found them there, I had to find a new hiding place. From experience, I knew it couldn't be in my room, or the playroom or in the piano. In Brownies, we made Christmas lanterns from empty oatmeal boxes. I brought my lantern home and put my stories in it and hid it in the pantry with the other cereal boxes. I finished a new story the night before about the Deacon, and I wanted to hide it before Mama woke up. I searched all the cereal boxes and even opened up a shredded wheat carton, but

I couldn't find my box. I was fixing to ask Trulee when I heard Daddy in the kitchen.

"Morning, Trulee. That sausage sure smells good."

"One of Mr. Jack's better years. I think he's got a new spice blend. Tastes like a bit more cayenne pepper and even a dash of cinnamon. You want some eggs?"

Familiar sounds and smells came from the kitchen: the sizzling of butter in Trulee's other cast iron skillet, the crack of egg shells against the bowl, the rattling of the metal whisk whipping the eggs into a frothy yellow liquid.

"Marsh, I want you to be careful now. I'm hearing things, talk around the Quarters." Trulee's voice was lowered.

"What kind of things?"

"Some of those people in the country heard about the group up in Dorchester. Getting a bit antsy. You know Gus has a group of the Freedom Riders camping out in the old missionary school and going around to the different towns. They been talking to some of the older boys. Right now, they're just pushing people to register to vote."

"I know. That's what Jack is doing this summer, helping Gus. Trulee, I want them to vote. I've promised them changes, and I'm making them. Everything can't change at once. I've just been on the City Council three years, and you know this is my first term as mayor. Little steps, my daddy always said. Little steps, and before you know it, you've crossed the whole field. First it was my office, then the hospital. This fall, the elementary schools."

A chair scraped across the floor tiles. I peeked around the pantry door to see Trulee sit down next to Daddy and put her hand on his arm. "I'm worried, Marsh. Gus has heard talk about some beatings and other carrying-ons. Some of them people are joining up and hassling the coloreds. It's like when

Mr. Willis was a boy. They're trying to get the old groups up again."

"I need to talk to him. See what I can do to help."

Trulee pushed back her chair, stood and turned to the bubbling eggs.

"Just promise you'll be careful."

"What can happen to me today? Rounds at the hospital, patients, and then a meeting at the Library."

"Daddy! Can I go to the hospital with you today?" I came out of the pantry. I don't think I was supposed to notice the look Daddy gave Trulee over my head.

"Not today, Princess. I've got to see patients, and then go to the Library for a Library Board meeting." He smiled at Trulee as she handed him his breakfast plate.

"Daddy! Can I go to the Library with you? I want some new books to read. Mama says I need to read more books. Please?" I gave him my best pleading look. "Mama's got Bridge Club, so she can't take me. Please?"

"I can drop her off, Dr. Marsh, on my way home. Then she can come back with you. If that's not a problem."

***

"Twenty-one, twenty-two, twenty-three, twenty-four, twenty-five," I skipped up the white granite steps of the Liberty County Public Library. I swung Trulee's arm with each step. I loved the big old library, with all the little nooks to curl up in when you want to read a book. The tall windows were shaded by oak trees, with the gray tendrils hanging from the branches, swaying in the off shore winds. "Come on, come on!"

"Slow down, child, you'll plumb wear me out. Some of us worked all day," Trulee grumbled, but she swung my arm, too. I pulled her through the big double doors and down the hallway to the children's book section. There was a new Madeleine L'Engle book I wanted to check out. I knew it was coming in this week and Mrs. Taunch, the Children's Librarian, promised to save it for me.

"Lan' sakes!" Trulee stopped short at the Distribution Desk. "Oh, dear." She eyed the group at the desk. Six little colored girls about my size, dressed up in their Sunday dresses and braided hair, waited in line with three older women. Each of the girls held three books. I smiled and started to wave at Tansie before I remembered that Trulee didn't know about my Wednesday night adventures.

"You girls know the rules. One book each. Go put the others on the book cart. It's going to take me an hour to reshelve those books. I don't understand why you're trying to do this." Mrs. Taunch stood behind her desk, arms folded over her chest, guarding her red pencils, date stamps and card catalog.

"My little girl, she wants three books. She reads up the one book you let her have in just a few days. Then she cain't get no more for two weeks." The first woman, shoulders slumped, still dressed in a grey uniform with white apron, placed her daughter's three choices on the desk. "These books, please, Miss Librarian. Cain't she have three? She treats them good. She likes to read. It keeps her out of trouble." It was Tansie's mama, and I knew her. Her name was Cora, and she swept up the colored ward at the hospital. Tansie stood next to her, head bowed, staring at her feet.

I looked at her and remembered the promise I had made on Wednesday. I must have squeezed Trulee's hand, because she looked down at me, as I was watching the girls waiting in the line.

Trulee looked at the line of little girls, all quiet, almost holding their breath. They looked at the floor, at Trulee, at the books in their arms, everywhere but at the librarian. Trulee guided me over behind a nearby bookcase, then she straightened up, smoothed her skirt and stepped up to the desk. "Mrs. Taunch, can't you please let the girls have three books? It's so hard for their mamas to bring them here, they all work. Children need to be able to read. These are all good girls, they go to my church. They take proper care of the books. I speak for them and their mamas."

"Trulee, I'm ashamed for you, and I know Dr. Hayworth would be too. Now I don't make the rules, but I am obliged to follow them, and you should know better than to try and make me bend those rules. Colored children can check out one book every two weeks."

"Mrs. Taunch, I've looked up the rules, and they don't make no difference between white children and colored children. I don't see why you can't find the kindness in your heart to let these children have three little books. Didn't you like to read as a child? School is out and the library is the only place they can get books. They parents, they can't afford to buy books; they's struggling to feed their babies. We should be welcoming all the children, not excluding them."

My heart just swelled up as I watched Trulee do what I had promised.

"You high steppin' yellow girls think you can just march in and tell me what to do. And you, Trulee Hayworth, you think you have a greater right than anyone. Well, you don't. Just because you can read doesn't mean you can tell me what to do. I know what the rules are, and I don't care how you interpret it, that rule is still going to be one book for each colored child. No exceptions. And if you don't just quiet down, right now, I'm gonna call down the security guard and he'll escort all of you out. Then none of those pickaninnies will have any books.

Is that what you want? Do you want to be responsible for depriving those children of any books?" Mrs. Taunch's voice got real ugly to match her face. Her mouth scrunched up and her lips were tight and her eyes were just about squinted shut. She slammed her hand down on the desk, rattling the pencils in the cup and the stamps on the stamp racks.

Tansie started to tremble, and her mama whispered into her ear. I was close enough to hear her.

"Don't let that mean skinny white woman scare you, baby. You take control of how you feel, and you keep that control inside of you." Tansie nodded, her face still pale. She tried hard, but three or four tears still ran down her cheek. "Now wipe your face."

"I'm beggin', Mrs. Taunch, as a Christian woman, to please let these children to check out three books. You aren't losing anything and..."

She cut Trulee off with an imperial sweep of her hand. "That is enough! I will be speaking to Dr. Hayworth about this, you...you...country trash! You children! Put those books over on that cart. You may bring one book. Do you understand? Do I need to speak any more clearly? One book. Now..." Mrs. Taunch turned her back on Trulee and reached for the first book, held out in shaking hands by Tansie's mama. Mrs. Taunch stamped her date stamp on the little card, which she slid into the pocket of the book. "Due back two weeks from today. Wash your hands before handling the pages. Do not eat or drink when reading this book. This book is the property of the Liberty Library. Next?"

"Brittan Lee?" Trulee gently shook my shoulder. I buried my face in her skirt and sobbed. "Baby, what's the matter? It's alright. Ever' thing's alright."

"But Trulee, she was so mean to you. She don't have no

right to be so mean." I looked at Trulee, my eyes full of tears. "She goes to the Methodist Church every Sunday. Her and Dr. Taunch, they come to our house for parties. She always smiles so pretty to me, and she buys her clothes up in Atlanta. How can she talk like that to you and those girls? It just ain't right."

"Shh, now. Pretty is as pretty does, I tell you that all the time, now don't I?" Trulee pulled a tissue out of her pocket and wiped my face. She held me close. "Baby, I've had people talk nasty to me before. Words ain't gonna to hurt me. Usually, people mean like that, they's afraid."

"Afraid of what?"

"Well, change. There's going to be some changes, and people are afraid. Now, listen to me, Brittan Lee. I'm going to drive these ladies and their little girls home in the station wagon. You go right over back there and look at the books. Your Daddy is upstairs at that meeting if you need somethin', but I should be back before he comes out. Stay right here. Promise?"

I looked past Trulee at the small stack of books, abandoned on the book cart. "Trulee, it's just not right for her to do that, is it? It's just not right."

"Honey, just because it ain't right doesn't mean it ain't done."

"Trulee, why ain't people fair? Doesn't Jesus say for all the little children to come to Him? Red and yellow and black and white? Don't Methodists believe in Jesus?"

"Brittan Lee, people ain't always fair. That's just life. What's important is for you to be fair to everybody. Now you stay right here and wait for me."

I waited until Trulee walked past the Distribution Desk, her back held straight and her head high. Mrs. Taunch stopped stamping books to glare at Trulee as she gathered up the girls and their mamas.

"Mrs. Taunch?"

She jumped about three feet up. "Oh, Brittan Lee. I didn't see you come in. How is your Mama? I meant to call her about the Ladies Medical Auxiliary Guild Meeting. That's a pretty dress you have on today? Did your Grandmama make that one? She has such a way with smocking."

"Mama's just fine, Mrs. Taunch. Thank you for the compliment on my dress. These books are mine." I pushed the stack of books across the counter, my name printed with neat precision on twelve check-out cards.

"These are a lot of books, Brittan Lee."

"Yes ma'am. My mama says I should read more."

"I think you have checked some of these out before. Yes, yes you have. Look here, this was two summers ago, July 2, 1962," she pointed to where my name on the card from earlier. "I think you are reading at least three levels above most of these books."

"Yes ma'am. I must really like the stories. To read them again, I mean."

"I surely hope you aren't trying to be a 'Miss Smarty Pants' with me, young lady?" I don't know how she spit out the words. Her lips were pinched so tight you couldn't see any of her Tangee Pink lipstick. "I certainly don't think your father would want that."

"No, ma'am. He certainly wouldn't want that. Thank you, Mrs. Taunch." I picked up the books and walked down the hall. I hoped my back was as straight as Trulee's.

Tears streamed down Leigh's face. "How could people be so horrid?" Leigh asked. "Trulee was so brave. You were, too. The librarian was an educated woman; how could she act like that?"

I wiped my eyes again. "Having an education didn't necessarily make one a social egalitarian. Trulee was the brave one. As far as I know, that was when she came out of the closet with her real work. I found out later that she had been working with her church, and with Daddy and his friend Gus, and the people at Dorchester. Where Daddy and Trulee grew up, at HomePlace, everyone was treated about the same. It sure was a shock to Daddy when Trulee and Gus couldn't come with him to the University. But Granddaddy sent them to college in Atlanta. Gus went to Morehouse, and Trulee went to Spelman. A lot of people don't know it, and they try to put her down. When she works with the black families, she has to talk like them so they don't feel like she is making fun of them."

"Trulee went to college?" Leigh almost tripped over a tree root, too busy staring at me to pay attention to her feet. "Why was she a maid?"

"There weren't a lot of job options for black women back then. Black wasn't yet beautiful," I said to Leigh sotto voce. "Everyone thought she was just a maid. But she held classes at night at the church, helping teach the black adults to read and do math. She was a substitute teacher at the colored school. I've got to get over saying *colored*. It's just that was the preferred term in those days. I showed my backside once and said the 'N' word, and I thought Mama was going to tear that backside right off of me." I rubbed the backside in question. "I never, ever said that word again."

Leigh started laughing. "I just can't see Grandmama whupping you."

"She did. And it wasn't the first time, and it wasn't the last time." I climbed in the car, buckled my seatbelt and turned to Leigh.

"So," she said as she started the engine, "Just how old is she?"

"Which one? Verna Hamilton is your grandmama's age. MeMaw Beeker is her mother, so that would put her about ninety-five or so. The new Mrs. Hamilton would be in her mid seventies." I looked back at the little church and the Cadillac parked in front of the door. "I wonder how long she has been Mrs. Hamilton."

Leigh pulled the car out onto Grace River Road and started back for Liberty. "It's getting dark. I hope it doesn't rain for Grandmama's party."

I looked at the cloud front. "Weather Channel has a tropical storm alert, but it isn't supposed to hit for several days. I hope it holds off until after the funeral. This may just be the daily thunderstorm."

"Is it named yet?" Leigh asked.

"Daphne, I think," I said. "Listen, pull over will you? I need to get something to drink." I motioned to another of the little store-diners. A small white building, a faded advertisement for *Coca-Cola available in bottles* was painted on the side. A path from the back porch meandered down to a small dock. Two steps made of concrete block and two-by-eight boards led to the front porch and screened doors. "This was another one of my Uncle Frank's stops."

The parking lot was empty except for a pair of trucks. "What exactly did you and Uncle Frank do?" Leigh asked as she sat at one of the three little tables. Her eyes darted around the room, watching out the window.

"Just drove around and visited with people," I said.

"He'p you with som'pin?" A woman called over from the back of the store. She came out from behind a row of shelves, wiping her hands on the towel tied around her waist. "Got some fresh oysters, just pulled this morning. Just mixed up some crab cakes. Iffen you already had your lunch, I can toast some pound cake. Tea's ready, or co-cola or coffee." She looked at me. "You from around here?"

"Not for a long time," I said. "We're just here for a funeral. I think some tea please and some of the pound cake."

"The same," Leigh said.

The woman nodded. She walked to the back of the store where we heard her talking to someone. After a brief period, she returned with two glasses of tea, six slices of toasted pound cake and a bowl of blackberry jam. "You don't talk like you was from around here, but just a bit. Call if you need som'pin else," she said.

I watched her walk to the back of the shop. "I'm like Trulee and Tansie. My voice has a split personality. When I come home to Georgia, they say I talk like a Yankee, that I've lost my southern voice. When I am up north, they tell me I talk like I have sugar melting in my mouth."

Leigh spread jam on one of the pieces of warm cake. "You do talk a little bit funny. Faster than Grandmama or Daddy, but underneath it all, I can tell you grew up here." She took a bite of her cake. "Heavenly," she said. "Okay, back to Uncle Frank. He had to have some kind of job, didn't he? How come nobody talks about him, even Auntabelle, and he was her husband."

"I loved doing things with Uncle Frank. He had a red convertible, and we would drive around and my hair would blow in the wind. I always felt special when I was out with him," I stopped and sipped at my tea. "He had a lot of jobs. Usually selling something. He was actually a very good salesman. People enjoyed talking to him. Mama always said he could sell refrigerators to the Eskimos."

"Like I loved doing things with you," she blinked, sipped her tea, then continued. "So why did Uncle Frank have so many jobs?" she asked as her eyes flickered over to the door and back.

"He had a, uh, mental illness of some type. I don't think I ever knew exactly what it was. But every now and then he would have a spell, and he would go over to Milledgeville, spend a few weeks or a month there. Then he would come back and start over." I looked around the little store. I could still hear voices from the back room. Crabs scuttled around in a large metal tank by the door. Baskets of muscadines, peaches and tomatoes spread bright color in racks by the door. The fragrances competed with the sharp, salty scent of the crabs. If I closed my eyes, I could be nine years old and eating toasted pound cake and watching the crabs race.

From outside the battered screened door, I heard the sound of tires crunching on the oyster-shell parking lot. A car door slammed. A few moments later the springs on the door creaked as it was pulled open and a man entered. He looked to be in his sixties, a perpetual farmer's tan on his arms. A thick roll of soft belly hung over the waist of faded work pants. A worn straw hat rested just above a pair of Ray-bans. He stood inside the doorway near the counter and watched us.

"What's at Milledgeville?" Leigh grabbed my attention back. "Except for the college?"

I looked at the man, who was now leaning against the wooden counter. He looked at me, then spit on the floor. Still watching me, he pulled a hunting knife from a leather sheath on his belt and picked at his fingernails. After spitting on the floor again, he resheathed the knife and walked past us heading towards the back of the store.

I swallowed more tea against the sudden dryness in my throat. "Uh, nothing. Uncle Frank went to Milledgeville State Hospital. It was the state mental hospital. Anyway, every now and then he would check himself in, get some shock therapy, come back home. I think he would have been classified as bi-polar these days. On his manic days, he would drive around, talk to everyone; it was when he was depressed that he would have to go to Milledgeville."

Silence hung in the room; the only sound came from the crabs scuttling in the big zinc tub. I looked up to see Leigh staring at the back of the room. She jerked as she turned back in her seat and brushed the cake crumbs off her lap.

"Oh, I remember reading an article about the hospital when I was helping Grandmama with some genealogy research," she said. "So what was Uncle Frank selling that summer? Do you want that last piece of cake?"

I gestured for her to take it. "I thought he was selling insurance. Sometimes, he would pull up in front of a store like this and give me an envelope to take inside. I thought it was somebody's policy. I didn't know that I was passing messages for the Klan. Notes about meetings and plans and things."

Leigh spewed her tea over the table and started coughing.

I got up and started pounding on her back. "Enough, enough!" she gasped. "That's just so hard to believe. My aunt, the civil rights activist, a secret spy for the KKK."

"I don't think I would call myself an activist, and it wasn't the KKK, just a group of wanna-bes. Are you about ready?"

She agreed, and we left after leaving money on the table for the food.

"How about letting me drive?" I asked.

"Can you drive a stick?" Leigh asked.

"Have you forgotten who taught you?" I said as I slipped the keys from her fingers. "Climb in." I had forgotten the fun of driving a fast car on the old back-roads. The Porsche met every advertising slogan it had ever boasted. Tires gripped the road as I steered into the curves; the suspension was perfect. The accelerator responded smoothly to the slightest pressure. All I needed were black leather gloves and a pair of Todd's driving loafers. I flashed a grin at Leigh.

These were familiar roads; memories of previous trips flooded my consciousness as signs for Little Creek, Harris Neck, Carnegan, Mud Cat Creek came and went in the blur of wind. I knew when to slow for the little communities, and when it was safe to open up the speed. When I concentrated on driving, I didn't have to think about Beth Ann or Daddy or Ebon.

"Aunt B!" Leigh shouted over the roar. She tapped my hand, which rested on the stick shift. "Who do you think was driving the car with Beth Ann? And if Beth Ann was in the car, then why did that young man die in the fire?"

I glanced at her, then in the rear-view mirror. "That, my dear, is going to be the million-dollar question. And I think that is why the FBI is really here."

I looked in the mirror again. A large, dusty, black truck was tight on our tail.

Leigh saw me look up. "He's been following us for a while," she said.

"Probably just one of the local farmers or fishermen," I said. I sped up to increase the distance between the two vehicles, but the truck stayed right behind us. I slowed to allow him to pass us, but he didn't. The truck just dropped back a few yards and continued to pace us.

"Who is it?" I shouted. "Do you know the truck?"

"No," Leigh said. "Was it in the parking lot at that store?"

"Can you see the driver?" I looked at the rear- view mirror, but the angle of the truck cab was too high.

"No, it looks like he has a ball cap pulled down over his eyes. Those aren't Georgia plates," Leigh said. "I don't know why he has those sunglasses on. It's getting darker."

She was right. The heavy cloud cover darkened the sky. There was a crisp clearness in the air that usually preceded a thunderstorm. "I think we need to stop and put up the roof," I said.

I decreased the speed even further to well below the forty-five mile per hour limit. The truck slowed to match my own speed and hung back just far enough that we couldn't see the driver clearly.

"Maybe we should just keep driving. Maybe we can beat the storm home," Leigh said, her eyes wide. "Besides, I don't know how to put the roof up."

"Hold on," I told Leigh as I hit the accelerator hard then made a quick left turn at the Ardoch State Historical marker and headed south on the old State Road. Even over the engine noise, I could hear the truck's tires squeal as the driver braked and made the turn following us. I kept my foot on the pedal as I pushed the convertible for more speed. Ahead, I saw the marker for Old Carnochan Creek Road. I didn't start to brake until I was three quarters into the turn, hoping the truck driver would fly past us. The car tried to cling to the road, but despite best efforts, we skidded sideways, kicking pea gravel and grass clods several feet into the air. I kept going.

"He missed the turn!" Leigh screamed. "Faster, Aunt B!" She reached to the floor and pulled up her purse, rummaging through it with one hand.

I slammed on the brakes and made a right turn into the driveway of an abandoned gas station. Behind the old oil bays I followed the tracks of the alley back to the River Road and headed east again. The sky flashed with heavy forks of lightning followed almost immediately with loud rumbles of thunder. Heavy rain drops hit the road. Our speed kept the dampness out of the car.

"Why isn't there any other traffic?" Leigh said.

As if by prophesy, when we rounded the next curve, a large John Deere tractor pulling a round baler took up his lane and half of the other side of the road. As we came up behind the tractor, the driver waved and motioned us around him.

"Oh, geez," Leigh let out her breath. "I thought that guy was chasing us. I started wondering if we had forgotten to pay for the tea or something." She let out a half-hearted laugh and waved her cell-phone. "I was just about to call Daddy."

I kept driving and taking quick looks into the rear view mirror. The rain was sheeting across the highway. "This is worse than the usual summer afternoon storm," I yelled at Leigh. We had made it about another two miles when I saw a flash in the mirror. "Damn!" I kept my foot on the accelerator as we entered the next curve. Letting my foot off the pedal, I allowed the car to slow down as I searched the roadside for familiar landmarks. When I spotted one, I turned the car onto an old farm driveway, sliding between the fence posts. We bounced over the cattle-grid covering the culvert and cut a new path down the overgrown driveway. I turned off the headlights and steered by the flashes of lightning. Long stems of grass beat against the undercarriage of the car and whipped the sides. Just past a row of huge oaks, I cut the engine and held on for dear life as the car crashed to a stop in the ruins of old Mr. LaCroix's broken-down tractor shed. We sat there in silence watching the road through the gaps in the broken boards, rain dripping from the holes in the shed roof. The black truck sped past our hiding place heading south on the River Road.

A brilliant flash of fire lit the shed through the veil of kudzu, followed by thunder so loud it drowned the sounds of our labored breath.

I looked at Leigh. Her wet hair was plastered to her skull and her teeth were chattering.

"I guess he was following us," she said.

CHAPTER EIGHTEEN
The Ridge, North Liberty County, Georgia, August 2005

Leigh's teeth chattered as we sat out the rainstorm in the dilapidated old tractor shed. The remnants of the rusted tin roof and the thick layer of kudzu kept out the worst of the storm, but the heavy gusts of horizontal wind lifted the leaves on the sides, allowing rain to drench us.

When the rain slowed then stopped, I started the car and tried to back out of the shed. One back tire spun on the matted grass and the engine whined. Slight movements of the car caused branches and pieces of shed to shift their balance and scrape the sides of Quince's prized possession. I stopped the car and opened the door, but it would only move a few inches before it caught on the debris. "I don't believe I'm doing this," I muttered as I stood up on the leather seat and hiked my skirt up to my thighs. Sitting on the back of the seat, I swung my legs around to the boot of the car and slid down to the ground. I opened the trunk and rummaged through the collection of beach towels, looking for anything to wrap around Leigh, to dry her off and warm her up.

"Wrap these around you, baby." I shook off most of the sand and handed two of the towels to Leigh.

"Quince is going to absolutely kill us. We've trashed his upholstery," Leigh dabbed at the leather dashboard with her towel. "Lordy, he is going to be so mad."

"I wonder what kind of insurance Quince has," I said, thinking about the gouges and scrapes I saw on the previously immaculate red finish.

"I think he has one of those specialty policies because of his speeding tickets." Leigh finished towel-drying her hair, then looked at me. "Aunt B, why was that man chasing us?" When she leveled those green eyes at me, it was just like Mama all over again.

"I don't know," I admitted. "I have no idea who it was or why. Did you get a close look? Was it someone we saw today at the church? But that still doesn't make any sense." My sense of righteous indignation took over. "That idiot could have killed us! Why in the piddle-pants was he driving like a bat out of Hades?"

"Move over, I'm coming out," Leigh stood up on her seat, clambered over the back and slid down the trunk. Her skirt slid up her thighs as she climbed out. "Yuck! My heels are stuck in the mud." She took a few careful steps, placing her feet on grassy areas.

I stared at her, at the large fist size bruises on her thighs. "Leigh? Honey, what happened to you?"

She straightened up, smoothing her skirt back down to her knees. "Nothing!" Her face flushed and the jaw trembled just a little. "I'm a little clumsy sometimes. I think I tried to sit down and missed the chair. Anyway, do you think he knows where we are? In fact, where the hell are we?"

"Hmm, this used to be old Mr. LaCroix's place. He was old when I was little. I imagine he's passed now. Don't know if it was inherited or sold. Doesn't look like anyone has taken care of this field for a long time. That grass thatches over, gets thick. Makes it really hard to plow. I think we're safe here though. The rain and wind blew all over the tracks we drove in on, can't tell we drove there. The car is hidden in the shed. We can duck back in if we hear traffic." I looked at the farm lane and out to the road. "There is a fresh water ditch by the road; it winds back to the river. I used to catch tadpoles there."

"So where are we exactly?"

"Um, Sapelo Sound is about three miles that way," I pointed. "Where we merged at that curve—if I had turned left instead of merging right, we would have ended up at Sapelo Sound."

"So why didn't we?" Leigh walked around the tractor shed.

"I was going too fast to turn left. I'm hoping that whoever that was thought I did go to Sapelo Sound. We would be safe there." I turned to her.

"So, Aunt B, why is Daddy so worried about you? And with good cause, it seems!"

"Like I said last night, there were a lot of Klan wanna-bes back then. Agent Zeller said the FBI is re-examining a lot of the civil rights cases. People are finally coming forward. New evidence is being discovered or old evidence re-examined. I always said that some of those friends of Uncle Frank were involved in that big fire in 1964."

"I thought the hurricane did that," Leigh interrupted.

"That's what they want everyone to believe. I know they beat up on Ebon at least twice, and he hadn't done anything. Neither had the other black people. Well, anything other than challenge the status quo. Ebon didn't take Beth Ann, and he wasn't responsible for Daddy. Don't believe what they say. Ebon was an angry young man. He was a good looking man and that's something else that scared the white men." My throat got raspy and closed up when I talked about Ebon. I followed Leigh to where berry vines climbed the shed. ""I call those dewberries. I used to pick baskets of them, and Trulee would make cobbler Think we can talk Trulee into cobbler?"

Leigh laughed. "Grandmama and Trulee are into nouvelle southern cuisine. They might make tiny berry tartlets with mint leaf decor. What do we have to put them in?"

"Go look in Quince's trunk. I think I saw a garbage bag. And see if you can reach your cell phone. We need to call somebody to come pull us out." While Leigh went for the bag, I walked a bit further.

"Aunt B? Aunt B?" Leigh was shaking my arm. "Earth to B!"

"Oh, sorry. I was daydreaming."

"Thought I had lost you there. I was trying to remember the signs of shock. I think we're both in it. Why else would we be looking for dewberries at a time like this?" Leigh took the berries from my hand and placed them gently in the bag to prevent bruising. "What were you looking at?"

She looked over at the giant oak stump. Dozens and dozens of old faded beer cans lay half buried in the ground surrounding the tree roots. Red and green shotgun casings decorated the area like left-over Christmas ornaments. The remnants of a metal lawn chair lay crumpled like the skeleton of an unknown animal. "Litterbugs! What was this? Party Central?"

I stared at the stump and the accompanying paraphernalia. "It was no party."

CHAPTER NINETEEN
The Ridge, North Liberty County, Georgia, August 1964

I hate this heat," Mama complained as Daddy steered the big Chevy from the farm lane onto the highway. "I don't see what was so important that we had to come up here. Oh, this wind is going to ruin my hair for church tomorrow." She tried to keep the ends of her pale hair tucked into her French twist against the gusts blowing in from the window as the car speed increased.

"Arabella, you know I try to come up at least once a week. Mr. Jenkins seemed to think it was important enough to call me." Daddy stared straight ahead at the road home.

The Shell Road ran from Savannah to Brunswick following the original path worn down by the feet of the Guale Indians and the Spanish monks sent to civilize them. It is an old road, with the history of the coastal region spelled out in black letters on the green roadside markers. Daddy would stop and read the markers to me almost every time we drove up to the farm. *See here, Brittan Lee, this says that in 1736 General James Oglethorpe established Fort Darien on the Altamaha River for the protection of the colonies against the threat of Spanish Invasion.* Every turn, every tree and most of the side roads between Liberty and the farm are ingrained my mind. Even now I can close my eyes and follow the green canopy of the live oaks swaying with heavy fringes of moss as it curves from the manicured lawns of the in-town homes, past the Witch's Tree, the stands of old growth pine and the roadside stands stacked with red tomatoes, green turnips and yellow corn, follow it all the way to the turn at the big iron gate at River Place.

Daddy was a gentleman farmer, took after his own Daddy that way. Granddaddy owned most of what used to be Long County, his daddy before him, and I imagine his daddy before that. One male child in each generation stayed with the farm, one became a doctor and one became a lawyer, like in the rhyme we used for jumping rope. Girl children were expected to marry well, and if more than three male children survived childhood, then they could choose to do what they wanted. Daddy was the number two male; he was the doctor. But he loved the feel of rich Georgia dirt on his hands and the taste of vegetables so fresh you wanted to slap them. Daddy had barely even set up his medical practice when he bought six hundred acres on Mud Creek off North Sound, in the very north-east part of Liberty County. Sapelo Sound became Daddy's refuge from work, from Mama. And ever since I was big enough to say "Me go, too," I'd been coming with him. Once a week, sometimes twice a week. It was my refuge, too.

"Well, and just what was so important? Nothing. I don't know why I came up here with you. There's nothing but bugs and heat and dirt. Look how dirty Brittan Lee is. The car just gets filthy, and then I have to get Raymond to clean it out before we can use it for church. "

This was a familiar litany; it came with every trip. I stopped listening as soon as she started. I opened the white bag I had tucked beside me on the back seat and counted the large red and white striped peppermints inside: twenty fat puffy peppermints, bought with the twenty cents Four had given me, bribe money I had used to buy this special treat at the candy-counter at McIver's General Store at The Ridge.

Daddy always stopped and bought us a cold Co-cola at the store. It wasn't much of a store, but then the people who lived there didn't have much money. They traded fresh vegetables, oysters and shrimp for the grits and cornmeal and salt Mr. McIver stocked.

Mama looked in the rear-view mirror. "And where did you get money for that candy, young lady? Don't you eat all that candy; you'll be sick for sure. And don't get that book all sticky and dirty. What book is that?"

I ignored her, pretending that I didn't hear her over the rush of wind.

"What in the..? What's he doing? We don't run chain gangs anymore!" Daddy pulled the car over to the side of the road, pulling up the parking brake as the car coasted to a stop. He climbed out and walked over to where a deputy sat, cool in the shade of one of the live oaks. A pump shotgun leaned against the trunk of the tree, and the ground was littered with cigarette butts and empty beer cans. The deputy, young but already sporting a beer-induced pot belly, was watching eight colored men working in the field alongside the road. Some of the colored men were just boys, not much older than Four or Jack. They were all hunched over, not looking at the car or Daddy, chopping at the mat of grass with hoes, trying to break the thatch. Metal cuffs and chains attached one bloody ankle to another, limiting the progress of one man to that of his partner. The striped shirts and pants were dirty and heavy with the sweat of fieldwork. Black flies and horseflies swarmed, diving and biting the men.

"Brittan Lee, get back in here right this minute," I heard Mama call after me. When I looked back at the car, Mama was busy rolling up the windows and locking the car doors.

"I'm just going to look for dewberries, Mama. So Trulee can make a cobbler," I went over towards the culvert that allowed cars to drive over the ditch and turn into the old tractor lane. Dark red and black berries hung from vines that clung to the rotten fence posts and tumbled down to the ditch. Hidden from view, I could still hear bits and pieces of Daddy and the deputy talking.

"….we don't run chain gangs anymore…"

"…special case, picked 'em up last night….gotta put 'em to use…wrong place at the right time." The deputy spit. "Hey, better tell your little gal there to stay clear. These's dangerous niggers, murderin', thieving lot of 'em."

Daddy's voice dropped, and he started talking like Mr. Jenkins does, sort of like he didn't have much schooling. "Hell, deputy, you know they ain't dangerous! I bet you not one single man out there did anything you and I ain't done. Trouble is, they's colored and did it."

"Yeah, you got that right, Doc. Anyways, since the Admin-is-trative office is closed 'til Monday, can't book 'em in, can't bond them out. So'se I thought, maybe I'd help Mr. LaCroix break out this field. Him being such a big donor to the sheriff's campaign fund. You unnerstan' how hard this shit is to plow." The deputy bit off another plug of tobacco. "You know the sheriff; he likes to help his supporters. He don't see nothing wrong with a little work out of the jail pop-u-lation. Keeps 'em quiet at night, stops 'em from fighting in the cells."

From the ditch, I could see Daddy looking around. "You think it's a good idea giving them all this beer?"

"Hee, hee, hee! That's a good one, Doc. Hey, you want one," he gestured to the few remaining unopened cans. "I got a church key here somewheres. Anyway, this is my beer. I ain't wasting it on no niggers."

"I don't see any water buckets. You been working them all day without water?" Daddy asked.

I knew that tone of voice. That was Daddy's real quiet mad voice. That deputy didn't seem to know he was getting himself into real trouble.

"Cain't check 'em in, cain't get no food tickets for 'em," the deputy said as if that explained everything.

"I see," Daddy nodded. "But you do know that if you work 'em in this heat, without food or water, they're gonna seize up on you?"

Straightening from his slouch, the deputy reached for his shotgun. "Seize me? Nobody's gonna seize me when I got this here."

"No, I mean seize up like having a fit, and they can die. You're a good Christian man, right, deputy? Go to church and all?"

The deputy spit on the ground by the empty beer cans. "Ever' Sunday, 'cept when I'm working or hunting. I'm a deacon at Old Grace River Freewill of Prophesy Baptist."

"And you like your job? Working with the sheriff?"

"Purty well. He can be a hard man, but fair, genr'ly. Why, Doc? You thinking of runnin' for sheriff?"

"No, no, the Sheriff is a good friend of mine. But if you can't give these men some food and water because it's the Christian thing to do, then do it because I don't know how you can hide a dead body from the sheriff. And you're gonna have at least one dead body in this heat."

The prisoners were closer to me. I could see them chopping, and every second or third chop, I could see a hand reach down and grab a dewberry. The hoes flashed bright splashes of reflected light, and I realized they were moving together, in harmony. Coming low over the field, hushed voices sang, the steady pace of the words timed to the downbeat of the hoes. I knew that song. I had heard that song on my Wednesday night forays...*Dan-iel in the Lion's Den, Dan-iel, in the Lion's Den, Dan-iel in the Li-on's Den...*

The white paper bag crackled in my grasp. A prisoner looked up from the ground, glancing over at me. His left eye was swollen shut, caked blood dried on his face, and a line of fresh wet blood ran from where a cut over his eyebrow had torn open. Flies crawled over the crusted surface, but whenever he tried to rub them off on his shoulder, the cut reopened. There was more crusted blood on his lip and chin. I could hear him breathing through his open mouth, ragged, gasping. He wiped his mouth on the dirty, stained shirt sleeve and looked me full in the face. It was Ebon.

"Brittan Lee? Where are you?"

I straightened all the way up. "Here I am, Daddy. I was looking for dewberries, and I found some tadpoles in the stream in this ditch."

Daddy looked at the deputy, then over at me. At some point in their conversation, Daddy had become the superior, the determiner of the rules. "How much water is in the stream, Brittan Lee?"

"I don't know. About to my ankles, I think."

"Is it flowing? Drop a leaf on the water and see if the water moves."

The deep green of the dewberry leaf floated for a moment then disappeared down the stream. "It's going pretty fast, Daddy."

"Good girl. Now go to the car and have your Mama give you those empty Coca-cola bottles and put them by the ditch."

I performed my assigned task and got back into the car. Daddy gave the deputy a long look and said something I couldn't hear. The deputy looked every which way except at Daddy, but he nodded as he examined his boots.

"It's about time," Mama complained as Daddy started the car and pulled back out on the road. The front window went down, and the wind filled the backseat. "I don't know what you thought you could do. You're the Mayor, not the sheriff, and this isn't the city." She sat back and rested her head on the fake velvet headrest.

"Mama, you're squashing your hairdo." I turned and watched as the prisoners became smaller and smaller in the back window.

"Brittan Lee, pass me up one of those peppermints, please. My mouth is as dry as beach sand, sitting here in this hot car."

Images of puffy red peppermints came and went in my head. I could taste the sugary-sweet tang, and the coolness that would go all the way up and down my windpipe when I took a deep breath, clearing my nose and sinuses. My ears started to buzz, and the inside of the car went dark. "There aren't any more, Mama."

Mama turned and looked at me. The last thing I heard before everything got hot and went black was Mama.

"Stop the car, Marsh, stop, now! I told you she was going to be sick if she ate all those peppermints."

CHAPTER TWENTY
Liberty, Georgia, August 2005

Unusual sounds woke me from my sleep- heavy footsteps, pots clanking, men shouting from beyond the bedroom window. Darkening sunlight filtered through the drapes, letting me know that I hadn't slept through Mama's party.

"I was just fixin' to wake you up," Trulee said. She sat on a low chair near the foot of the bed, waiting. Guarding, protecting me, I thought, as she had many times before. "You about got enough time for a quick shower, put on a little make-up and come on down."

"How long have you been sitting there?"

"Long enough," she said. "Knew you might need some watching over. You know, it's about time you moved back down to Liberty. Your Mama needs you here. She's getting old, needs someone to take on some of her burden. I'm getting old, too. Need someone to take on for me, too."

"What about Jack and Four? Why can't they do it? Or any of the grandchildren?"

Trulee rolled her eyes at me. "Girl, Jack is a judge; he's doing all he can at that level, but he can't work outright like he used to. Four is doing what he can, but his help is different. He runs a free clinic once a week, gives away lots of free medicine. He guilts them other doctors into donating time and supplies. But them grandbabies need someone to follow. You be that person. Liberty needs help. We still got some of the old problems, and we got new problems- battered women, abused children, homeless. You done good up there, but now we need you to come back. Your Daddy would want this."

I must have made some sound, some gesture, for Trulee glared at me for a minute before continuing.

"Your Mama had a practice studio put in that house next door for you. She had the walls specially soundproofed so that no one could complain about the noise, not that anyone would. Your piano playing is one of God's gifts to us. She's ready to move your piano over there. You can live here, go out on your concerts from here, make them CDs and help the people here. It's time now. Yes, Marsh would want this." When Trulee slipped into the dialect of the coast, I knew she was serious. She stood up and went to my closet and started sorting through the dresses handing on the rod.

She said the magic words that made my eyes tear up. *Your Daddy would want this.*

"Trulee, why didn't you come with us when Mama married Mr. Walden?"

"Honey, you ask me that every time you come down here and my answer hasn't changed yet. My work here wasn't done. Still isn't. With your Daddy gone, I had even more to do. Your Mama had to get you out of Liberty. It wasn't safe for you right then. But God needed me here to help his children," she said. "Child, you have to quit blaming your Mama. Your Mama believed you. She made a lot of people mad when she up and married that man and moved away just six months after your Daddy died. But I think Mr. Walden really loved her. Your Mama changed after all that unpleasantness. Go read your Bible. Malachi Chapter Three, Verse Three. *In the heat of the fire, God saw his image in her.* Your Mama is a good woman. She didn't keep me here; I kept me here. Your Mama helped me all those years she was gone. She sent books for the school and clothes for the children. She gave the start-up money for the grocery store in the Quarters, so the people wouldn't have to walk so far to get food. When she moved back here to Liberty, she started doing things herself." Trulee gave me a little wink. "When you got money, people forgive you real quick. Your Mama has worked with the Art Guild, the Historical Society, the Library Board. Most of them people will be here tonight." She looked at her watch. "Real soon, in fact. You need to get fixed up."

"Trulee, did you hear about Beth Ann? That it is Beth Ann?"

"Yes, honey, I did. You know word spreads fast. We prayed for that child." She selected an outfit and laid it on the chair. She came over to the bed and patted my foot.

"Trulee, who do you think took her?"

"Well, you always said it weren't Ebon, and I believed you. I know your Mama believed you. Who do you think did it?"

I clutched my fingers to keep them from trembling. "I still think it was her Daddy. She had been going off and seeing her Daddy on those Wednesdays. Did you know he married my old choir director, Miss Darton?"

"No, can't say as I saw her much after all that happened. But honey, I thought he moved to Detroit. How would he be seeing that child?"

I looked around my room, then jumped out of bed and opened the closet doors. I surveyed the contents: my black concert dresses lined up at one end, smooth black ballet slippers below them, then my extra dresses, shoes lined up on the rack, folded sweaters on the shelves. I turned back to Trulee.

"Mama said she kept all my things from when I was little. Do you know where they are?"

"What?" Trulee wrinkled her brow as she thought. "Honey, you have more important things to worry about right now, like getting dressed for your Mama's party." She stood and walked to the door. "People will start arriving in thirty minutes. I'm going to check on the food." She paused for a moment. "Four has a big storeroom in back of his carport. I think he still has some of your Mama's boxes there.

***

I made it downstairs just as Mama's guests started pulling into the parking area. Mama stood tall and elegant, draped in folds of soft peach silk as she greeted her guests. Trulee waited beside her in a pale silver dress that reflected the silver in her hair, also welcoming those arriving. Music from an ensemble was floating on the breezes coming in off the marsh. Waiters in starched white shirts and black pants carried trays of fragrant hors d'oeuvres. In the corner of the living room, a bartender waited to mix or pour the beverages of choice.

"Aunt B, don't Grandmama and Trulee look just beautiful?" Morgan came up from behind me to slip an arm around my waist. "Sorry I didn't stick around last night, but honestly, you would think that a man Daddy's age would have better taste in women. It's not like he didn't have a good role model, with Grandmama and you and Mama and all," she chattered on. "And he has dated lots of other women that weren't so bad, especially compared to Desiree."

"Morgan, honey, play nice. Move back into your bedroom at your Daddy's house. Always be around. Fix them breakfast. Always be respectful. That will drive her crazy because I imagine she wants to get your father alone. Now we need to go make nice to everyone." I gave my niece a quick kiss and aimed her in one direction while I took the other.

"Dr. Stevens, Virginia, so nice to see you both." I stepped up on my tiptoes to do the air-kiss with my father's medical partner. "Virginia, you didn't even mention you were going to be here. We didn't have much time to visit yesterday. How is everyone doing? Where's Cynthia?"

"Fine. Hear you may be back to stay?" He looked down at me, an eyebrow raised.

"Well, I don't know about that quite yet," I started, but he cut me off.

"Think hard about it. People have long memories," he said. "I'm getting a drink. Virginia?" He left for the bar without waiting for an answer from his wife.

"He's had a hard day," Virginia Stevens said in lieu of an apology for her husband. Out of character for her, she seemed deflated, worried. "Lost a patient. Excuse me, I need to go…" She gestured down the hallway and left me watching her leave.

"Oh girl, I heard the news!" Another set of arms encircled me in a tight hug. "Child, when I heard about that, I 'bout died. I said *Thomas, what in the world,* didn't I, Thomas?" Tansie kept her tight grip on me as she looked for her husband.

"I know, it was so scary. I kept telling Leigh that it was just a mistake. It must be a farmer or something and…"

Tansie released her grasp and pulled back a little bit to look at me. "Girlfriend, I am talking about them saying it was Beth Ann. I wasn't talking about you. It isn't always about you. It doesn't always have to be about you. What in the world are you talking about?"

"Oh!" I deflated a little bit. "Some idiot chased us about ten miles down the highway, and I crashed Quince's car into an old tractor shed."

"You what! That car that boy's baby. Does he know? Of course not, you're still standing here alive. Girlfriend, do tell. Thomas, go get us something to drink," Tansie directed her husband as she took my arm and led me over to a pair of chairs.

"Now do tell," Tansie said. "Oh, wait a minute." She looked over my shoulder, a frown marring her face.

I turned to see what was disturbing her. Four was standing in the middle of the hallway, anchored by a bosomy bleached blonde. One of her hands clutched his arm, the other waved a drink, spilling droplets on Mama's pristine antique hardwood floors. She wasn't as young as Morgan was worried about. In fact, I think Desiree was valiantly losing in her attempt to even be my age.

"Tansie! Don't tell me you're jealous. I thought you got over Four thirty years ago," I giggled at the thought.

"That woman," she said. "Girl, I know I'm black. I've been black all my life. I don't care that I'm black. But that woman makes me feel like a Negro." She shuddered. "I just can't believe Four would be interested in a woman like that. Old Alabama money, my black behind! She must be something else in bed!"

"Tansie!" I was scandalized. "You don't think!" I couldn't finish my thoughts, then I scolded myself for being a prude.

"Nah, she's just a big ole tease. Far as I can tell she's using the guest room."

Desiree's eyes skimmed over us, then moved on to other guests.

"Who is she looking for?" I wondered aloud. "I should get up and introduce myself; she acted like she didn't have any idea who I was."

"And your Mama with the Holy Shrine to Brittan Lee over in the piano room. Never mind, honey. That woman just gets on my last nerve. I found out her real name is Dorene. I guess that wasn't sophisticated enough to be a stage name so she changed it to the unique *Desiree*." She emphasized the word *unique* and grinned at me. "If I wasn't a good Christian woman, I would snatch her blonde hair out by her black roots. Watch this," Tansie said.

She walked over to the doorway. As she approached Four, Desiree pulled back away from Tansie, a tight twist to her smile. Four looked down and reached out to give Tansie a big hug.

"Hey girl! How's that husband of yours?"

"Just fine. He's getting us something to drink." Tansie flashed one of her most charming smiles at Desiree. "You haven't brought your friend to hear us sing, Four. We'd love to get her professional opinion."

Desiree's lips tightened even more and her white-knuckle grip on Four's arm caused his jacket sleeve to crease. "Uh, yes, uh certainly."

"Here comes Thomas," Tansie said. "We'll talk to you later, set something up." She nodded her good-byes, met Thomas with the drinks and led him over to where I was sitting, fascinated by my eavesdropping. "Now tell us about what happened to the car."

"Brittan Lee!" Trulee walked over with the phone, holding the mouthpiece flat against her hand. "Sorry, Thomas. Brittan Lee, have you seen Leigh? Her boyfriend is on the phone again. He's called four times today, says she won't answer her cellphone. It's getting a bit annoying."

I shook my head. "Haven't seen her in about half an hour. Let me talk to him," I reached for the phone. "David, how are..?"

"Where the hell have you been?"

The voice on the phone was so loud Tansie and Thomas turned to look at the phone.

"And why haven't you been returning my calls? Do I have to come down there and straighten out a few details?"

"Excuse me, this is Leigh's aunt, Dr. Hayworth," I said. "I believe we met at Christmas."

The caller quieted down. "Excuse me. I thought the maid was getting my fiancée. I need to speak with her immediately."

Although calmer, the voice still held a whiny tone that I didn't like.

"I'm sorry, but we're in the middle of a family party. I'll let her know that you called," I said.

"You better make sure she calls me back." The phone clicked to a dial tone.

I stared at the phone for a minute. "I'm not believing he hung up on me."

"Who?" said Tansie.

"Leigh's fiancé, although he sounded more like her stalker."

"Leigh has a stalker?" said Thomas. "What is it with this family? So what's this other stuff Jack was telling me? I want the details."

I told Tansie and Thomas the entire story. "So I'm not sure if I over-reacted or if he really was following us."

"Sounds to me like he was chasing you. Why didn't anyone call my office? Didn't either one of you have a cell-phone? Have you told this to that FBI agent?" Thomas asked. "Tansie told you to be careful. Hard-headed women."

"I was careful. Leigh even had a gun," I said. "I'll tell Agent Zeller." I wasn't enthusiastic about it. He would probably try and make Jack put me on a tighter leash. But I needed to find out what happened to Beth Ann. "I was supposed to go see him this afternoon, but when we finally got home, I was so tired and achy that I just went to bed instead. I'm going to go to the Courthouse tomorrow morning." If I hadn't been watching Tansie, I would have missed the look she shot Thomas. "Okay, what's up?"

"Nothing, honey. Don't worry about it. So how did you get back home?"

"She called Jack, Jack called me and I went over with one of the tractors from the farm."

I jumped at the sound of the voice from behind me. "Trey!" I turned to greet him. "And Joanie! Thomas, Tansie, Joanie makes the beautiful glass things at the Pier Market. Oh, gosh, Joanie, I owe you money!"

"I heard about your accident. Trey told me. I'm so sorry I didn't hear you fall in the river. I just thought you had left to go look at other things. I would have called the emergency people," she said.

"You didn't know. I'm okay now," I said. "It was an accident."

Tansie shot me a look filled with doubt.

"Excuse us," Trey said. "I think Mama just came in." He put his arm around Joanie and led her over to the foyer.

"Fell in the river? When?" Tansie asked. So I had to tell that story, and by the time I was finished, Thomas had locked his jaw real tight and was looking around for Agent Zeller.

"Umm, umm, umm, Brittan Lee, I do not believe in coincidences like this. Finding Beth Ann was one thing, but twice now somebody's hurting on you. I do think you need some watching over until all this is over."

"Thomas, I'm going to be fine. I'll have Leigh around, and probably one of the boys as well. And I haven't forgotten Agent Zeller. But I need to find out what happened to Beth Ann. Tansie, why did you tell me to be careful? What stink do you know about that's going to get stirred?" I asked.

She looked at her husband. "Thomas, go take a walk." He protested, but stepped back a few feet. Tansie leaned in toward me. "People want the FBI to make a full investigation into what happened that night. The old people never believed Ebon had one dang thing to do with Beth Ann's disappearance. He was beat up; others were hurt for nothing more than being the scapegoat for those racists. Ebon was murdered and so was your Daddy. A lot of people lost their homes in that fire. So we think it's time something was done about it. It's pretty clear now Ebon couldn't have been dead in the building and in that car at the same time. We want the truth to come out."

"You really think so?" A flood of relief came over me. What I had said, what I had believed all my life, others believed it, too. I wasn't crazy.

"Yes, I really do." Tansie was resolute.

"So what can I do to help?"

"Just keep telling the truth. The truth is going to set us free. Do you remember the night the Freedom Singers came to the church?"

CHAPTER TWENTY-ONE
Liberty, Georgia, August 1964

The skateboard wheels dragged, squeaked and caught on every sidewalk crack, but the makeshift wagon was still easier than trying to carry all those books from the First Baptist to Tansie's church. In addition to those twelve library books I had checked out, I had ten Baptist hymnals.

"Miss Darton's gonna just kill you. She's just gonna kill you. This is stealing. You can't steal from God and go to Heaven." Beth Ann puffed out the words from the back of the wagon. Her face was all red from pushing, and she slowed down to wipe sweat from the tip of her nose.

"They aren't stolen; they're loaned," I clarified. "And it's not like I took them from the Sanctuary. They were in a box in the back of the Adult Choir Room. Under a table. Nobody was using them or anything. They were just going to waste back there."

"Well, they must be there for some good reason, or they would've just thrown them out."

"You can't throw away things with Jesus or the flag on them. It's against the Constitution. Jack told me." My big brothers knew everything. "Where are you going?" Beth Ann had started across the street at Courthouse Square. "We've got to get over to the church."

"You keep going. I'll meet you back here." Beth Ann kept walking.

"Beth Ann? Are you mad at me? What are you doing?" Beth Ann had been acting real funny. She looked over her shoulder more than usual, and she acted like she had a big secret. Beth Ann never keeps secrets from me.

"I just want to get a cold Co-cola. I'll meet you back here at eight. You go on over to the church." Beth Ann didn't ever look back at me. "I'll get you a cold Co-cola, too. I've saved thirty cents."

"I've got my own money," I hollered at her back. "Beth Ann, are you sure..." She just kept walking. "Don't worry about me. I can get there just fine without you. I can pull these books all the way there." She didn't turn back, so I balanced the books in the wagon and left.

The sounds from the Liberty African Methodist Episcopal Church carried even further in the wind than usual. I could hear the clapping and the music two blocks away. The music pulled me faster down the broken sidewalks, until I joined a crowd of colored children sitting outside the open doors of the church. I saw Tansie swaying and clapping to the music.

"Tansie! What's going on?"

"Shh!"

I sat and listened, and I felt the power of the music fill me until I was swaying and clapping with the others. "Glory, glory, Hallelujah, I'm gonna lay my burden down."

"What chu know about burden?" one child asked when the music stopped. "You ain't never had no burden. Not like my mama and daddy, and my mama's mama. They got burdens."

"Well, this was a burden." I pointed to my wagon and the box of books. "Who was that singing? They were just wonderful. I wish I could sing like that."

"White people can't sing like that. You got to feel it way

deep inside you. These songs, they says them here songs is our story. They's a gospel group from Atlanta. They been going around singing in the churches all over the place."

"They's the Mayfield Gospel Singers, Freedom Singers," Tansie said. "Where you get these?" She started to pull out the books. "These is the books from the libr'ry." She stared at me. "Hey, she got's our books from that ole libr'ry lady."

"I suppose you think's we should just be grateful you got our books?" one of the older girls asked as she looked through the box. "And what's these?" She removed a hymnal.

"What's going on out here?" Tansie's mother came down the pathway. "Music going to start again real soon. Where them boys gone to?" She looked at the back of the building. "Them boys back there? You…go get them worthless things right now. Music's starting and these people come all the way from 'Lanta to sing and them boys go talkin' in the back room. Shame!"

"That's what they doing in the back room, Mama," Tansie said. "Talking to the big boys. Mama, Brittan Lee got us our books."

Cora came over and, first wiping her hands on her skirt, selected a book from the box. "Well, baby, so she did. Did you say thank you to her?"

"It's okay, Cora. I wanted to do it. Trulee said I should always do the right thing and not just what everyone else is doing because they're doing it. Mrs. Taunch was wrong to talk to you like she did. My daddy's not going to let her do that anymore."

"Umph," Cora looked at me, at the book in her hands, at Tansie, then back at me. "Well, I thanks you for helping these chilrun. You like them singers?"

"Oh, yes. I think it is just beautiful."

"Well, y'all sit down. They's startin' again." She looked at me once more, then handed her daughter the book. "You keep them clean. We take them back next week." She turned and went back into the main church building.

"Brittan Lee? How come you call Tansie's mama 'Cora,' but we gotta call your mama 'Mrs. Hayworth'?"

"That's just the way it's always been....oh!" The piano drowned out anything else I might have said. I sat down, overcome with my thoughts but filled with the music.

"What do you want?" A man called out.

"Freedom!" the congregation answered.

"What do you want?" he asked again.

"Freedom!" they answered.

"Freedom! Freedom now! Freedom now! Freedom now! And before I'll be a slave, I'll be buried in my grave, and go home to my Lord and be free, and be free. And before I'll be a slave, I'll be buried in my grave, and go home to my Lord and be free and be free. No more segregation, no more segregation, no more segregation over me.... and before I'll be a slave, I'll be buried in my grave and go home to my Lord and be free..."

We all held hands out on the sidewalk and swayed with the music flowing from the church. I turned to see Tansie's lip trembling and tears streaming down her face.

"Tansie? Why you crying? They can't make you a slave anymore. There ain't been any slaves for a long time. What kind of freedom do you need?" I asked.

Tears kept rolling down her cheeks, and her shoulders started to shake.

"Tansie, don't cry," I said as I looked in my pockets for a handkerchief.

"I want to be free to go to the libr'ry every day myself," she sobbed.

"Oh, Tansie," I put my arms around her and started crying with her. "Please don't cry. My daddy, he's gonna get you into the library."

The cheering and applause startled us. Churchgoers poured from the open doors blocking the light, and milled about on the sidewalk, talking to one another as they gathered up their children.

"People, people," Deacon Johnson appeared in the doorway with the gospel group. The Deacon clapped his hands. "Peoples, we needs to thank the Mayfield Gospel Singers for they wonderful courage in bringing they music here to us. And we need to offer our hearts up in prayer for they safe passage home through the troubled roads ahead."

"Amen!"

"And peoples, we need to empty our pockets and pocket books to helps them on they joun'rey back home. We don't have much, but they has even less. So gives what you can now."

The Deacon took off his black hat and passed it to the nearest person. That man looked at the empty hat and reached into his pockets and pulled up a few coins. He looked at the coins and over at his wife. She nodded, and he dropped them into the hat. This continued until the hat had made the rounds of the congregation and was back in the Deacon's hands. With great care, the elderly man counted the change. "Thanks you all. We has collects three dollars and twenty t'ree cents to help the Mayfield Singers back home to 'Lanta. This will help gets them back to the Ridge with our friends. Now, it's about de curfew time, so gather up your chi'ren." He looked out over the congregation and his eyes fell on me.

"Chile, whut for you be here?"

I was still crying. "I came to listen to the music. Deacon, I have thirty cents. Can I give that to the singers?" I held out my three dimes. "Please?" I placed the coins into his hand.

Thunder rumbled overhead, and the congregation started to move off in the directions of their own homes. The old man looked at me and nodded. "Surely, chile, surely. God provides even thru' de words and deeds of the lil' chilrun. Ebon! Come over to heah!" he gestured to one of the teen-aged boys. "Come heah and walk Miss Brittan Lee ovah to the Baptist Church. Be quick now. He'p her with that wagon."

"But Grandaddy, I..."

"Jus' do what I say, boy. And be back quick. It's almos' the curfew."

Bowing his head to the Deacon, but glaring at me, Ebon took the handle of the makeshift wagon. "Come on."

The thunder continued to rumble overhead, and occasional flashes of lightening sparked fire across the sky. Ebon led the way back to Courthouse Square staying as close to the bushes and overhanging trees as possible. He was moving so fast I could hardly keep up. Every time I slowed down he would grab my hand and pull, then drop my hand as if it were too hot to keep hold of, wiping his own on his pants.

"Brittan Lee! Brittan Lee!"

"Wait, Ebon. That's Beth Ann. Where is she?" There wasn't any sign of her in the Square, but I kept hearing her voice. In the near distance, the thunder seemed to be continuing non-stop. The chattering of a flock of gulls was almost loud enough to block out the rumbles. A summer storm was going to come crashing down on us. We needed to make it back to our church. "Beth Ann? Where are you?"

A pair of patent leather shoes, then legs in white socks came down out of the Liberty Oak, followed by Beth Ann.

Looking both ways, she ran across the street and pushed Ebon and me into the bushes.

"Get back!" She pushed harder until we were surrounded by azalea leaves. "Stay in here. Hush!" Beth Ann was out of breath and trembling. She kept looking up and down the Square.

"Oh, Beth Ann, where's my Co-cola? You should have come with me; you wouldn't believe it. There were the most wonderful singers at Tansie's church, and they came all the way from Atlanta. And they sang, and we all clapped and it was…"

"Shh!!" Beth Ann grabbed me and put her hand over my mouth. Her eyes were real wide. "He said there's bad men out. With guns. And they're driving around and they're going to make trouble if they find anyone out. He said they would hurt people if they found them out. Hurt good people like the Deacon. We gotta stay in the bushes all the way back to church. And be real quiet. They already drove by about a thousand million times. Lots of them."

"Who said that? What men…" My words were muffled as Ebon helped Beth Ann drag me even further into the bushes.

"My da…"

"Din't you hear her? Hush! They's bad—I knows."

"Hmmph," I twisted my head free from his grasp. "How do you know?"

His dark eyes stared at me. "I just knows." His hand tightened around my mouth.

Headlights came around the side street behind the courthouse. The truck tires screeched as they rounded the corner real fast. From the light of the street lamps, we could see three men in the back of the truck, holding shotguns in the air.

"Over there! Did'ja see anything?"

A second truck came up another side road, more men yelling in the back. "Head over that a ways. Earl said they was gathering behind that nigra church. Frank, he's out on the Coast Road to the north, and Luce, he's checking out to the south. Whoo!" A deafening clap of thunder resounded.

I felt Ebon and Beth Ann crouch lower in the bushes. My legs got weak, and I got down, too. I hid my face in the dead leaves on the ground.

"Come on. Stay low, be quiet," Ebon led the way, staying in people's yards, avoiding the sidewalks and the light from the street lamps and porches. "Down!" We dived flat onto the grass, as another car full of yelling men drove past. "Just leave the waggin. You kin get it later."

We could only move in short spurts, hiding bush by bush, staying in dark. We made our way almost another two blocks. I thought the thunder kept rolling. It wasn't thunder; it was the raised voices of men.

"Brittan Lee! Look! Ain't that your cousin Trey?" Beth Ann pointed to a blue and white car moving in our direction. "What's he doing out? Can he get us home?" She dodged out into the street in front of the car.

"Beth Ann, come back here!" But the car had stopped. It was Trey.

"Brittan Lee, what in the Sam Hill are you doing out here? Aunt Belle is going to be so mad at you! Y'all are filthy and covered in those leaves and trash, and it is fixin' to be a gully-washer! Get in here!" He reached over and opened the passenger side of his car. "Brittan Lee, get over here."

"Trey, what's going on? What do all them men want?" Beth Ann ran over to the car.

"You ain't...Beth Ann, where's Brittan Lee? She out here with you?" Trey looked over at the bushes, then up and down the street.

"Here I am," I stepped out of the leafy cover to the sidewalk. "What're you doing out here?"

"Never mind about me, get your little hiney in this car right now!" He looked up and down the street, then gestured to me once more. "Now, Brittan Lee, or I'm gonna tell your Mama where I found you. Dang you two!"

"What about Ebon?"

"Who?"

"Ebon Johnson. He was taking us back to church," I gestured to the young man hiding in the bushes.

"Oh, damn, oh damn, oh damn! What are you doing out with a colored boy? Do you want to get yourself killed? Get all of us killed?"

"Trey! You said bad words! Ebon was taking us back to church. I went to hear the music at Tansie's church and the Deacon made him..."

"Oh shit..." headlights were bouncing from across the Square. "You, boy, get in here."

I could see Ebon pause in the shadows, then he ran over to us and the car.

"Get in, quick. Lay down on the floor. Brittan Lee, cover him up with that old beach towel, then you two get in there. Hang your legs over him. Quick now and shut up." Trey turned on the car radio and the music of the Beatles blasted through the car. Beth Ann and I grabbed each other as the car jerked forward. "Y'all!" Trey looked at us through the rear view mirror. "Sing to the radio."

Beth Ann and I held hands. "She loves you, yea, yea, yea, she loves you, yea, yea, yea."

An old red truck pulled out at Mulberry Street and stopped in front of Trey. "Hey, you kid. Pull over."

"Oh damn, oh damn, oh damn," Trey kept muttering and looking in the mirror at us. "Y'all just keep singing, you hear?"

Two skinny men in overalls jumped out of the back of the truck and sauntered over to Trey's car. "Boy, what you doing out here?"

"Yessir, I, uh, we're going home. After church."

The beam of a flashlight roamed over Trey's face and into the back seat. "Turn off that junk. So you girls was at church? That's not church music."

I looked at Beth Ann and answered for us both. "Yessir. First Baptist. We had church supper and then Children's Choir practice. But we heard this on American Bandstand."

"First Baptist, that's in the other direction. What're you doing down here?"

"Um, we wanted a cold Co-cola. Trey said there was a machine in the basement. Mama don't let me have cold Cocola at home. She says all that sugar will rot my teeth and the dentist bills are..." The flashlight blinded me, and I put my hand up to shield my eyes.

"That right, boy? Ain't you Frank Littleton's boy? You got them boats over at the marina?"

"Yessir, that's me. Um, I'd appreciate it if you didn't tell my mama about this. It's a little thing I do on Wednesdays. As a treat for the girls. Their mamas are real strict about them drinking Co-colas." Trey was rigid in the front seat, staring at the people still in the red truck ahead of him.

"Uh huh. Git them girls out of here, boy. And git yourself home. Things is gonna be happening round here."

"Yessir, thank you, sir."

Trey watched them in the rear view mirror until the men had climbed back in the truck and the old truck had turned around, and then, in silence drove us home.

CHAPTER TWENTY-TWO
Liberty, Georgia, August 2005

I s this a private conversation? May I join you? Ladies, can I freshen your drinks?" Andrew Zeller stood tall over us, his smile making his dimple even deeper. "Deputy? How are you doing this evening?"

Thomas stood and held out his hand. "Agent Zeller. I think you may need to circle the wagons around this one. Maybe call in the elusive Special Agent in Charge."

"Andy, please." Andrew sat down. "What's she been up to? She missed an appointment with me this afternoon." He looked down his nose at me.

"And just where were you, Mister Agent Man, while my girlfriend here was crashing her car, trying to escape some crazy idiot?" Tansie shot him her most stern look, the one that quelled even the most rambunctious five year old.

"Dr. Hayworth?"

Thomas nudged his wife. "We've heard this story. Come on, sweetness, Jax is trying to signal us to mingle and schmooze. Miss Belle has most of Liberty society here tonight. Best we be taking advantage of it."

Tansie nudged him back as she looked over his shoulder. Auntabelle was entering the room followed by Trey and Joanie. Almost ninety, she still had the soft brown hair of her youth, although that could have been helped by her beautician. She had the same cheekbones as Mama, but her smile never had

Mama's soft sweetness. I know that she saw me, because her cheeks flushed a soft pink and she turned away. Mama may have forgiven her, but I hadn't. It made me a lesser Christian, and I prayed over my weakness, but I hadn't forgiven her.

As Thomas and Tansie stood up, I realized that the sound level in the living room had indeed picked up. The room was wall to wall people, with more spilling out in the hallway and out on both the front and back terraces.

"I've got to go meet and greet, too," I apologized to Andrew as I rose from my seat. "Mama will skin me alive if I just sit here and monopolize your time. "

He caught my arm and pulled me back to my seat. "We need to talk. What did they mean?" His eyes were as cold as his hand.

After freeing my arm, I picked up my glass and shook the last bits of ice into my mouth. I chewed the crushed cold, swallowed and looked at Andrew. He was still watching me, green eyes fixed on my face.

For the third time that day, I told the story of the mad dash through the country roads. "But the more I think about it, the more I believe it was just my imagination gone wild. Leigh and I just fed into each other like a pair of school girls watching a horror movie. No one would be chasing us. It was just somebody trying to beat the storm." My casual assurances aside, my insides were churning like Trulee's Mixmaster.

Andrew watched my eyes as I talked. "Did you run into anyone you know at the wake?"

"These were old women, fragile spindly little old ladies. I probably met some of them when I was a child. I nodded and smiled and did the social thing with all of them. Mama brought me up right. But there were only two or three I could put a name to, except Verna and the Hamiltons."

"The Hamiltons?"

"Yes, as we were leaving the church, they were arriving. And look, Auntabelle is over there. You wanted to talk to her about the office finances. In fact, I think you ought to check into everybody's finances. Money being the root of all evil and all. Oh!" I jumped about six inches in my chair when a hand was placed on my shoulder. I turned in the seat and looked up. "Dr. Bruce! How are you?" His long arms surrounded me in a hug when I stood up. His blonde hair had faded to a sandy gray, deep worry lines accentuated his face, but his blue eyes still sparkled when he talked. He held his trademark Panama hat under one arm. "How is Miss Zora doing? Andrew, this is Dr. Bruce Wensley. He was one of Daddy's partners many years ago."

The men shook hands before Bruce Wensley answered my question. "She has her good days; unfortunately, tonight isn't one of them. She made me promise to come home with stories of what young man you are with, what all the ladies are wearing and what delicious food Trulee has made. So what can I tell Zora? I understand there is rumor out regarding your return to Liberty. You know Zora would love that. She really appreciates your visits to her. She has every CD you have made and plays them all constantly." He turned to Andrew. "Whenever Brittan Lee comes to town, she almost always plays the piano or the organ at the First Baptist, and Zora insists on coming in to the service."

"Brittan Lee does play well," Andrew agreed. "Your wife..."

"Zora doesn't leave the house too much anymore," Dr. Wensley said. "Excuse me, someone is calling me and I must go check out the ladies' outfits. I have to give a full report."

When his tall frame was out of earshot, I said, "Miss Zora

has polio. Everyone thought it was a mild case; she spent six months in Crawford Long Hospital in Atlanta back in the '50s. She had a relapse back when I was eight or nine and spent months at Warm Springs. Anyway, the polio left her really weak, and she doesn't have much use in her left hand, arm or leg. Mama says that what Miss Zora has now is called post-polio syndrome. It's an all day affair for her to leave the house. I try to go over to play for her, so she doesn't exhaust herself trying to go out." I reached for my empty glass. "I need something else to drink, then I really do need to go visit with people." I made my way through the crowded house, nodding and greeting Mama's friends, the ladies from the Sewing Club and the Bridge Club, members of the Historical Society and the Liberty Tourism Board. I chatted as I circled the buffet table, exchanged hugs and air kisses in the music room, and made my way down the hallway to the terrace, Andrew Zeller following close behind me.

"I feel like a slab of prime beef," he whispered. "All those women giving me the geriatric eagle eye."

"Calm down, Casanova. Most of those women have been waiting thirty years for me to bring home a man. Their biological grandmother clocks are ticking. They don't know our relationship is strictly professional."

"So, where are your friends?" he asked. "These all seem more your mother's age, or your brothers'."

Swallowing, I turned to him. "I, uh, really, uh, I don't have much contact with the children I knew back then, just Tansie. It's mostly, like you said, Mama's and the boys' friends."

"Really?"

"Before it happened, I had Mama and Daddy and Trulee and Beth Ann, and the boys, of course. I knew other children from school and Brownies and Sunday School, but Beth Ann and I were inseparable. After the hurricane, I didn't have Beth Ann anymore, then Mama moved us away."

We made it to the end of the hallway. A large white tent covered the terrace so the gentle raindrops wouldn't chase the partygoers back inside.

"Aunt B!" I followed the call over to the brick barbecue where several of the nieces and nephews were standing.

"Here," Jax said, handing me a plate of shrimp. "Sustenance. You're going to need to get your speed on when Quince finds you, personal bodyguard not withstanding." He punched Agent Zeller on the shoulder. "We told him she fled the county, but I don't think he bought it. So, you two engaged yet or just expecting a love child?"

Andrew choked on his glass of ginger ale. Jax obliged him by pounding on his back, until Andrew gasped and grabbed Jax's arm. "It's okay," he coughed. "I'm still alive. So Quince knows about the great land chase? Unusual name, Quince?"

"Nice music," I said in a desperate attempt to change the subject. The musicians were in a corner of the terrace; the quartet flowed seamlessly from jazz to Broadway to southern ballads. "Where did Mama find them?"

"Music students. Grandmama can find anything. Quince is short for Hayworth Marshall the Fifth. Doctor Hayworth Marshall the Fifth," Jax explained. "Lord help us when he gets married. I think calling a child 'Sex' would make all of the tacky name lists."

Everyone laughed at the idea.

"Well, at least he wouldn't be named for Georgia counties. Madison and Morgan. At least it wasn't Liberty and Columbia," complained Madison.

We sat on the high stools, ate shrimp and listened to the

pure music, crisp notes floating out from the tent until the musicians excused themselves for a break.

"Well, I better socialize some more. Two of the ladies I met at the Pier Market are here. With your father, if I remember correctly," I turned to Jax. "They said they were staying at the guest house at Sapelo Sound. Seemed really nice."

"Daddy could do worse," Jax agreed. "Either one of them. Except I think one of them is more interested in Uncle Trey."

"Oh, you're right," I said. "Joanie came in with Trey. I didn't put two and two together. How stupid of me? And you, young man, be a little more gentle with your sister. She's a lady, and we ladies bruise more easily than you brutes."

"Oh, God!" Jax said. "Sorry, Aunt B." He nudged me towards the door.

"And Jax, you won't believe the call I just took for Leigh," I whispered. "I don't think I like her boyfriend much anymore. He seemed nicer at the Christmas party. Oh, my piddle, what is that?"

"Oh, Mrs. Walden, I just love your house. Marshall has told me just about everything, but he failed in his attempts to describe just how lovely it was!" A shrill voice rose over the conversations of the other guests, a shriek that sent chalkboard shivers down my spine. "We have driven past it, of course, going to his home. But driving by doesn't do it justice. You must tell me your interior decorator; we're going to have a few things done. How nice to have this party for us!"

"I told her it was for the Historical Society and the Tourism Board. Morgan told her it was for you. But Desiree is just a diva-want-to-be. She believes every party is for her." Leigh drained her wine glass and held it out for a refill. She flicked a quick look over her shoulder at the cars parked along the old alley. "She's hoping Uncle Four will pop the old question."

"He's not," Jax said. "That woman is deluding herself."

"I don't know. Dr. Hayworth seemed happy last night," Andrew said.

"Yeah, but he was here, and not at his house with her," Morgan said. "Don't you wonder what she does all day when he's at the office or the hospital?" She stomped back to the house.

"I wanted to put security cameras around the house, like NannyCams, just to make sure she wasn't getting into stuff," Jax said. "But when I started to bring it up, he floored me. Not actually, but I thought he was thinking about it. Quince says she's not as bad as Morgan thinks she is. I'm not saying I think Uncle Four should marry her, but then I don't have to be around her very much. She just sucks the energy out of a room."

After returning my glass to the bartender, I took a deep breath. "I am going to finish greeting everyone. Mama and Trulee are probably overwhelmed at this point. You are all going to join me or risk being deprived of Trulee's biscuits at breakfast."

"Whoo who! Grandmama and Trulee overwhelmed? Aunt B, you've lost it!" But they followed me into the house.

The party had started to thin out a little. There was moving room between people, and the servers' trays weren't emptied quite as quickly as they had been earlier. Individual conversations were more distinct as the overwhelming sounds of the crowd softened.

"Agent Zeller, Andrew," Mama approached us. "I haven't had a chance to talk to you tonight, but I am so glad you came by. Did you have the opportunity to speak to a lot of the people?"

"We've kept him pretty occupied, Grandmama," Leigh

said. "He's been appointed the official Aunt B nanny. It's so cool, he knows these purses that have a special gun pocket in the bottom, so you can legally carry and be able to find your weapon when you need it. He's going to show me tomorrow on the Internet."

"Uh-huh," Mama wasn't fazed. "Did you have a chance to speak with my sister, Annabelle? Brittan Lee, did you introduce Agent Zeller to your aunt?"

"She seemed to be busy elsewhere, Mama," I deferred the direct answer.

"Brittan Lee? Has anyone seen Trey?"

"I just saw him heading out to the terrace with one of those ladies from Sapelo Sound," Jax said. "Mama, you've had a great turnout. Thomas and Tansie have been doing the meet and greet for the past two hours, making some good contacts. Thanks."

"I think that young man will make an excellent sheriff. Liberty needs to move further into the twenty-first century." The crash of a mis-fingered chord resonated from the piano room. "Lord, help me, what is she doing now?" Mama followed the sound of the discordant notes.

My back went through the chalkboard-scratch again. People without perfect pitch don't seem to understand how much it hurts the ears and head of those who do have it. I closed my eyes against the sound.

"You don't like show tunes?" Andrew asked.

"I love show tunes. I made pocket money playing in piano bars. I just want them played well. That isn't. People who can't play well shouldn't try to play other people's grand pianos without permission. They just mess them up. That's my piano." I felt my lower lip start to form a pout.

"You have to share your piano, Brittan Lee! You have to share."

I jumped when I heard that. It took me back to Beth Ann and that first night at the AME church. Memories ran rampant through my head, one settled there.

"Oh my…piddle!" I searched for Andrew. "We have to go to Four's house. Right now!"

CHAPTER TWENTY-THREE
Liberty, Georgia, August 2005

W e can't just run out on your Mother's party," Andrew whispered, looking around the room. "That would be rude. Your brothers would kill me. I could take one, maybe both of them, but throw in the nephews and Miss Trulee and they would cream me."

"Come on. Marsh Pointe is just two blocks up. We'll only be gone a few minutes. Nobody is going to miss us. We'll be right back, but we have to go now," I tugged on his arm.

"Why now?" Andrew smiled and nodded at a pair of elderly women who were watching his progress.

"I have to find something. Right now, while it's still in my head." I succeeded in getting him out the door, rather subtly, I thought, and out to his car. "You drive. Go to the end of the road and turn right. Marsh Pointe is the subdivision out on the hummock."

"What is so important? Don't you think you should have mentioned it to your brother if not your mother?" he said making the turn onto Marsh Pointe Way. "Wow!"

The narrow road seemed to vanish at the end, dropping off like it was the end of the earth. Lights twinkling from the far-off islands reflected on Liberty Sound. The red and green steering lights on the buoys added a holiday air. The almost full moon came from behind the dense cloud cover and shone a straight path across the water; the car could have continued on the steady beam until we reached Little Tolomato Island.

"Isn't it beautiful?" I said. "Oh, here. This is Four's house. He moved here when he married Elaine back in 1970. They got it from her parents when they retired to Florida." The house was sleek and low, a carport on one side, a dock and pool in the back. It was a style once modern, cutting edge architecture that was now having a revival.

Andrew parked the car in the driveway, almost under the carport. I pushed open my door and jumped out before he had even turned off the engine. The back wall of the carport held hangers for the rakes, shovels and edgers. A lawn mower squatted over an opened newspaper, small drippings of oil made splotches of greenish-black. Two bikes were parked next to the mower. Hanging baskets lined the edges of the carport, trails of tropical flowers swaying in the off-shore breeze. The storeroom door opened into the breeze way between the carport and the house. Or, it would open if Four hadn't locked it. I felt along the edge of the doorframe, dug up the soil in the two clay pots by the back door, lifted a few of the larger rocks.

"If you were Four, where do you suppose you would hide the key?" I asked Andrew as I continued to look under rocks, flowerpots and the door mat.

"If I were Four?" He looked at me, hands on his hips. "I wouldn't hide a key, and I doubt he did. The man has a lot more common sense than his sister."

The window in the storage room door was dark. I framed my eyes with my hands and tried to peer inside. "I can't see anything. Maybe around back. I'm going to try those windows." I opened the gate in the chain-link fence and walked around to the back windows. There was a rustling from the padded chaise lounge on Four's deck. Something launched from the chaise, barking and yipping, a miniature hurricane of fury.

"Dang it! When did Four get a dog!" I made it out the gate inches before the dog reached me.

"What's the matter, don't you like dogs?" Andrew knelt in front of the gate. "Hey fella! What's your name? What are you doing out here? You could get eaten by an alligator, little fellow like you." He reached in and scratched behind the dog's ears.

"I'm not really a dog person. I mean, I probably could be, but I traveled so much it didn't seem fair. Quarantine and all that. There was always a big hound or two at Sapelo Sound, descendants of Granddaddy's dogs. Jack still has some there, but Four never had a dog. I bet it's hers." I blathered on.

"Him. It's a him. Looks like a Cairn terrier, but I bet he's a natural blonde. Nice little guy."

The little guy in question was wagging his stubby tail so hard his entire body shook as he burrowed under Andrew's arm, trying to climb into his lap. "Get down, fella. We have a party to get back to." He stretched up to his full six feet. "Are you ready, Brittan Lee?"

"No, we still have to get into the storeroom. Can't you jimmie the lock or something? I thought police were supposed to know how to do things like that." I tugged at the door.

"Law enforcement trade secrets," he pulled out his wallet and selected a credit card. Sliding the card into the space by the door knob, it clicked and the door swung inward. "After you, my lady!" He bowed. "Now, what are we looking for?"

"You could have done that when we first got here and saved me a lot of stressing." I walked inside the storeroom and searched for a light switch. "I'm looking for a white box, shoe box size. It was a Brownie project. The outside was covered with white lacy looking contact paper and the inside was lined with pink velvet. We made little slits in the sides and wove pink ribbons through them, and they came out the top to tie the lid in place. It was a Mother's Day project, I think. I gave mine to Mama, but later she let me use it to keep my stories. It shouldn't be too hard to find. I hope it's here. Trulee said most of my stuff was stored here."

Andrew found the light switch and flicked the room into brightness. "Wow! Someone went to a Rubbermaid fire sale." The entire back and side walls had been built out into shelves, which were packed with dark green plastic storage tubs. At least thirty bins lined the wall; each bin had been identified with care as *Mama's Boxes.* "Easy? Where do you want to begin?"

"Oh, double-piddle! Do you think there is any organization to them, or was everything just dumped in a container?" I surveyed the rows of matching tubs. "This may take longer than I thought."

"You know your family better than I do. Is this normal or is this anal-retentive even for them? Let me get one or two down, and we can see if there is any time-line pattern here." He hauled down a green tub from the end of the top shelf and pried open the lid. "Okay, what are these?" He held up a handful of soft fluffy material.

"Oh! Those are cashmere sweaters. Vintage cashmere sweaters. Those were Mama's from the forties and fifties. Look at the colors! And the little beaded buttons! I bet the girls don't know these are here or they would have been long gone!" I held up a celery green sweater, then a rosy pink one and measured them against me for size, then put them down again. "Focus. We've got to focus. I'm going to mark the boxes we've opened, so I can come back." I pushed aside the bin and searched my purse for a pen.

"Here, what's this? It's really heavy," Andrew's shoulders and arms bulged in his jacket as he lifted down another tub and put it on the worktable.

The lid was jammed down; I was tempted to cuss when I broke a fingernail and scraped one of my knuckles prying it loose. "Books and sheet music from the eighties."

"Well, that rules out the sequential order for the boxes. We may as well start at one end and work our way down." He pulled down another box and opened it for me, then one for himself. We continued the routine and began to sort through almost forty years of my life. Andrew's new best friend curled up in the box of sweaters and fell asleep, snoring with an occasional yip and scurrying of his feet.

"So tell me about your friends here?" Andrew looked over as he pulled down the next box.

"Nothing much else to tell; I already told you everything earlier." I sorted through the box, added the contents to the label and resealed the lid.

"What about high school?"

I opened the next box and rummaged through the old summer clothing. "I was in boarding school after Mama married Mr. Walden. He traveled a lot, and Mama went with him. I wasn't into lacrosse or the equestrian stuff, so I spent a lot of time in the music room." *In the music room, I could lose myself in my piano and pretend it didn't matter that I was all alone.*

Andrew removed the tub and handed me another one. "So did you come home very often?"

"Where was home? Sometimes Chicago for Christmas, or for the summer. Sometimes, I would join Mama and Mr. Walden wherever they were. All I wanted was a piano to practice on. Most of the hotels were happy to let me practice. A few times I even made money at the piano bar until they found out how old I was. Hong Kong was my favorite; very 'thirties elegant.' This was before it went back to China. Mama and Mr. Walden were there for nine months, and I got to fly over three times. The general manager at the hotel let me practice as much as I wanted to on the grand piano in the banquet hall. Mr. Lee had it re-tuned when he found out I was coming the second time. I would play for hours, until my hands were stiff. Hong Kong was where I learned about hot paraffin dips for achy joints. Mr. Lee's mama took me to a little place where they dipped my hands and let the warm wax sit, then they dipped them again. It felt so good. Then she fed me hairy crabs and chopped fish and little rice balls." My stomach rumbled as I remembered the food, and my eyes got a little teary when I remembered Mrs. Lee.

"So you really do have million dollar hands?" Andrew remembered Jack's comment from the previous night.

"Not really, that was just a long-standing family joke. I rarely do formal concert work now, maybe a CD every couple of years. I spend more time working with the choirs and doing my volunteer stuff. Maybe quarter-million dollar hands," I smiled. "I think the insurance policy may still say that though. I need Jack to check it out." I sifted through the box, made notes on the label and went to the next box. "What about you? How long have you been with the FBI? Did you join for the adventure?"

"I had enough adventure in Viet Nam. I was with the military police there. After my two tours there, and some time in Japan, I came home, went back to college. The CIA offered me a position, so did the FBI. I saw enough CIA overseas, so I went with the Bureau," he paused. "I retired in 2000 after I was wounded. So now, I can choose to help out on various cases."

I fumbled the books I had pulled from my tub and dropped them back in. "Wounded? What happened? Are you all right now?"

"I was shot, smashed up my hip. One of those white supremacist groups had taken hostages—a group of school children who were putting on a Kwanza pageant. Supremacists thought Kwanza was inappropriate—should have been a Christmas program—and grabbed six of them. They had already killed one little girl by the time we were called. We had to try and take out the terrorists before they could injure any more of the children. We got the children out safely, two of the supremacists were killed, and two of us good guys ended up with a few holes."

"Oh my heavens! Well, you walk fine. In fact, some of the ladies seemed to really enjoy watching you walk."

He blushed. "I've been told that a slight limp can be sexy."

"I'm embarrassed. I didn't even notice a limp," I said. I sealed the lid on the box in front of me, pushed it over and opened another one. "Leigh mentioned your brother." I looked over at him.

Andrew pulled down another tub and put it on the work table, then moved the two resealed ones back to the shelf. His mouth had a grimace and I wondered if it was pain from his leg or the mention of his brother.

"My older brother disappeared in the summer of 1964. He had taken a year off from college and was working with the Freedom Riders and the SNCC. Did you know that between 1950 and 1970 over a hundred civil rights volunteers were reported missing?" He opened another box, then paused, looking out the window to the lights on the distant island. "The FBI has been getting a lot of leads. People who were scared to talk back then are talking. One man was convicted and sentenced to life in prison for brutally killing three young men who were helping the black people register to vote. He claims to be too ill to go to prison, but he can drive his Cadillac to the VFW bar every afternoon. I'm trying to find my brother. I want my mother to be able to visit his grave. She's about your mother's age; she needs to be able to say good- bye to her eldest son."

I couldn't see what was in my container; my eyes were all blurry. I tried to think it was dust from the boxes, but I knew it was because I felt the same sense of loss he did. Of incompleteness.

After about an hour, Andrew was opening the twentieth box when he groaned. "Oh, my back. We may have to come back tomorrow." He stretched and rubbed his lower back. "So tell me, why didn't Four go into practice with Dr.Wensley and Dr. Stevens?"

"I'm not really sure. I was in boarding school in Switzerland at the time. I'm kind of surprised they stayed in practice together. They didn't always seem to get along."

"Really? Personality clashes? Financial problems—one person bringing in more than the other?"

"You would have to talk to Auntabelle about that. She could probably tell you to the penny how much each one booked. Most of the patients were Daddy's." I put about half of the papers in my lap back into the box. "The other two had been in practice with Daddy for nine, maybe ten years. One had been in the Navy, and one was doing all kinds of residency work at Yale or Harvard, some Yankee school. I always thought they got along until one afternoon, when I was there...I really got in trouble that time. Mama spanked my bottom good." I could laugh now, but I was really upset at the time.

CHAPTER TWENTY-FOUR
Liberty, Georgia, August 1964

I wasn't pouting. I was curled up in my corner of the back seat of Daddy's black Chevy with my eyes scrunched closed, pretending to be asleep. If I was awake, then when Daddy looked into the rear view window and said "Let's sing," I would have to. Otherwise, he would think I was pouting.

Daddy always wanted to sing on long trips, and I sang with him. Our voices harmonized with my treble working into an alto and Daddy's bass. Sometimes Mama or Four or Jack would join in, sometimes not. I knew all of Daddy's favorite hymns by heart, and the songs he knew from when he was little. One of my favorites was about the little poor girl who was going on the train to find her poor, dear old blind father in prison almost dead.

> *"The east-bound train was crowded,/ one cold December day,/ the conductor took up his tickets/, the same old fashioned way,/ a little girl in sadness,/ her hair as bright as gold,/ she said 'I have no ticket,'/ and then the story she told,/ my father, he is in prison,/ he's lost his sight they say,/ I'm going for his pardon,/ this cold December day,/ my mother's daily sewing,/ trying to earn our bread,/ my poor dear old blind father,/ in prison almost dead./"*

Daddy would start this song and by the time the little girl had her poor dear old blind father on the train, tears would be streaming down my face. In my mind, I was that poor little girl trying to help her Daddy.

On that day, I just wanted to sit in my corner and be quiet, so he wouldn't notice me. My head vibrated against the hum of the windows, and my left shoulder burrowed into the crevice between the seat and the door. White stripes on the black asphalt led the car north-west. We were going to Daddy's hometown, Hillsborough, in middle Georgia for the annual family reunion. I watched the stripes disappear under the car, my head nodding with the stripes until exhausted from a long night of crying. I didn't feel like singing. I was still mad at Daddy for not defending me when Mama spanked me. It wasn't my fault she didn't know where I was when I had told everybody where I was going. It wasn't my fault I got locked in Daddy's office and everybody looked everywhere but there for three hours. It's not like it was the first time I ever got locked in somewhere. Auntabelle accidentally locked me in her house three weeks ago. She forgot I was sitting on the floor behind the sofa reading, and she left to go shopping.

"I'm going down to Daddy's office to fetch him home from work," I had announced to Mama as she was discussing the welcome party for the three new doctors in town.

"Crab puffs, you know everyone loves Trulee's crab puffs. I won't let her tell anyone the secret, but I bet she told Mattie anyway. I'll send her down after lunch to get fresh crab from the dock." Mama scribbled some notes on her little pad that had her initials in dark blue at the top. When I get restless in church, sometimes Mama will give me one sheet of her paper, and I would write my stories. "That's nice, dear, just don't be any trouble."

Daddy shrugged his broad shoulders into his suit coat and adjusted his tie. "I should get out early. I told Louise not to schedule anything after three. I want tonight to go well."

Mama's face tightened and she looked down at her notes. "I'm sure Trulee will do her best. And the new divan looks just exquisite in that alcove in the living room."

"Arabella, that's not what I was talking about and you know it." Daddy picked up his black doctoring bag and walked to the door. "We have to set the example of what's right."

After lunch, Trulee folded up her apron, gathered her shopping lists and drove off in the old Chevy to buy the fresh crab and a few other last minute party supplies. Mama finished up her list writing, started up her Cadillac and headed for Carla's Cut and Curl to get her hair-do done up for the party. I climbed out from under the big azalea bush, wiped the old pine straw off my skirt and started the three blocks down to Daddy's office. I was wearing my second best Sunday dress and new white anklets with my patent leather shoes. I had my Sunday purse with two tissues, a dime and my Sunday School class lesson just in case I had to wait for Daddy.

"Hey there, Mr. Hall," I waved to the corner neighbor, pulling his mail from the box. "I'm going down to Daddy's office. Can you please see me across the street?" I wasn't allowed to cross the street by myself. "Thank you kindly, sir," I said as he took my hand and escorted me to the opposite corner.

"Should you be out by yourself, Miss Brittan Lee?" he asked as he tipped his straw hat.

"It's all right, Mr. Hall," I assured him. "Trulee's gone shopping and Mama's getting her hair done. I'm supposed to make sure Daddy comes home on time." I think Mr. Hall could have been laughing at me as he wiped his face with his big white handkerchief.

"Good afternoon, Miss Louise. Isn't this just a lovely summer day?" I dropped a slight curtsey as I bobbed in front of the reception desk. My nose wrinkled as I looked around the large room, full of green plants and a big fish tank. I always associated the same odor to medical offices and florists because of Daddy's green thumb and insistence that a cheery waiting room brightened people's souls. "I've come to make sure Daddy gets home on time."

Her lips set in professional nurse mode, Miss Louise leaned out over the reception counter. "So far it's been a nice day, Miss Brittan Lee. I can't speak to later. So you're here to get your Daddy? Well, he has a few patients still. Why don't you go fetch that latest issue of Highlights, and we'll just put you in an empty room to wait for him."

I did as I was told, and Miss Louise took me to an empty examination room in the fourth wing of Daddy's office. Daddy had his offices and examination rooms in the first wing; Dr. Wensley and Dr. Stephens had offices in the second and third wings. The fourth wing waited for a new physician and was used for overflow.

Miss Louise deposited me at the little desk, and I opened my magazine. Eventually I had found every hidden cup, solved all the puzzles and read most of the stories. The fun stuff over, I looked in my pocketbook for my Sunday School lesson book.

"Suffer the little children to come unto me, for such is the Kingdom of God. Luke 18:16." I repeated my Sunday School Bible verse several times. The minute hand on the big wall clock had only moved twelve minutes. I tiptoed over to the door, cracked it slightly and peered down the hallway. Voices murmured and echoed down the tiles. I closed the door and turned to inspect the room. The tall silver cabinet had glass doors, which screeched when I opened them to count the cotton swabs, the bandages and the bottles of iodine, alcohol and peroxide. Removing the glass blue tipped thermometer, I held it and rotated it in front of the light, trying to find the silver flash that Miss Louise said was the patient's temperature. I grasped it and snapped my wrist just as she did. "Open your mouth and put this under your tongue and don't say anything for three minutes," I instructed my imaginary patient. "I have to prepare a shot for you." I searched for the glass syringe and box of needles that I knew must be there. I couldn't find any, so cautioning my patient to not move, I moved over to the little drawers under the bed on the examining table. They were empty too, so I opened the cabinet doors under the bed. I saw something in the back corner of the large space, and I stretched to reach it. My arms weren't long enough, so I climbed inside to grasp the piece of paper. Once inside, I realized that I fit very well if I sat Indian style and bent my head and neck and tucked one arm under my knee. I could even reach over and pull the little door shut. My right leg started to cramp up and I couldn't untwist my neck, so I pushed the door open to climb out. The door didn't move.

"Daddy! Daddy?" My shoulder banged against the cold metal door. I pressed my face against the little vents in the side, so I wouldn't die of suffocation like the little children in the old abandoned refrigerators. "Miss Louise? Daddy?"

"Bruce, did you hear something?"

The click of footsteps and clinking of metal against metal came closer. I tried to peer through the vents. It sounded like Dr. Stevens, and I wasn't sure I liked Dr. Stevens. He and his wife had three daughters, all older than me and he talked to me like I was three years old instead of almost ten. When he smiled, it didn't make it all the way up his face to his eyes.

"Bruce, can you step in here for a minute?"

Another set of footsteps resounded down the tile hallway. This set had a slight hesitation. I knew that had to be Dr. Wensley. He had a limp from when he played football for

Liberty Academy. He was the quarterback. A tackle from Johnson County High had deliberately roughed him on a play in the last thirty seconds of the game. Johnson High got a fifteen yard penalty; Liberty Academy made a touchdown on the next play and won the Class A championship. Bruce Wensley tore three tendons in his left knee. He never got to play football for the University. I liked Dr Wensley. He always asked me my opinion on how to talk to sick children, and he always had peppermint gum in his pocket.

"What can I do for you?"

"In here."

The metal door lock clicked shut and the little desk groaned under the weight of one of the two men. The roll of sheet paper on the examining table rustled as the other doctor leaned against it up over my hiding place.

"I've got patients waiting. What do you need?" I never heard Dr. Wensley angry before, but he sure sounded mad. Something slapped against the palm of his hand. Squinting through the vent slices, I saw him holding my Highlights magazine rolled up in his hand.

"Listen, you've got to stop him," Dr. Stevens said. "He's going to lose us patients. Folks are getting stirred up. There's no call for this. You have to talk to him."

"Why? What if I agree with him? It isn't going to hurt our business, and those who leave, we probably don't need them anyway."

"Then I guess you're just a nigger lover, too."

"Well, that's taking it a step too far. I just happen to agree that we need a contagious waiting room more than we need a colored waiting room. I don't want some child with mumps or chicken pox sitting out in the waiting room with some of our older patients. I don't think anyone would be stupid enough to find another doctor because we made them sit in the same waiting room as a colored patient. In New Haven, they stopped segregating the waiting rooms five years ago."

"Dammit, this ain't Yale; this is Liberty. I'm just starting to build my practice, and I've got a mortgage and three kids to support. I can't afford to lose a single patient. And what about the hospital board? You saw their reaction when he suggested letting colored people use the same rooms as white patients. Those colored wards are plenty good for them. They don't need semi-private rooms." Dr Stevens kicked back against the metal cabinet, just inches from where my face was stuck against the vents.

"Dammit, don't you understand? This is just the start of it all. Next'll come the restaurants, then the schools. I don't mind eating their cooking, but I don't want to sit down to dinner with them. He isn't from around here, but you and me, we grew up here in Liberty. We know our people. He doesn't."

"Hank, I'm not going to discuss it any more. I agree with Marsh. And even if I didn't, I respect him enough to go with his judgement on this. He's lived here close to twenty years. I 'spect he's got a pretty good understanding of the people. I got my own bills to pay, too. Insurance doesn't even come close to covering Zora's treatments."

The little desk creaked as he must have leaned against it. I tried to see out the little slits again, but Dr. Stevens' leg blocked my view.

"The hospital board is going to go along with it. If they don't, he's going to build his own hospital. So go find someone else to do your dirty work!"

"Well, you're just plain foolish! He's going to take us down with him! I'm going to find some way to stop him if

I have to..." Dr. Stevens pushed off the exam table so hard it rocked on the floor.

The shouting was echoing off the tile walls. I tried to cover my ears with my hands, and discovered I was holding my breath. The door slammed into the wall behind it, sending little pieces of tile across the room.

"You're going to regret this, Bruce! And so is he!" Loud footsteps got quieter as he must have gone back to his own office down the hall. When I heard Dr. Wensley's slow limping step leave the room I was finally able to exhale. I curled up tighter in my little metal cave, and eventually fell asleep. When I woke up, it was dark in the room. I pushed and jiggled and the little cabinet door popped open. I rolled out onto the floor, my feet and legs just flopping like a gigged frog. The numbness passed into pins and needles, and I started crying it hurt so bad. When I could move, I crawled to the door and stood up holding to the handle.

"Daddy? Miss Louise?" The hallways were dark, only the little safety lights glowing. Fading sunlight filtered through the side door, so I knew it couldn't be too late. I tried to open the door, but it was locked. Daddy had a modern office made of cinder block, with no outside windows except the glass doors. Those doors had to have a key to turn the bolt. Feeling my way along the wall, I walked up to the front office and found Miss Louise's telephone. I dialed our home telephone number. I had known it since I was four. And from the sound of Mama's voice when she answered, I knew I was in big trouble.

CHAPTER TWENTY-FIVE
Liberty, Georgia, August 2005

Andy Zeller laughed at me. "Seems like you got into your fair share of trouble as a child. Skipping out on Wednesday night church, getting locked in people's houses and offices. How did you end up so, well, so nice, and not a spoiled brat?"

"Years of boarding school, where I wasn't one of the chosen princesses. A lot of therapy. Bruce and Hank must have worked it out and done well. Hank and his wife have a beachfront house on St. Simons. Bruce has a nice place out near Mudcat Creek." I sorted through the stack of paper in my lap. "My stories. These are some of my stories." I read the first one, a story about seashells on the beach printed with care on lined paper from the tablet given us by the Coca-Cola bottling plant. I shuffled through the other stories.

"Here, here! See this! Look!" I waved the papers in front of Andrew. "See, I knew. I knew. I was right!"

"What?" Andrew squatted next to me. He reached for the papers with one hand and patted the dog with the other.

The little terrier sat up in the tub of sweaters, his hackles raised. He was growling low in his throat.

"Hey, what's the matter, fella?"

The dog took off running from the storeroom, his toes scratching on the concrete. For a small dog, his barking was fierce and protective.

"What the hell?" Andrew stood up and took a step after the dog. "Oh, well, let the alligator get him. So what am I looking at here?" He reached for the papers again. He bent over to take them from me, just as the bin behind his head made a resounding *thwack*!

Diving, he landed on top of me, flattening me against the concrete floor. The window looking out to the back and side yard dissolved into a thousand cracks blurring the view but not shattering into pieces. A second *thwack-clang!* Overhead, the hanging light fixture started to gyrate in wild circles. Out on the lane at the entrance to the subdivision, a car backfired.

"Uhh, get off! You're squishing me!" I wiggled, trying to get free. My right hip ground into the concrete floor and the scabs on my arms reopened as I scraped them on the rough floor.

"Shh! Be still, no, get under the worktable. Go on, get back under there. All the way." He pushed me, then pulled two bins to block me in. "Stay here and be quiet!"

"Where are you going? It was just a bird! Sometimes they get blinded by the light and fly into the windows! Get me out of here!" The tubs grated on the concrete floor as I tried to push them out. I looked around for what must be a mortally wounded marsh wren.

"Idiot! That was a gunshot! Now stay down and quiet." Andrew had drawn his gun and was moving out the door before I realized he was gone. He waved his free hand behind his back. "Stay here!"

Glory to God in the Highest...

Glory to God in the Highest, and to the Son and to the Holy Ghost...

My cell phone was ringing. Stretching my left arm as far

as I could, I was able to snag my handbag from the floor and drag it under the table.

"Hello! What?"

"Brittan Lee, where in the hell are you? Mama knows you aren't here, and so does everybody else. They want you to play the piano, and I keep making excuses," Jack ranted.

"I'm at Four's and…"

"What the hell are you doing at Four's? Get your hiney back here right now!"

"Jack, I can't come play the piano right now. Somebody's shooting at us!" I kept talking but soon realized I was talking to a dead phone. The dog came back in, whining, and joined me under the work table where we both shivered despite the heat. After a long two minutes, I heard the wailing of the siren from Thomas's deputy sheriff car and the scrunch of tires on the oyster shells. Several car doors slammed and the urgent voices of the men rose over the sounds of the incoming tide slapping at the boats moored to docks behind the houses.

"Set up a perimeter."

"Go find that hump!"

"Could you tell the direction?"

"Where's Brittan Lee?"

"Come on out, Brittan Lee. He's gone." Jack and Four blocked the door to the storeroom, crushing each other into the door frame in an attempt to be the first into the room. Four reached in with a practiced hand and flipped the light switch.

"Hey, what happened to the light. Look out! Be careful; there's broken glass all over the floor." He pulled the tubs out of the way and helped me to my feet.

I clung to the dog with one hand and my stories with the other.

"Who was it? Why were they shooting at us?" I looked from Four to Jack then out the door for Andrew.

"They're checking everything out. Probably stray shots from gator poachers. We've got a ten footer in the estuary," Four said. "Let's get you back to Mama's. Thomas and Andrew have everything in hand, and they've called in an investigative response team." Thomas said we could get you out of here. They'll come talk to you at Mama's. Come on, Snickers." He took the dog.

"Answer me! What the hell is going on?" I dug my heels in the yard. "Why do they need a response team for a poacher?"

Four snatched me up as easily as if I were a child and carried me and the dog to his car. "This isn't the time to show your backside! We'll talk back at the house."

***

"Now, what was so all fired important that you had to leave Mama's party and go break into my storeroom?" Four hauled me through the foyer and down to the kitchen at Mama's. Most of the guests had gone, but a few old friends lingered in the living room or out on the terrace. Trulee saw Four dragging me through the door and came after us; Mama's back was to the door. Four tried to keep his voice down, but he held me so tight the dog and I both squirmed to get free.

"I had to get something," I said. "Leigh said something, and it reminded me and I had to go find it. See!" I waved the sheaf of papers under his nose. "I had to go get my stories."

Four stared at me. "Have you lost what's left of your pea-picking mind? In the middle of the party? What were you planning on doing- a dramatical recitation of forty year old stories? They weren't even that good then. We just humored you to shut you up!"

My eyes welled up again. "They were good stories! But that wasn't it. Look!" I waved the papers again. "Look!"

"Four, hush up! You know that isn't true. Honey, what exactly am I supposed to be looking at, other than the stories?" Trulee asked as she took the stories from my hand and replaced them with a glass of ice water.

"This! This! Oh," I said. "Ya'll weren't there. At the pier yesterday. Those divers who saved me. They had been doing some diving near the crash scene. One of them found a Zippo lighter with this medallion on it." I pointed to the top of one of the papers. "This letterhead! From Beth Ann's daddy's office. Doesn't that prove he was there?"

Trulee stifled a gasp with her hand. "Oh, sweet Jesus!"

"Four, darling, there you are." Desiree walked into the kitchen followed by Bruce Wensley. "You just disappeared. Trulee, get me another drink." She looked at me, then glanced away, dismissing me, as if she thought I too was a maid. "I was having the most fascinating conversation with Bruce and some other people out on the terrace. Did you know that this part of the state is one of the most rapidly growing and that property values are tripling? God knows what that old house of yours is worth now! Snickers!" She gave the dog air kisses. "What are you doing here? Did you follow your Mummsie all the way over from Daddy's house?"

I eyed Four with alarm. *Daddy's house?* I mouthed, overcome by an urge to giggle despite everything that had happened. Snickers and I had been through a rough evening together. We were buddies but *Daddy's house?* I looked at Trulee, then at the papers in her hand. She nodded, backed up a step to the kitchen counter, reached behind her to pull open a drawer and slid the papers inside.

Bruce Wensley was looking at me, checking my arms and hands. "Brittan Lee, are you all right? You're bleeding? What happened?" He led me over to the kitchen sink. "We need to clean this up. Four, do you have a bag here?"

"I've got it under control, thanks, Bruce," Four said. "Brittan Lee tripped yesterday and scraped herself up. I've got some antibiotic cream for her. Honey, I'm going to be here a bit longer. There was a little problem over at the house. Why don't I run you home?"

"I thought I heard sirens earlier heading over towards that area," Bruce said. "Everything all right?"

"Poachers off the coast. Been some big gators in the Sound," Four said. "Shot out a window in the storeroom. Thomas is over there with a team. Never can be too sure."

"Well, yes, of course. Listen, uh, since you're going to be tied up here, why I don't drop your lovely fiancee off at your house. If you think it's safe to leave her there, of course," Bruce offered.

"Oh, honey, wouldn't that be just too nice of Bruce?" Desiree clutched Bruce's arm while batting her eyelashes at Four. "Let's just go say good-bye to Miss Arabelle." She tripped down the hallway, her stiletto heels leaving tiny scuffmarks on the hardwood floors.

"Bruce, hang on for a minute. I need to check with Thomas and Andy," Four pulled his cell phone out and hit a preprogrammed number. "Yeah, Thomas. Four. Listen, do you think it's okay to send Desiree over for the night?"

He listened for a minute. "I'll let them know. Thanks." He looked at Bruce. "Thomas thinks it's safe. No signs of entry or attempted entry into the house. Alarms were still on. Doesn't think there was an intruder." He waved me down as I tried to protest. "He knows there was a shot-out window, but he thinks it came from a distance. So tell Desiree not to leave the house. Everything is marked off with crime scene tape, and the team is going to do another grid search tomorrow."

Bruce tipped his white Panama. "I'll take good care of her." He made his good-byes and left down the main hallway.

"Poor Miss Zora. What that woman's been put through," Trulee said through tight lips as she watched them leave. She glanced over at Four. "Yes, poor Miss Zora."

CHAPTER TWENTY-SIX
Liberty, Georgia, August 2005

Something woke me from my sleep despite the little white pill I had taken. I sat up in bed and looked around for something out of place. My nightlight cast enough of a glow that I could see my room was just as I left it. The voices in my head were quiet, a miracle enough in itself. Perhaps that was it. I wasn't used to quiet, and it was too quiet. Instead of the usual night noises, there was silence. There were no tree frogs croaking, no chittering of little marsh creatures. I climbed out of bed and went to the window.

With the draperies parted just a few inches, my hand froze. There was someone on the terrace, sitting on the edge of the brick wall, partially hidden by the swing. Motion sensors failed to detect his presence, failed to cast the bright forbidding lights over the front and back yards. I glanced at the illuminated clock by my bed. Four a.m.

I looked back into the yard. The man was gone. *I'm not crazy, there was someone there.* I told myself. But the voices started in my head. *You are crazy. Crazy children go to Milledgeville. This is all your fault. Beth Ann wouldn't be in the river if it wasn't for you.*

"Stop it!" I said aloud. "There was someone there, and I'm going to find out who." I grabbed my robe and went downstairs. Trying to remember the best Barney Fife moves from old television, I walked down the hallway sideways, clinging to the wall. When I reached the terrace door, I peeked through the glass at the edge of the lace curtain. There was no one there. Moving from room to room, I peeked out the windows and rechecked locks. No sign of anyone. The clock in the kitchen displayed the time as four-thirty. For thirty minutes I had wandered through the house checking and rechecking locks. I was stronger than this. I went back to my bedroom to try and get a few more hours of sleep.

***

The root doctor's ointment stunk to high heavens, but it did make my hands feel better than Four's antibiotic cream. When I woke up the second time this morning, what few muscles hadn't hurt the day before did now. I put the smelly concoction on my hands and arms after reading my morning devotions and went down to my piano. If I go two days without practice, I can tell. If I go three days without practice, my coach can tell, and if I go four days, Mama can tell. I didn't want Mama and her friends to be disappointed, so I grabbed a hand towel and went down to the music room.

The tiny scrapes and cuts on my hands stretched and hurt as I started my fingering exercises. Scales, then more exercises until my fingers and wrists were limber enough to risk actual music. I was still so tired from my disturbed sleep that I was playing from sheer muscle memory. Notes of the meditative largo from Dvorak's Ninth Symphony filled the room. Mrs. Parrish claimed the Symphony for a New World was based on the African-American music Dvorak had loved during his visit to the United States. Nevertheless, I was glad that Dvorak appreciated the syncopated rhythms and pentatonic scales of the old gospel and field music. The New World Symphony was one of those pieces of music I planned to trace for the new CD.

"Beautiful, darling!" Mama was standing in the doorway with Trulee. "I wish you could have played last night for us. Play something else!"

I thought for just a brief second and started the entrance for *After the Ball.*

"Many a heart is aching, if you could read them all, many the hopes that have vanished, after the ball," Mama and Trulee joined in.

"And whose heart do you think was broken last night?" Leigh asked as she walked in with a cup of coffee and sat next to me on the piano bench. "I think Agent Zeller looked awfully happy."

I poked her in the side.

"Careful," she scolded. "Don't make me spill coffee on your piano. Grandmama, you saw her poke me."

"Both of you stop that. That piano has survived a lot more than a cup of coffee, but let's not tempt fate. Brittan Lee, what?" Mama was interrupted by Jack shouting into his cell phone as he stomped up the front steps followed by his son. "What do you suppose has him riled so early in the morning?"

"Stupid, ignorant idiot! I was there! I heard Thomas tell her to stay in the house," he yelled. "So she takes the stupid dog out a different door." He slammed the cell phone shut. "I don't know which one of them I'm going to kill first! Damn!" He looked up to see four pairs of eyes watching him. He froze, then attempted a weak smile. "Good morning, Mama. Ladies."

"And good morning to you," Mama said. "Would y'all like some breakfast or at least some coffee? A little sugar to sweeten up that sour attitude?" She gave them both a hug.

"Mama, the idiot woman opened the back door and walked all over whatever evidence might have been in the backyard. And what she didn't walk on that blasted dog crapped—I mean did his business on. I was there. I heard Thomas clearly tell her to only use the front door," he explained.

They gave us all hugs, and we wandered back to the kitchen.

My nephew caught my arm and held me back. "I was gentle, Aunt B," he said. "I didn't want to bruise you." He grinned at me. "Listen, I called an old friend in Columbia after the party. He told me that Leigh kicked her boyfriend to the curb. And I get the feeling he wasn't too happy about it."

"Oh, she must be devastated. Your mother thought they were the perfect couple," I felt a pang of anguish for Leigh. "He came from the right family background. Which of course, according to your mother meant they had money. And he was a lawyer. And so good looking."

"Well, Bradford had a mean streak a mile wide when we were in elementary school, a real bully. After I moved back here to live with Dad in junior high school, we kind of lost touch," he said. "I'm glad Leigh wised up."

"Bradford? I thought his name was David. Do you think he made those bruises on her arms?" I asked. "And she has some big ones on her thighs as well. I wonder how long that had been going on? She hasn't mentioned a word of it, bless her heart."

"David Bradford. If I find out he did, I'm going to rearrange his pretty face," Jax gave me a menacing scowl, then ruined it by grinning. "Shh, now. Don't upset Grandmama." He slipped his arm around my waist as we caught up with the rest of the family.

"So why is this wandering around going to be a problem?" Mama asked as she pulled down coffee cups from the cabinet. "I admit that Desiree isn't my ideal daughter-in-law, but I want my children to be happy. But just walking in the yard? Was she naked or in some filmy, vulgar lingerie?"

Trulee choked on her coffee, and Leigh had to turn her back to Mama and put her hands over her mouth. I felt her shaking as she tried not to laugh out loud. Jack shot me a look, and I realized that no one had told Mama the whole story about the night before.

"Mama, somebody tried to shoot me last night. Me and Andy Zeller. We were over at Four's looking for something. Somebody tried to shoot us through the storeroom window."

A crash resounded through the kitchen when Mama's coffee cup slipped through her trembling fingers and shattered on the granite countertop. "That's three. The river, the car and now this! Oh, baby, I'm so sorry I made you come back." Tears rolled down her face and she clutched Jack's jacket. "It's supposed to be over. I thought it was all over once Frank passed. It's been so long. We have to protect her. They have to find out who is doing this now."

"Mama, it's all right. I'm fine," I helped her to a seat at the kitchen counter. "There are plenty of people protecting me. I've got Agent Zeller and Leigh, and Jack and the boys. Don't worry."

Trulee put a fresh cup of coffee in front of Mama and a tissue in her nerveless fingers, then she wiped down the table. "Nobody's gonna hurt this child. God has watched over her all these years, he's gonna watch over her 'til this is all over. Truth's gonna come out now."

Mama wiped her eyes. "I can't bear it if anything happens to you, Brittan Lee."

"Well, you aren't giving me much credit there, are you, Mama?" Jack sat down with his cup of coffee. "I got the FBI, a deputy sheriff..."

"She still got shot at!" Mama glared at him.

"Yeah, with an FBI agent at her side!" Jack glared back. They sat there for a few seconds like a pair of Granddaddy's hounds squaring off, before Jack relaxed his posture. "Mama, we're not going to let anything happen. But you're right. We have to find out what this is all about. Dang!" He started patting down his pockets looking for the vibrating cell phone. "What!" He listened for a minute. "Yeah, I heard. I'll tell her. Listen, you aren't making any Brownie points with my Mama." He listened a few more minutes. "All of us? What time? All right, I'll see what I can do." He closed his phone. "That was Andy Zeller. Brittan Lee, you're supposed to meet him at ten at the Courthouse and bring whatever it was you found last night. Mama, he apologizes for almost getting his butt shot off, too. He wants to see all of us at the Courthouse this morning." He looked around the kitchen. "Now can I get some breakfast?"

Mama cut him off. "Brittan Lee, what did you find over at Four's?"

I went to the kitchen drawer and slipped it open. Four pieces of paper with the story of the old oyster man. I took them out and gave them to Mama.

Her face softened. "One of your stories. Honey, what in the world does this have to do with anything?" Her eyes widened as she focused on the papers. "Oh!" Her hand went to her mouth.

"Mama? When did he marry Miss Darton? Trulee didn't remember."

"I didn't know that he had. I thought he left Liberty the month before Beth Ann disappeared. He came back when they were looking for y'all, then left again. I've haven't seen him in forty years," she said, still looking at the story.

"He's back," I said.

"My breakfast?" Jack asked, as he reached over to take the papers from Mama.

Attention, coastal residents!

Mama's weather radio blasted at high volume. Leigh must have jumped a mile in her seat. Her coffee cup sloshed all over the table.

The Severe Weather Team is tracking Hurricane Daphne in the Atlantic Ocean. She has been upgraded from a category one to a category two hurricane with current top sustained winds of one hundred and six miles per hour. Anticipated storm surge should Daphne make landfall as a category two hurricane is six to eight feet. There is a good probability that the hurricane will increase and make landfall as a category three Hurricane with winds ranging between one-hundred eleven and one hundred thirty miles per hour and a storm surge of nine to twelve feet. As a reference, Hurricane Jeanne, in September 2004, hit east central Florida as a category three storm. Hurricane Daphne is tracking in a similar path to Jeanne, but three hundred nautical miles north. Anticipated landfall is between Jacksonville, Florida and Savannah, Georgia. Anticipated landfall is Friday night or early Saturday morning. The Southeast Emergency Disaster Management Team will be meeting today to discuss evacuation plans for coastal residents. All residents who live within three blocks of the marsh coast and all island residents are encouraged to initiate evacuation and property protection plans. Travel advisories will be posted for non-residents. Stay tuned for the latest in severe weather coverage.

The weather report was still being announced when Jack's cell phone went off again. He glanced down at the text message.

"Dang it," said Jack. "Can I please get some breakfast before I go to my Emergency Disaster Management meeting?"

CHAPTER TWENTY-SEVEN
Liberty, Georgia, August 2005

So what do you think your agent wants to talk to you about?" Leigh said, as we left Mama's house. "Why didn't you tell me someone had shot at you? Do you think Desiree can use a gun?" She giggled. "Never mind, I think she was on the terrace with Dr. Bruce the whole time you were gone. I wonder what Uncle Four thinks about that?"

"He's not my agent. Four and Thomas are trying hard to believe that it was a poacher going after gators, but I know that's just talk. They don't really believe that. Not after what happened to us on the way back from Verna Hamilton's. " I concentrated on keeping the car in the correct lane.

"Do you think the hurricane will really hit here? Daddy was joking, but I think he was a little bit worried," she asked, as we watched the wind buffet the big flag outside the Dodge dealership on Highway 17. A sign mounted six feet above the sidewalk on the flagpole announced: *The storm surge from a Category Three hurricane would reach this point.*

"The last semi-direct hit was forty years ago," I said. "Hurricane Dora. Those duplexes Mama bought were flooded up to the porch. The houses on Marsh Pointe Park had just been finished and they all flooded. A whole bunch of the old oaks went down, taking roofs with them. The wind was awful; it shrieked and howled like banshees for three days. Down on Jekyll, the storm surge buried half of the beachfront motels.

That's when the state took back all the leases and made it a state park again. Those new million dollar condos on St. Simons Island, that's what worries me. Those things are hanging off the seawalls. I don't care that a computer program said they were safe up to a category four; those computers haven't been through a real hurricane."

"Oh, come on, Aunt B, tell me what you really think," Leigh teased. "I know you're just dying for one of those big pink places with the ocean view."

"Right," I said. "Those things are expensive. One of those real estate magazines said they started at one million five. You buy one, and I'll come visit."

I noticed Leigh got real quiet again. "Honey, you want to tell me what's going on with you and David?"

Silence.

"I forgot to tell you he called last night. Several times. Said you weren't answering your cell phone."

"I turned it off," she said. "It has a GPS unit in it."

"And that's a problem because?"

"Because I don't want him to find me," she said, her chin wobbling. "I broke up with him. It's over. And that's how I want it. He doesn't seem to think I mean it. He doesn't understand the word *no*."

"Well, honey, on the bad side, he's found you," I said. "On the good side, we're evacuating the city and you will be surrounded by uncles, brothers and cousins who would probably beat the living tar out of this guy if he came near you."

She laughed and wiped the tears off her face. "I think they would, too."

"I, of course, have to protect my hands," I said, knowing it would make her laugh again.

As we drove along the Coastal Highway, we noticed workers starting to board up the big plate glass store windows. The highway traffic was heavier than usual, with more cars heading away from the islands than towards them. The air was dense and crackled with excitement. Across the marsh beyond the barrier islands the sky was dark gray. The marsh grasses were already bending from the wind.

"Lot of cars. Is this where Daddy's meeting is?" Leigh asked as we pulled onto Courthouse Square.

The parking lot was full, and the cars lined the street-side parking. I found a place on the next block. With some clumsy maneuvering of my aching shoulders, I managed to get the car parallel to the curb. I thought I heard the dull rumbles of distant thunder echo in the sky as we approached the building. Once we were closer to the front sidewalk, I realized the sounds came from the crowd of people massed in front of the granite steps.

"Are they all here for the meeting?"

Maybe fifty or sixty people gathered in front of the building, divided roughly into separate but equal groups by the sidewalk. On the south side of the walkway twenty-five or so white men dressed in rough work clothes, straw hats or ball caps milled about in clusters. On the northern side were three even lines of elderly men and women, dressed in Sunday best. They stood shoulder to shoulder. The tension was palpable between the two groups; I could feel it out where we stood.

"Oh, no! Tansie's protest!" I tripped over an uneven place in the sidewalk.

"What do you mean *Tansie's protest?*" Leigh asked as she caught my arm to steady me. "What's going on?"

"Freedom!" Someone yelled from the crowd.

"What the hell you talking about?" A tall, lanky man in overalls stepped to the front of one group. "What the hell freedom you talking about? We ain't got no slaves!"

"We want the freedom of knowledge. Why were our homes burned to the ground. Who did this?"

I recognized the woman speaking as Cora Howard, Tansie's mama.

"Why were the authorities never brought in to investigate? Why has it taken forty long years?" Her voice rang out, still as powerful as when she sang with Trulee in the Liberty AME Church.

I looked into the neat line of protestors and saw Tansie, saw Mr. Willis, saw so many of the children I had played with on those long ago Wednesday nights. They stood arms linked in front of the Courthouse.

"What you bring up this old shit for now?" yelled the lanky white man. Emboldened by the crowd behind him, he took a few steps closer to the opposing side. From behind his back, he pulled out a sign tacked to a two-by-four post. *Get Over It* was painted in large red letters. "You talking about sixty years ago."

"Aint't nothing happened to any of them people. Git the hell back to where you came from! Or something might happen to you!" A burly man, the man from the diner up near Grace River, stepped up beside the first one. "What the hell you talking about? Get out of here. Get back to work!"

From my distance, it looked like a chess game in play. On one side was the black queen, with her king, bishops, rooks of every color and hue. On the opposing side were a melange of white pawns, each jockeying to be the leader. The disorganized mass of agitators tried to cross over the sidewalk. From the back of the group, more makeshift signs of cardboard, of old barn siding and even what looked like a piece of tin roof were passed forward to be waved overhead or staked into the grass.

"Go back! Go back! Get over it! Get over it!" they chanted.

"Freedom and Truth! Freedom and Truth! Freedom and Truth!" Cora led her group of protestors. They linked arms and swayed with their chants. "Freedom and Truth! Freedom and Truth!"

I could hear sirens approaching. I looked back at the street and made my decision.

"Leigh, go wait in the car for your Daddy." I started to walk towards Cora and her friends. Leigh grabbed for my arms.

"I can't leave you. Daddy would kill me! What are you doing?"

I kept walking. I knew the truth, and I was going to tell it again. I had to tell it again.

"Your daddy, men like your daddy," Mr. Willis shouted in a quivering voice as he pointed to two of the white men waving signs. "Men like that beat my brother. My brother died. And no one cared. No one did anything."

"Freedom and Truth! Freedom and Truth!"

"You keep my daddy out of this. He's a good man. He's a granddaddy," the burly man's face was red, and he sprayed spittle as he yelled. "You keep my daddy out of this. Your brother had what was coming to him."

The din became overwhelming as I got closer. Angry screams from one side of the sidewalk were deflected by the steadfast chanting of the other side.

"Brittan Lee, you came!" Tansie moved out of the crowd and came to my side.

"I didn't expect it today! Dang it, Tansie, we've got a

hurricane coming!" I yelled into her ear. "We've got to get people home to get ready."

"We had a hurricane forty years ago, too. The community was ready for this. They been waiting forty years for this. It's time someone was held responsible for what happened!" she shouted back.

"They are! That's why the FBI is here," Leigh yelled.

"Leigh, you need to go over there behind the building," Tansie shouted. "Get out of the way. No telling what's going to happen next."

"Go on, Leigh," I said. "Tansie, you know this won't help! This might keep other people from coming forward with information. And we've got a hurricane coming!"

"Do you think I'm an idiot? I know it won't help. But Mama and Mr. Willis and some of the others, they're just aching for this. Something brought the FBI here, and Mama, she don't want them leaving without some answers."

"Tansie, who knew about today?"

"No one! I wasn't even sure til this morning. When I looked at what Mama did, and Miss Trulee helped her, I just got chills. She said it was like what Miss Trulee planned back in the fifties and sixties. When everything had to be kept quiet. Your Mama's part of all this; she got the permit for a concert. You ready to sing?"

I must have given her a funny look.

"Really! Remember the singers? Jack and the others up at Dorchester? They moved people from place to place like they were on the Underground Railroad. Mama and her group had these secret signals and notes and all that. Under other circumstances it would be funny."

"Well, it wasn't enough. Somebody found out. How do

you suppose they found out." I nodded towards the screaming red-faced men. "They even have signs made, so they didn't just find out today. Oh well, come on. Please promise me Cora didn't invite the TV reverends."

"No, I convinced her that they would just be in it for the publicity. The minute they show up, the reporters forget about the cause and focus on the latest sex scandal. Mama, she and Mr. Willis are in it for the soul. You know Ebon was Mama's nephew? Her sister's baby?" She stood a little straighter. "We're doing this for him."

I took her hand, and we worked our way through the crowd to the front. I linked my arms between Cora and Mr. Willis. Leigh took Mr. Willis's other arm, then linked up with the young black woman next to her. From my other side, I saw Tansie moving in between her mother and the new pastor at the AME. Her full vibrant voice rang out over the crowd.

We shall overcome, we shall over come
We shall overcome some day….
Deep in my heart, I do believe
We shall overcome some day.

I joined her, as did Cora, Mr. Willis and the others, all of our voices raised together.

God is on our side, God is on our side
God is on our side this day….
Deep in my heart, I do believe
God is on our side, to-day.

We sang the verses over and over again, swaying with the rhythm, our arms linked. It was hot, humid, muggy, already over ninety degrees. I could feel the perspiration stinging my eyes and the scrapes on my arms as it dripped down my face. Cora stood tall next to me, not a hair out of place, not a drop of perspiration on her face. Mr. Willis stood as tall as he could, a look of joy and serenity on his face. I tried to help support him, but he didn't need my help. Out of the corner of my eye, I saw my nephews, Quince and Jax, helping Mama and Trulee over the grass to join the other singers. More cars pulled up and people poured out of them adding to the masses on the Courthouse grounds. I like to believe that most of them came to our side of the sidewalk.

The sky darkened as the wind escorted more storm clouds in from the ocean.

We shall not, we shall not be moved
We shall not, we shall not be moved
Just like a tree, planted by the waters
We shall not be moved

"Attention, attention!" Someone was at the top of the Courthouse steps with a bullhorn. "Attention, may I have your attention?" Jack was standing there, along with a red-faced Sheriff Ungler. The elderly sheriff was yelling directions to the younger officer holding the bullhorn.

"Please disburse immediately." The officer turned to the sheriff. Ungler waved his arms, shook his fist at the crowd then looked at the blackened skies. He said something else to the officer, who nodded.

"Please disburse immediately or you will be arrested for disorderly conduct," the bullhorn crackled. "Please disburse immediately. This is an illegal gathering. You must leave and return to your place of work."

As we continued singing, I saw people coming out of the

Courthouse. The porches were packed. I saw Andrew move near Jack, saw them both scanning the crowd. At the street end of the walkway, deputy sheriffs stood by their cars. At both ends, people waited, listening.

I felt a heavy weight on both my arms. Cora and Mr. Willis had both sat down on the grass, pulling me with them. Within seconds, there were almost one hundred people sitting in the Courthouse Square singing *We shall not be moved.*

From the opposite side of the walkway, the men continued to yell and jeer, first content to wave their signs, then they started spitting on us. Brown smears of chewing tobacco juice stained the sidewalk, some of it splashing up onto our clothing.

And before I'll be a slave, I'll be dead and in my grave,
And go home to my Lord and be free,
Yes, and 'fore I'll be a slave, I'll be dead and in my grave
And go home to my Lord and be free

"Damn it, give me that." The entire crowd heard the Honorable Judge Jackson Hayworth curse on the Courthouse steps as he snatched the bullhorn from the officer.

"Attention! Folks, we have a category three hurricane approaching the coast of Georgia. We have less than twenty-four hours to prepare our homes, gather our families and evacuate. We don't want a repeat of what happened in 1964. We have members of the Emergency Management Team standing by to pass out the Disaster Preparation Checklists. Please take one as you leave. If you think you will have any problems with the preparations or evacuation, please tell me or one of the members of the Emergency Management Team. For those who do not drive, we will have buses making rounds of every neighborhood starting at four o'clock this afternoon. This isn't going to be a repeat of New Orleans. We want everyone to be safe. We have made arrangements to use the Wayne County High School Gymnasium. Please make sure everyone has a one week supply of personal medications and at least two changes of clothes. Pack any important personal papers. Bring along some snack foods, granola bars, things like that, and a few bottles of water. Thank you for coming to this public meeting for hurricane preparedness."

For a brief minute, I thought Jack was going to pull it off. Then all hell broke loose.

CHAPTER TWENTY-EIGHT
Liberty, Georgia, August 2005

Heavy black clouds blotted out the sun. The Reverend Avondale stood up next to Cora and flourished his gilt-engraved Bible, his vestments billowing in the wind like the sails of a giant maroon ship. Fat heavy raindrops spattered down onto us.

"The Holy Spirit of the good Lord works within our hearts and within our souls, so that we can be more like him. Take this forgiveness the good Lord is offering to you now. Pray for this forgiveness for your sins against our people," he prayed. "Iffen these people don't repent, then the good Lord will smite them down." The reverend raised his Bible again, gesturing to the sky.

The odor of ozone filled the air, and a metallic taste in my mouth made me salivate. Electricity made my hair stand up in prickles. I knew what was going to happen, and I threw myself over Mr. Willis. I don't know if I was trying to shield him or if I just wanted to get as low as I could. I pulled on Cora's arm and caused a domino-like effect down the line of protestors, toppling them into a heap.

The ragged little bursts of lightning which had been flickering against the dark sky merged together. With a blinding flash, a giant bolt shot from the black cloud bank and exploded into the electrical transformer behind the courthouse, the crashing boom coming so closely behind it seemed simultaneous. Several more brilliant flashes crackled against the sky, each followed by its own deafening crack. Heavy drops of rain, supercharged with energy, pelted us. Our clothes were saturated within seconds of the down burst and little rivulets of rainwater rushed down the sidewalk onto the street.

"Shit! That was close!" The men ran for the protection of the oak trees. Daddy always said *Never stand under a tree in a thunder storm,* but I guess he never said it to them.

The wind whipped the branches of the trees, and the heavy rain knocked leaves and old acorns to the ground. A powerful gust caught at the edge of one of the larger homemade signs, tearing it from the stakes holding it and sending the sheet of tin flying into our midst. The heavy sign crashed into Reverend Avondale. He crumpled to the ground, blood streaming from his temple down his face, mixed with the rain. His Bible, dropped when he fell, lay sodden on the grass.

"They killed the Reverend!" A woman screamed. "They killed the preacher!" She threw herself on his prostrate body, shielding him from the rain. "Somebody help us!"

Cora crawled to his side and tried to stop the bleeding with her handkerchief. I saw Mama, Leigh and Trulee trying to get out from under Jax and Quince. They all crawled through the rain and the muddy grass to join Cora.

"Brittan Lee, call 911!" Mama shouted. "Here, Cora, use this." I looked back to see Mama ripping the lining from her skirt and wadding it into a ball. "You, you, you," Mama pointed to different men. "Get the Reverend under the porch."

Under the trees, the agitators stood silent and watched. A few made apprehensive steps towards us, then perhaps thought better of it and stayed under the tree. But those steps seemed to indicate a signal to the wet men standing guard over Cora, Mama and Trulee.

As if directed by a messenger from God, they turned in unison and headed over to the trees. Wiley Bryant, still as big as he was when he played offense for the Liberty Colored School in 1962, led the line. Pride and fear alternated in my heart when I saw my nephews right beside him.

"Stop!" Cora stood up. "Stop! It is God's place to avenge this. Beware his wrath!"

The rain continued to pelt everyone, although the force of the winds had lessened. The men and women from the Courthouse ran down, hunched over from the rain and wind to help us get the reverend to safety. I saw Jack grab Mama and Cora and Andy, right behind him, reach for Trulee and Leigh.

I was bent over helping carry Reverend Avondale, so I didn't see who landed the first blow. I did hear the sounds of the fight, the yelling and screaming, the thuds of men pummeling each other.

The skirmish was brief and decisive. When I looked up from the reverend, I saw a large number of the agitators running in the direction of the parked cars. Catcalls from Cora's team punctuated the sounds of car engines starting. The men started to wander back over to the Courthouse, swaggering and slapping each other on the back, rain water dripping off their faces.

"Quince," I yelled to my nephew. "Get over here and tend this man. Dang it, this is where you needed to be."

My even-tempered mother swatted her thirty year old grandson. "What were you thinking?" she said. "There's a time and place for everything."

Quince knelt over the pastor and looked at the still-bleeding gash on his forehead. He ran experienced fingers over the back of the unconscious man's neck, then his arms and legs. "Reverend!" he said, as he took the pastor's wrist to check the pulse. "Reverend!"

Mr. Willis knelt on the steps of the Courthouse and clasped his hands. "Heavenly Father," he prayed, "look down on us, your children. Give our reverend strength, heal him, please, O God. We thank you for this victory over evil that you gave your children this day. We beg you for this miracle, too, that you save our friend."

"Reverend," Quince said. "That's good; open your eyes!"

"Thank you, Jesus," Cora said. "He's alive. He's moving! Listen! The ambulance is coming."

The people moved out to form two long lines to guide the ambulance in to the steps. The rain had passed. The emerging sun glinted off the droplets of water remaining on the leaves and grass and steam started to rise from the pavement.

Directed by Quince, the emergency medical technicians made quick work of checking the Reverend and loading him into the ambulance.

"Cora, Mr. Willis," Jack said. "Please get everyone to go and get their homes boarded up. Get everyone to pack three days of clothes, important papers and some food. We'll have school buses coming around starting this afternoon to pick up people that don't have cars. We have to get everyone in-land to higher ground."

Cora smiled at him. "Judge Jack, they are on higher ground."

She turned to the people waiting on the grounds. "You heard the man. We got packing to do."

CHAPTER TWENTY-NINE
Liberty, Georgia, August 2005

Jack and Andrew escorted us to the temporary FBI offices in the Courthouse.

Jack tried his hardest to get us down the sidewalk and back to the car, but Mama dug her heels in.

"We have something to talk about," she said.

"Mama, I think later's better," Jack said as he tried to turn her around. "We have a hurricane to deal with."

"Now, Jack!" She continued in her resolute march, shoulders back, dripping rainwater on the dingy linoleum. "Andrew, please lead the way."

The offices loaned to the investigators were in the basement of the Courthouse. The hallway was painted a dingy institutional gray as was the room we entered. Little slit ground-level windows didn't provide much additional light. Three desks were crammed together, with rolling chairs at each desk and wooden arm chairs next to the side. Two other agents were in the room, one murmuring into an oversized phone receiver as he rolled a computer mouse on the desk; the other one sorting through pages in a thick file. Both of them looked up when we came into the room, then dropped their eyes back to their work.

"Agent Forsyth, Agent Green." He gestured to the other men. Agent Zeller took us through the office to a glassed-in cubicle in the back. Jack showed up with blankets he had scrounged from somewhere.

"Can't we at least move this up to my office?" he asked.

"Jack. Let's get this over with," Mama said as she took one of the blankets. She sneezed twice.

"Mama, we need to get all of you home and dry. See, you're already sneezing."

"It's not the rain; it's the cigarette smoke," I said. "I thought you couldn't smoke inside the Courthouse."

Andy gestured to one of the slit windows. "The smoking area is right there. The frames aren't sealed. Sometimes the smoke filters in."

I watched the legs and feet of people standing in the smoking area. Uniform pants and polished black shoes. Someone had tanned legs in flat sandals. Ashes were flicked on to the ground. Bracelets jingled when a chubby wrist stubbed a butt into the sand filled urn.

"Brittan Lee?"

"Brittan Lee?"

Jack poked me in the side. "Brittan Lee, pay attention."

"Most people think we are here to investigate the disappearance of Beth Ann Hamilton. Actually, we were here already when the remains were found. As I've told some of you, our division frequently gets sent leads regarding past potential civil rights crimes, hate crimes. When we get them, we search the records we already have for those areas, and when possible, go out and do the investigation. " Andy picked up a thick manila folder. "This file was started in 1985. The Special Task Force in Washington received this in April of that year," he extracted a piece of yellowed paper and slid it across the desk.

Telephone Call Report
Date: 15 April 1985
From: No name given.
Phone: No number given.

Message: It was an accident. The doc wasn't supposed to die. Nobody was. It was just to scare them, the fire. I'm sorry. I'm real sorry.

"The caller didn't identify himself, or his location or the time and location of the incident. It went into a tickler file while the Bureau waited to see if the caller made any additional contact. The only thing we had to go on was the fact that this caller specifically asked for the task force on Civil Rights, he mentioned a fire and he mentioned a physician. The file was updated in 1990. Since then, the Task Force has investigated 182 incidents, which were designated as potential civil rights violations. Ninety-six involved a fire, forty-three mentioned a physician. Liberty, Georgia wasn't even in the radar scope until last month." He paused, opened the folder and removed another sheet of paper.

Telephone Call Report
Date: 26 July 2005
From: No name given
Phone: 912-265-0615

Message: The fires in Liberty, Georgia in 1964 was deliberately set as a threat to the black community. The doctor and the other man weren't supposed to die; that was an accident.

*** Note: phone traced back to a prepaid cell

"Oh my God! Who...?" I couldn't even think of the questions to ask. I reached out to take Mama's hand.

"Now we had a time and a location, so we came to Liberty," Andy said. "We've reviewed the sheriff's report from 1964, and we're in the process of interviewing everyone who can tell us anything about that night."

"What have you learned?"

"The official report"—he tapped the file on his desk—"the official report lists Beth Ann Hamilton missing and presumed dead. Kidnaped by a young black male, who was later found dead, burned to death, when a building collapsed. It is believed that Beth Ann's remains were lost in that fire."

I flinched at his words. My eyes were closed as I tried not to hear, not remember that night. A tear ran down my face. "No, no, she wasn't there."

"The second casualty was your father. The third, of course, is believed to be Ebon Johnson," Agent Zeller continued, as he thumbed through the reports. "The sheriff's report is incomplete. Full of blanks and what is clearly guess work. No arson investigation. No full autopsy of the two bodies found. Whoever signed off on these reports is either an idiot or was hiding something." He glanced at the door, checking who was standing nearby.

Andy looked straight at me. "I was very concerned about the poor quality of the investigation that had been conducted, the lack of clear evidence identifying the bodies. Coupled with the two messages we had received, it showed a pattern of negligence or deliberate obfuscation. I took it to the Special Agent In Charge and discussed it with him. Then I went to your mother and obtained her consent to exhume the remains of your father for a forensic autopsy."

They're going to dig up my father! I stared at him. The voices escaped, oozing their way from the box in my head, entwining around my brain. *You were such a bad girl. It's all your fault. They are going to dig up your father.* I started to shake. "It wasn't my fault. It wasn't my fault." I tried to drown out the voices.

"Brittan Lee, nobody said it was your fault," Mama said. "Brittan Lee, listen to me. We know it wasn't your fault."

"Brittan Lee, it is really important that we can accurately identify not only your father and the other man, but we need to know how they died." Andy tucked a paper napkin in my hand.

"You said you were my friend. But you want to dig up my daddy." My voice broke.

"Brittan Lee, I already gave him permission," Mama said. "Your father was exhumed last week and taken to the GBI Forensic Laboratory in Decatur."

"They already did it! And all this while you acted just like there was nothing on?"

"Well, child, you never asked us, and we thought it might be better to wait and see," Trulee said.

"Wait until what? I went to the cemetery, and he wasn't there? There would be nothing but an empty hole?"

"Brittan Lee, we knew that wasn't going to happen," Jack said. "This is something that had to be done, and it's been hard enough on the rest of us. Stop showing your backside and give Mama and Trulee some support. You think it's been easy on them?"

I opened my mouth then shut it again. Jack was right as usual. I hadn't been to the cemetery more than ten times in the last forty years. It wasn't Daddy's final resting place that mattered as much as his spirit and his soul. I knew where those were. This just made it seem so final. I couldn't pretend he was down on Alligator Alley anymore.

"I'm sorry," I said. "Agent Zeller, do you have any results from the," I choked over the words, "the examination?"

"We know it was your father buried there. Dental records," he said. "And more. An elderly man, a retired diener from the old hospital came to us. He knew where the pathologist had stored some of the lab samples from the original, uh, autopsy.

There was an entire lab that was just closed off after the new addition was built. The pathologist had an interesting collection of specimens. But there were some pathology samples that were never documented in the record. We sent those as well. We know now that Dr. Hayworth didn't die in the fire or of smoke inhalation. They can tell that from the lung tissue."

I closed my eyes, took a deep breath and reached out for Mama's and Trulee's hands. "So how did he die?"

"He was shot in the back of the head."

CHAPTER THIRTY
Liberty, Georgia , August 2005

"They recovered the bullet," Jack said quietly.

My eyes flew open. "You knew? Who shot him?"

"That we don't know. But for someone to get that close, it had to be a person your father knew and trusted," Andy said. "And that is where you come in back into play. I need to know exactly what you saw from the shed. Who you recognized, when they got there, when they left."

"I've told you and told you. I don't believe what I saw anymore." I stood up and squeezed past Jack to stand under the slit window.

"Agent Zeller, I'd power down your computer if I was you. I don't think the wiring in the basement has been updated since Oglethorpe built the place." The florescent lights flickered and hummed again, emphasizing my point.

The overhead light fixtures blinked once more then stayed dark.

"Damn it to hell! Phone's dead," Agent Green complained from the other room. "Geez, the computers!"

"It must be the ghosts. I've heard that they don't like the new modern things."

"Get away from the window, Brittan Lee," Mama said. "Lightning might strike again."

The rain started up, heavy fat drops beating on the sidewalk just beyond the smoking area. I watched as legs hurried against the wet, then delayed entry into the dry hallway in order to get one last cigarette.

"It was raining that night, too," I said, thoughts pouring out of the closed part of my memory. "Heavy thunder. Lightening. They had finished beating Ebon. We were sopping wet. The rainwater mixed with the blood on Ebon's face. They locked us in the tool shed, me in the front section and Ebon in the back. Had to separate us, you know. I stood on a box or something to try and see out the window. The window is on one wall and the door is on the other. I would run back and forth between then. I could see from one and hear from the other." I waved away some of the smoke that had drifted in.

"Deputy Ungler was there. Uncle Frank came, but I was already locked up then. I heard the man from the Gulf Station; he always filled Mama's gas tank and checked the oil. I think I recognized two other voices of some of Uncle Frank's clients." I paced three steps, turned and paced three more.

Jack started to say something, but I saw Andy shush him.

"Daddy got there. I could hear him. I beat on the door, but he didn't hear me. Somebody, I think it was Uncle Frank kept pointing to the building across the street. Nobody came and let us out of the shed. Daddy started across the street, and Deputy Ungler called him back and said it wasn't safe. Bruce Wensley was there, and Hank Stevens. I don't remember when they got there. Somebody said he would go with Daddy." I sat down and looked back at the slit window.

"I listened at the door, but I couldn't hear them talking anymore. I climbed on the box and saw Daddy going across the street, so I sat down to wait for him to come back. The shed was dusty, and the smell of gasoline from the mowers was making me nauseated. My eyes burned. My throat was raw from screaming." I wiped my eyes and blew my nose. "I never saw Daddy again. I heard Dr. Bruce shouting that lightning had struck the building and it was burning. Then everyone was gone. I waited and waited. The rains came even harder and the wind. And finally, Jack came."

Everyone was quiet. Andy broke the silence.

"Do you have any idea how many men were there?"

"Lots. I was nine. Ten men would have seemed like a lot. Oh," I remembered something. "Merle and Earl. Beth Ann and I saw them earlier that summer when we were out and about on a Wednesday. We thought it was funny that their names rhymed. They were there that night."

"Merle and Earl? Any last names?" Andy asked.

I shook my head as I watched the smoker's feet come and go. One set of feet, a woman, lingered. A manicured hand dropped one butt after another onto the ground, grinding it into the terrace with her high-heeled shoe.

The rain had slowed to a drizzle, but the skies were darkening again. Through the slit window, occasional flickers of lightning lit the sky followed by the rumbles of thunder.

"There was no flash," I said. "There was no flash! No flash! A crash but no flash!" I looked from face to face. "That's what was wrong. No flash! There was no lightning, I would have seen it! But I heard the crack. It must have been the gunshot. I always thought it was thunder."

"Someone set the fire," Jack said. "That's why the reports were incomplete. They were trying to hide the fact that the fire had been deliberately set. Why would anyone burn down an old office building?"

"To hide the murder of Dr. Hayworth," said Andy.

"Why would someone want Daddy dead?" I asked.

A door crashed into the wall behind me. "Why would anyone want my daughter dead?" Warren Hamilton stood in the doorway.

I think Beth Ann's father had aged twenty years in the last twenty-four hours. His face was grayed, his eyes swollen and red, and he didn't stand as tall as he had at the church. I must have made some sound, because his eyes turned to me.

"You!" he said. "I loved my daughter, Brittan Lee. You of all people should know how much I loved her. I helped search for my daughter after she was kidnapped by that black boy. I…I…"

"Mr. Hamilton," Andy stopped him. "I'm meeting with the Hayworths right now. Why don't you have a seat outside, and we can talk in just a bit?"

"Ebon didn't take her!" I said. "I told you that. She was with you. Almost every Wednesday night, she went off with you. She stopped coming with me."

Warren Hamilton's knees buckled, and he would have collapsed had Jack not jumped up and helped him to a seat.

"Not that Wednesday," he said. "Not that Wednesday. I had a meeting that went too long. Someone, someone else was going to meet her for me. When she went to meet Beth Ann, the alarm was already out. Beth Ann was missing."

"She went looking for you. We usually would sneak out after church supper, about six. I'd go over to the AME Church, and Beth Ann would wait under the Liberty Oak for you. About eight, she would join up with Ebon and me on our walk back to our church. We waited and waited for her that night, but she never came."

There was a pause.

"Agent Zeller, are you no longer considering my daughter's disappearance as being connected with the death of Marsh

Hayworth? Were the reports I gave you any help at all?" he asked.

"What reports?" I asked.

"I don't see how since Beth Ann's remains were in the river and not in the building," Zeller answered.

"Who was going to meet Beth Ann for you?" Jack, Mama and I all spoke at the same time.

"I've had private investigators looking for Beth Ann for years. I use them a lot for insurance fraud claims. I gave him their reports," Mr. Hamilton said, nodding at Andy. "They never picked up a single lead in all that time." His tall angular frame slumped in the chair.

"Private detectives?" I thought about my extra phone line, put in just for Beth Ann's call. I had always believed she would return, just as Warren Hamilton did.

"Warren, who was meeting Beth Ann for you?" Mama asked again.

Mr. Hamilton answered, "Cheryl Darton."

The electricity in the room crackled. I felt both Mama and Trulee tense up.

I must have gasped. "But she was supposed to be at Children's Choir. And she didn't like children."

"Warren! What in the world were you doing with Cheryl Darton? You were a married man, and she was, well, I'm not going to say what she was," Mama said.

"She's been a good wife for forty years," he said, his voice rising. "Verna, Verna and I just weren't getting along anymore. That hag of a mother did her best to constantly break us down, tear us apart. She was trying to poison Verna's mind against me, and Beth Ann, too. Beth Ann didn't believe her grandmother. Thank God she had a strong friend in Brittan Lee to support her. Cheryl would have grown to love Beth Ann over time."

"No, she wouldn't," I said. "She called us names. She didn't want us in the Children's Choir." I remembered the secret mean little pinches she would give me when she moved me from one place on the choir risers to another. I saw the bruises on the soft side of Beth Ann's upper arms. Cheryl Darton would never grow to love Beth Ann.

"Warren, the Cheryl Darton I knew did not like children. I talked to the Reverend about it once. He assured me that the children were just complaining because she was more strict than Miss Harper had been. I still worried about it," Mama said. "Brittan Lee was most unhappy. It almost turned her off music, and we know what a waste that would be. The Lord blessed us when he gave us those two beautiful girls and their music. Warren, I'm so sorry. I always felt so grateful yet so guilty that I still had my little girl."

Andy looked through the papers in a red file folder, then looked at Mr. Hamilton. "Mr. Hamilton, where exactly was your meeting?"

"Jacksonville. I was living in Jacksonville temporarily. I'd moved most of my office records there. I was just waiting for the permanent move back to Detroit. Why?"

"Warren, before you say anything else, I suggest you obtain the services of counsel," Jack said.

"Why? Am I a suspect? I don't need a lawyer. I'll tell you anything I can. I need to find out who could do this," Hamilton said, his eyes tearing up again. "I've been trying to find her for forty years. I've hoped and prayed that she was kidnapped by someone who just wanted a beautiful little girl, and not dead in that building."

My chest tightened, and I felt my own eyes filling up.

"Mr. Hamilton, you knew something about what was going on that summer, didn't you?" I asked.

"I don't know to what you are referring," he said through his hands.

"One Wednesday night, Beth Ann was hiding up in the Liberty Oak. When Ebon and I came to get her, she pushed us in the bushes. She told us that you said bad people were out that night and we had to be real careful going back to the church."

He sat up and pulled a handkerchief out of his pocket to wipe his eyes. "In my job, I heard people talk. Some people thought the black community was getting too uppity. I tried to warn Marsh about it. There was an unofficial patrol in the town to make sure the blacks stayed in their part of town after dark. Seems they weren't there in time; that black boy got her anyway."

Jack stood up and rubbed the small of his back. "Warren, that boy couldn't have been any part of this. Beth Ann was found in the river. Ebon Johnson was either in church or in a form of custody at the same time."

"So it seems, but still," Mr. Hamilton blew his nose. "It's hard to give up something you have believed, clung to for so long. They never found her body in the ruins. I had to have some hope she was still alive."

I understood exactly how he felt.

"Why does it matter where I was? Those reports, the investigators, they can tell you where I was all day, up until the phone call came at nine that night. That Beth Ann was missing," he said. "She went to pick her up, and Beth Ann wasn't there." His voice cracked. "We never had any children," Warren Hamilton hid his face in his hands. "I've lost my baby forever." His shoulders shook as he cried, deep sobbing cries.

Mama and Trulee moved over to comfort him, patting his shoulders and murmuring indistinguishable words of sympathy and support.

Andy pulled the three sheets of paper from the file.

"The car Beth Ann was found in had Duval County plates. Jacksonville Florida."

"Mine didn't. I had Glynn County tags. I was in my car," Mr. Hamilton sat back in his chair. "I was in my car."

"Whose car was Miss Darton driving?" I asked.

"Hers, I imagine. What car would she be driving?" He shrugged. "Afterwards we were in mine. I don't remember what she did with hers when we moved."

"We found some of the records from the agency where the Bel-Air was rented. Widow of the owner had them in a storage locker. Her husband died in the hurricane, and everything went into storage. The wife had been working that day. She remembered that the person renting the car was a white woman. She said the car was never returned. In the aftermath of the hurricane, everything was in turmoil, but when she did get around to reporting the car as stolen, the police found out the name the woman gave was fake."

"Oh," Mr. Hamilton thought about it. "But that wouldn't have been Cheryl. She had her own car. Cheryl loves me. She would have loved Beth Ann, too."

I watched him, a tumult of emotions sliding in my head. Flickers of thoughts flashed—memories of Beth Ann, her father and I going to the movies, him getting us getting ice cream Dilly Bars at the Dairy Queen, Beth Ann and I singing joyously at the AME. "She never would have loved Beth Ann," I said.

"Mr. Hamilton, where is your wife?" Andy asked.

"Out on the smoking terrace," he said.

"Now, Mr. Hamilton, this was in the debris found in the river area when the car was salvaged," Andy pulled a clear zippered bag from his desk drawer. "Does this look familiar?"

Inside the bag was the silver Zippo that Frankie had found and cleaned. On the side was the logo of the Greater South Insurance Group, the initials WGH, and the date 15 June 1963.

Hamilton looked at the bag and with shaking hands reached out and pulled it closer. Removing reading glasses from his inside jacket pocket, he put them on to examine the lighter. He traced the logo and his initials with one finger. Tears ran down his face again. "I misplaced this the summer I lost Beth Ann. I thought I had just put it into the wrong box or something."

I sat watching him, his obvious grief made me question my own long-held beliefs.

I looked at the feet of the smokers outside the window. Little curls of smoke filtered their way into the room through the cracks in the sides of the window, just as the little thoughts in my head filtered out through the cracks in the white box. I watched the wisps of gray dissipate in the room.

"You don't smoke," I said. I stood up and looked at Warren Hamilton. "You don't smoke. You never did. You never smelled like some of the other daddies. You never used the lighter, did you?"

"I,uh, no, I don't smoke. But what does that...?" He had a look of confusion on his face that cleared to concern. "Someone had my lighter. Someone wanted to make it look like I had stolen my own child. They tried to frame me? If I didn't have those reports, the frame-up might have worked."

"Who could have taken it?" I asked. I glanced up at the window.

Hamilton saw where I was looking. "No! Don't be ridiculous! Cheryl wouldn't do that. She swore that Beth Ann had already been taken when she arrived to get her."

"Mr. Hamilton, Beth Ann was waiting for you at six like always. There was nobody else under the Liberty Oak when I left her. Ebon was at the AME church when I got there just after six. He stayed there until almost eight with me and about forty other people, then the Deacon told him to take me back to my church, just like he did every Wednesday. We waited for Beth Ann back at the Liberty Oak for almost an hour. That's when we knew she was missing," I said. "We were the ones who reported it. For a long time I believed that Beth Ann was with you. I knew how much she loved you and you loved her—that's why she would leave me on Wednesdays to see you. But if she wasn't with me or you, where was she?"

"I don't know," he cried. "There had never been any problems like this in Liberty before. Children were safe. That boy must have taken her."

"I know for a fact that Ebon Johnson had nothing to do with Beth Ann going missing," I said. "Who else had a reason for not wanting Beth Ann or me around? I've been thinking about that ever since I was pushed in the river. Why would anyone want me dead?"

Silence filled the room as everyone watched Warren Hamilton. Grief etched deeper lines on his face.

Startled by a tap at the door, we all looked over. Agent Green stuck his head in.

"Sorry, but this lady is looking for her husband."

Cheryl Darton Hamilton, tall and elegant in a black pantsuit stood framed in the doorway. Despite the damp, her hair remained smooth in her chignon, her make-up was unmarred. She had no lines on her forehead, no tiny wrinkles around her eyes. Her smile was severe and cold. There was nothing soft about the former Children's Choir Director.

"Warren, are you about finished?" she said. She looked over and nodded at Mama. "Arabella, it's been a long time. Brittan Lee." Her lips pinched tight when she looked at me.

He stood up so abruptly he knocked over his chair. Starting towards her, he said, "Why weren't you there to pick up Beth Ann? Where were you? My baby was expecting you to meet her."

"No," she backed up into the door frame, and looked around for an escape route. "She wasn't there. I waited for over an hour, and she didn't come. I went over to the diner for a cup of coffee—that's where I heard she was missing."

Warren stood up, some inner strength pulling him straight and tall. "Cheryl, you didn't want Beth Ann to come with us to Detroit. You wanted to leave her here with Verna."

Cheryl Hamilton remained standing, looking over the group in the small room. "I thought the child should be with her mother, even that mother. I can't believe you spend thirty minutes with these people and you are willing to blame me all over again. I told you I didn't know anything about this. Now, let's go, Warren!"

"What do you mean *blame you all over again*?" Jack asked Mr. and Mrs. Hamilton. "What did you blame her for in the first place?"

Neither of them answered.

Andy stood up. "Mrs. Hamilton, I suggest you contact a lawyer. We will be needing to talk to you some more about this situation."

Warren sat slumped, shaking his head. "You didn't want Beth Ann? You didn't want her to come with us? My God, Cheryl, what did you do?"

She pulled herself to her full height and looked at Andy eye to eye. "I have nothing else to say on the subject. I gave a full report forty years ago." She turned to leave. "Warren, are you coming?"

"They have the car at the FBI Crime Lab" I said. "Don't forget about the fingerprints."

She stopped at the door and turned to look at me. "Brittan Lee Hayworth, you always were a nosey, interfering child with an overactive imagination. Warren?"

CHAPTER THIRTY-ONE
Liberty, Georgia August 2005

How could he stay with that woman if he had any thoughts she was responsible for that child's death?" Trulee shook her head in disbelief. "It seems to me he went from Hell to whatever is worse than Hell."

"Horrible. I couldn't do it," Mama said. "I knew she was on the hunt for a husband, but I had no idea she had set her sights on someone else's, although I remember someone mentioned her and another married man. Bruce Wensley as a matter of fact. I just put it down to nasty gossip."

"I saw them kissing once," I said. "They were in the ladies changing room."

"In the church?" Mama and Trulee were scandalized.

"Brittan Lee, why didn't you tell me?" Mama asked.

"I was some place I wasn't supposed to be," I said. "You would ask me how I knew, and I would have to admit I had cut choir practice. If there is anything the boys taught me, it was to cover my tracks."

"Shh," Jack scolded. "That was one of our secrets."

Mama studied her hands. "Isn't it amazing that fingerprints can last so long? Brittan Lee, how did you know about the fingerprints?"

"*CSI* on television," I said.

Andy thumbed through the papers once more. "Now about the investigation."

"Is there enough evidence against Cheryl Hamilton?" I asked.

He shook his head. "It's all circumstantial right now. We actually might be able to get fingerprints from inside the car. Maybe the woman from the rental car shop can identify Cheryl Darton as the woman who rented the car. I don't suppose any of you have a picture of her from those days?" He looked at the notes he had taken. "Brittan Lee, keep thinking about who you saw or heard that night. That reminds me, how is it..." Zeller was interrupted by someone rapping on the glass wall.

I looked up but the angle of my chair prevented me from seeing who it was. I tried to rearrange the facts in my head. Warren Hamilton had not been with his daughter that night. He had been having an affair with Cheryl Darton, and she could be responsible for Beth Ann's disappearance. How could any woman do that to a child? Mama's talking interrupted my thinking.

"Trulee, don't we have a picture of the Children's Choir from Vacation Bible School that summer?" she said. "I'm pretty sure Cheryl Darton was in that picture. It's one of the last ones of Brittan Lee and Beth Ann together."

Zeller excused himself and went out the door. He returned a few minutes later, apologizing. "Sorry, that was the Special Agent in Charge. We're going to comply with the evacuation procedures. We need to get everything packed up and moved inland." He turned to Jack. "Where are you sending your family?"

"The Homeplace," Jack said. "I think a hundred miles inland should be safe. Trey and the crew are already closing up the house at Sapelo Sound, loading up the horses and dogs. I want to get Mama, Trulee and Auntabelle off by this evening, before the traffic gets too bad." He looked at his watch. "At six tonight, we start blocking off the east-bound off-ramps from Interstate 95, making everything west-bound. Where will you be staying?"

"Jesup. The SAC thinks that will be far enough in-land."

"Well, good luck. I've got to get everyone home, then meet with the Emergency Management team." Jack stood up and held out his hand. "Come on, ladies."

"Jack! There you are," Bruce Wensley stood in the doorway, rain-water dripping from his Panama hat and the bottom of his raincoat. He looked over us, one by one. "I've been looking for your brother. See if he needs me for anything."

"Uh, Bruce, Four would be at the hospital. Are you sure you have time to help? I know it must be hard to get Miss Zora all packed up—what with her oxygen tanks and her medications and splints and things," Jack said.

"Oh, we're not evacuating. Our house is four miles inland from the coast. I'd rather keep her where she is comfortable," he said. "I figured Four wouldn't be evacuating with you. He'd want to stay and watch over the hospital. I was going to offer him room for himself and his ladyfriend. I know Marsh Pointe will most likely take some of the worst of it. Belle, y'all are all welcome to stay with us, too."

"But what if we lose power?" Mama said. "Is Zora's help going to stay with you?"

"We've got an emergency generator. I had to put it in when she started using that ventilator at night. Well, I'll be looking for Four at the hospital." He nodded, put his Panama hat on and went out of the room.

"I can't believe he would do that," Mama said. "Poor Zora, bless her heart. She hates being a burden. Well, let's get moving. We have a lot of packing to do."

"Wait, Jack, Brittan Lee," Andy said. "Brittan Lee, can you be spared for just a few minutes? Jack, I promise I won't keep her very long, but I would like her to show me that storage shed before everyone leaves."

Mama hesitated. "Brittan Lee? Are you sure you are up to that? I mean?"

"I don't, I mean, why right now?" I wasn't sure I wanted to go anywhere with Andy Zeller right now.

"I won't keep you very long," he promised again.

After reassuring Mama that I would be right along, I escorted the agent down the hallway and out the basement door into the lightly misted afternoon sun. The earlier rain still stained the flagstone path to the storage building. Only about a hundred feet away from the Court House, the building stood in the shadow of the Liberty Oak. Several of the massive limbs rested against the tin roof.

"So, Agent Zeller," I said, "has any of this helped your investigation? Are you any closer to knowing what happened?"

"Last night you called me Andy," he took my arm as we stepped over a large puddle.

"Last night I didn't know you were planning on exhuming my father." I allowed him to maintain his grip on my arm.

"I'm sorry. It was important, and it was the right thing to do. Now we know that Beth Ann's disappearance and your father's death were probably not related. And we know that someone killed your father; it wasn't an accidental fire caused by lightning," he said. "I didn't not tell you. I didn't even know you. We went to the next of kin, which was your mother."

We stopped in front of the old building. Gray Spanish moss swagged from the branches of the Liberty Oak to the tin roof and hung like draperies over the small windows set high and deep into the faded pink walls. The top of the slanted tin roof raised up maybe six feet over the ground. The front door, the only door, was made of thick wooden planks.

"Interesting, um, storage shed. It's a little more solid than I usually think of a shed as being. What's it made of?"

"Tabby," I said. "Tabby was made by the slaves from oyster shells and sand and water. Daddy said that this building was probably the first courthouse and jail in the colony."

"Brittan Lee," he said. "Why is it almost every conversation we have, you quote your father? Honey, he's gone. It's been forty years."

"It's how I keep him close," I said.

"Oh, honey," his arms wrapped around me and my head rested on his shoulder. "He's always going to be close to you. Your strength has always been your love for your Daddy."

It felt so comfortable, so right, to be held. It felt even better when he kissed me.

"Listen. Can you hear the singing?" I said.

"Um," he loosened his grip. "No."

"Listen closely, feel the wind, move with it and listen from inside of you."

I been in the storm so long,
I been in the storm so long, children
I been in the storm so long,
Just gimee little time to pray...

I sang the words to him, and we swayed to the breeze.

"It's the magic of this place. The coast is where you get your inspiration," he said. "I spent an hour listening to your CDs last night after the party. You need to come back." He looked at the building. "Tell me about this shed. Why isn't it locked?"

"I don't know. There used to be one of those hasp lock, hingy things here." I showed Zeller the triangular area of darker wood. Fingering the three tiny screw holes, I said, "It was right here. I wonder why they took it off? Historical preservation, maybe?"

"You would still need to protect whatever is inside," he said. Depressing the tongue latch, he pulled open the door. "What is in here?"

"Used to be tools. And for a while, they kept the cases of Cokes here. Full and empty bottles," I said as I followed him inside. "You could cash in the empties and get three cents each for them."

Tools lined the walls, hung from racks mounted on the ten foot long walls. Two lawn mowers stood in the middle of the damp earthen floor. The same empty wooden Coca-cola case was under the window—the box where I had stood trying to see my father.

"This is where you were?" Zeller said.

I nodded, trying to catch my breath, trying to keep my heart from racing and the knot in my stomach from erupting.

"And in there?" he pointed to the inner door.

"Ebon," I said.

Zeller pushed the door open and stepped into that tiny room. It was no bigger than five feet by eight feet.

"This was the jail part," I said. "I think the slaves were kept in here. Look over at that wall. The one without the window."

He cleared out some of the trash to get closer to the wall. "Shackles?" He touched the rusted chains still attached to the wall. "No way out except through the door," he said. "So how did Ebon get past you?"

"He didn't," I said. "He went out the window."

Zeller looked at the window then at me. "It's a single pane window. No hinges, no crank. It doesn't open. Is this the original window?"

"Are Jack's initials carved in the frame?" I asked. "And Marsh's and Trey's?"

Muttering under his breath, Zeller shoved aside trash, old empty fertilizer bags, and the broken sprinklers he had just moved from the opposite side. Swoops of spider webs caught in his hair, and he had to stoop to keep from dusting the entire ceiling. He got his face as close as he could to the worn and peeling window frame. "Where?"

I closed my eyes and tried to remember. Memory was my other strength. "Run your fingers in the lower right corner."

"Damn it," he muttered under his breath. "Splinters. Hey! There are initials here! How did they get there if this place was always locked up?"

"Gang initiation," I said. "Well, it wasn't a gang; it was a high school fraternity. You had to get in from the outside, without breaking the window or the door locks. If you made it in, you carved your initials in the window frame. If you look close, you'll find most of the initials of the current male population between ages of forty and seventy. It was spooky, had to be done at night. Everyone swore they could hear the ghosts of the slaves rattling their chains. You had to jangle the chains, too, just to make it a little more spine-chilling."

He came back out to me. "So do you know how they did it?"

I nodded. "Come with me." We went outside and around to the window. On this side, the window was only four feet off the ground and was sheltered by the hanging moss. I search my purse and found a nail-file. "Look on the ground and see if you can find any nails," I told Zeller.

"What the..." he went back inside and returned with two large nails. "Let's do it the easy way. We're running out of time."

"Look at this beautiful glass. See the waves and the little bubbles? This glass is original to the building. Two hundred years, that's pretty good," I pushed one nail vertically into the wood at the top of the glass on the left, and one on the right. Tensing my back and bracing my elbows against the tabby windowsill, I jiggled the window frame bit by bit. I would lift the frame just a slight bit and pull first the left side, then the right side forward in quarter-inch spaces. After over ten minutes of terminally slow progress, I had the window frame right at the outer edge of the wall. "Forty-five years of piano gives one a freakishly strong upper body," I said.

"Remind me never to arm-wrestle with you," he said. "So your brothers came over here, took out the window, carved their initials. All for a fraternity prank. So how did you know?"

"I followed Jack," I said. "By then Four and Trey had graduated. But they told him what to do."

"Okay, but what does this have to do with Ebon getting out?" he said.

"It's easier from the inside," I said. "There is more wood, so you can put your fingers against the frame and gently lift and push at the same time. Still takes a long time. I told Ebon what to do."

I pushed the window frame back into place, again bracing my elbows against the tabby and coaxing the wood into place. "See it can't slide smoothly because the tabby is rough. So you have to lift it just a tiny bit- about an eighth to a quarter of an inch. Pushing it is a lot easier than pulling it out." We went back inside the shed.

"Why did you help him?" Zeller asked.

"He was my friend," I said. "You know what they were going to do to him. They already beat him to a pulp, and it wasn't the first time. Ebon was bound for a better glory. He was here for a purpose, and I didn't want him dead."

"What did he do after he got out? Why did he leave you there?"

"I told him to. My side of the shed is where people were. His side of the shed had more branches and moss and stuff, so he had some cover. I had three dimes tied up in my hankie—it was my good one, with my initials in the corner and a little pink flower. And I had Jack's phone number at Dorchester. He gave it to me for an emergency. I figured this was an emergency. So I tied them all up together and slid it under the door. Told Ebon how to get the window out, and told him to put it back after he was free. To stay low, go to the marina and call Jack. That Jack would take care of him."

Zeller just looked at me. "Did he?"

"Yes. Jack and his friend, Tony, came down, fetched Ebon and took him back to Dorchester Academy. When he got healed up enough to travel more, Gus, that's Trulee's brother, and Tony, they got Ebon up north."

"Where's he now?"

"I don't know. Gus said it was better that way. But sometimes I would really like to know that he's still all right," I admitted.

"What about the other boy, Tony?" Zeller said, an urgent tone in his voice.

"I never saw him again," I said. "Ask Jack. Why is this guy important?"

"I think he was my brother."

Without a doubt I knew he was right. The so familiar green eyes, the same nose, the same wavy black hair, although Tony's was down to the middle of his back. Even his easy familiarity with Jack, as if they had known each other for years.

This time I reached up and put my arms around Zeller.

"What in the hell is going on here!" A man stood in the shadows of the doorway.

CHAPTER THIRTY-TWO
Liberty, Georgia, August 2005

Mama, I swear he scared me to death," I said as I boxed up perishables from the refrigerator into a portable cooler. "Just showed up out of nowhere. Said he was looking for Jack. Suddenly everyone's looking for Jack."

"Well, he is the chairman of that emergency committee," Mama said, her voice coming muffled from the interior of the deep freezer. "But Hank Stevens wouldn't hurt you. He loves you like his own daughters. That always did drive Virginia crazy, what with three girls of her own."

Trulee came into the kitchen with two more empty boxes. "Belle, get out of that freezer. If it stays closed, the food will stay frozen, even if the power goes out."

"I just want to make sure we have enough food." Mama backed out of the freezer, her nose pink and frosted. "I thought I had some more of those nice chicken casseroles. You know the ones, Trulee, with the little peas and the mushrooms. And the crab casseroles. You know Amalie loves those."

"When Amalie finds out you're bringing food, you might just wish you'd stayed to face the hurricane." Trulee shook her head. "Amalie takes big notice of her hospitality."

"Well, yes, but we're bringing, what, nine people? Vickie and Michael already left for her mother's in Atlanta, and they took Morgan and Madison with them. That leaves me, you, Annabelle, Brittan Lee, Leigh, Trey, those two women at Sapelo, Jax, eventually maybe Quince, Four and Jack," she ticked names off on her finger. "Oh dear," she said, a horrified expression on her face. "Do you think Four expects us to take Desiree with us? Since I just know he and Quince will stay here at the hospital. Jack will probably stay behind, too. Honey, flip the light switch, will you please?"

Jax and Leigh had bolted shut the hurricane shutters over the French doors to the patio, and the windows from the kitchen and Mama's bedroom. The interior of the house was dark and gloomy. I could hear their voices as they moved to board up the sides of the house.

I dragged the cooler to the porte-cochere door. "Mama. Don't you remember? Dr. Bruce offered to take in Desiree and Four? You know, I don't think that woman has spoken five words to me in the three days I've been here."

"Something's out of kilter there," Trulee said. "I doubt Miss Zora wants company. I'd be willing to bet she wants to get to high ground, too. Belle, you know his history." She handed me the box she had filled with staples from the pantry.

I stacked it on top of the cooler. "Mama, I'm going to make sure everything is picked up or tied down outside."

"Watch your hands, dear," Mama's voice trailed after me.

On the south side of the house, a ladder was leaning against the wall. Leigh was bracing the bottom of the ladder as Jax balanced at the top, reaching for the shutters.

"So what can I do?" I asked.

Jax looked down from his perch. "You can take all the chair cushions and potted plants and put them under the house. Those lattice things under the kitchen and bedroom windows are hinged. Put everything under there."

"Aye-aye, sir." I saluted. The wind was starting to pick up, not quite so hard as the Weather Channel reports had it, but still enough to blow the blossoms off of Mama's roses. The breeze was hard enough that I could only manage one lounge cushion at a time; it took me about nine trips to get them all secure. Mama had put little rollers under her big potted plants, so I rolled them to the edge of the patio and only had to lift them about two feet down to the enclosure.

I started to drag the heavier wrought-iron furniture over to the edge of the patio.

"Hey! Hang on, baby sister." Four came around the side of the house and grabbed one side of the chaise lounge. "This area is just wide enough to hold the furniture, stacked on each other. Mama was thinking ahead. She had steel eye bolts put in along the edge, so we can chain down the furniture."

We brought over the other chaise, six chairs, the two end tables and the larger dining table.

"I don't think this is all going to fit," I said, surveying what was left to the space to put it in. "Do we have some other place to put it?"

"I guess we can chain it to the columns in the porte-cochere," Four said. "Are y'all about ready to leave? Whoa!" A heavier gust of wind knocked loose several palm fronds and sent them sailing.

Lightning flashed over the islands, followed by a rumble of thunder.

"They've almost finished the mandatory evacuation of the islands. Daphne has turned into one of those freak storms. Already up to a category three. Didn't think this water was warm enough to build up a storm that much," he said. "Roads are going to be packed. I want to get Mama and Trulee out as soon as they can leave."

"Uncle Four!" Jax and Leigh came around the corner, dragging the heavy ladder.

"Hey there," he said. "You ready to get out of here? I need to run over to the house and get Desiree and some legal papers for Mama to take. Y'all go make sure the ladies are ready. Come on, Brittan Lee."

We climbed into his car to make the quick drive over to his house. Leaving the engine running, Four left the car door open and ran to the house.

"Desiree! Desiree?" He went inside and returned almost immediately with a file box of papers and Snickers. "She's not in there. No message. Not answering her cell phone. Here," he shoved the dog and the box at me. "I'm going to leave her a note."

"Snickers, where's your Mommy?" I said. I scratched behind his ears, and he twisted his head trying to lick my fingers. "Why would anyone go off and leave you all alone?"

"You have to take care of the dog." Four rejoined me in the car.

"Me? You know I'm not a dog person. Did you check to see if any of her clothes are gone?" I said. "Bruce Wensley came by the Court House this morning looking for you. Said you and Desiree were welcome to stay out there. Maybe she's already there."

"Humph," Four snorted. "Left the poor dog alone. Didn't bother to call me or leave a note. Probably for the better. I think she is with Bruce, they were real cozy at Mama's party. She must think he has more to offer. Wait til she finds out all the money is from Zora's family trust. Bruce can't touch it without her permission. That's why Desiree hooked up with me in Florida, she thought I was a doddering old fool looking for a trophy wife. I knew exactly what she was like, but I thought it was funny for a while. I mean, the looks on everybody's faces. Desiree kept hinting about things she wanted me to buy her.

I think she was annoyed that I wasn't moving faster. Yeah, she probably took up with someone else, she works fast, you know.. Kind of like the dog, though."

"Sentimental slob, aren't you?" I punched my brother in the arm.

He turned the car into Mama's driveway, and I noticed the car Jax was loading.

"Hey, where did you get this monster?" I asked. Mama drove a Cadillac, not a Hummer.

"About three hours ago," Jax said. "Shook hands with the manager and promised to do the paperwork after the storm passed. I wanted something real sturdy for the evacuation. Grandmama," he called, "you two ready?"

"Two?" I said. "Where's Leigh?"

"We're waiting on her. Right after you left, she couldn't find her purse," he said as he reached for Mama's little tote bag. "So she went to get it. Wish she would hurry."

Four tensed his jaw. "How long is she going to be? I want you to get on the road. Winds picked up just since we left."

He was right. The palm trees were starting to bend against the wind, which was bringing in cooler air. Spanish moss was being dragged from the trees by spiteful little fingers of the storm, to roll along the ground until they caught on the bushes. Gray-black clouds lined the skies, with the occasional backlighting of a flash. Pellet-sized bits of hail hit us, stinging with the same intensity of the blackflies.

"You go on," Four said. "I'll wait here and take Leigh to the hospital with me. That's where the Emergency Management Team is going to be, anyway. No, Mama," he said when she tried to protest. His beeper sounded, and he looked down. "Dang, they need me at the hospital. Leigh will be fine, but I want you out of here." He took my arm. "Brittan Lee, get into the car."

I pulled back. "Jax can take care of the ladies. I'll wait here with you for Leigh. Better yet, you can go on to the hospital, and as soon as Leigh gets back, I'll bring her over there."

Despite her objections to the plan, Four and Jax half-lifted Mama up into the high seats of the Hummer. They assisted Trulee to her seat, then slammed the doors.

"I'll stop by and get Auntabelle," Jax said as he climbed into the driver's seat, "then I'll be on the road. I've got a full tank of gas, plus two five gallon cans in the back, so we should make it all the way to HomePlace. Aunt B," he said, "make sure your cell phone is charged. Call me when you leave here."

I nodded, then looked up. "Jax, did she say where she left her purse?"

"At the Court House. Under some bushes by the front entry." He waved good-bye and turned the car out onto the oyster shell lane.

CHAPTER THIRTY-THREE
Liberty, Georgia, August 2005

Three minutes. Five steps. Five minutes. Five steps. Seven minutes. I alternated pacing in Mama's tiny mudroom and checking my watch. I could hear the wind still whipping through the trees outside and the rumbles of thunder.

Attention coastal residents! The Emergency Disaster Management Committee has declared a state of emergency for the coastal counties: Camden, Glynn, McIntosh, Liberty and Effingham. Mandatory evacuation is required for all residents who live within twenty miles of the coast line. All island residents are required to evacuate. This is a dangerous, rapidly progressing storm. Those who have not yet evacuated are strongly encouraged to do so now.

It scared the tar out of me when Mama's weather radio blasted its message of doom. I had to sit down for a minute and catch my breath. I had just recovered enough to resume my pacing when my cell phone rang and scared me again.

"I'm still waiting for her, Four," I said. "I'm sure she'll be here any minute."

"Aunt B?"

The voice was faint and barely distinguishable over the crackles of interference.

"...following me, Aunt B. He thinks..."

"Leigh! Leigh! Where are you? Honey, where are you? Leigh, can you hear me?" I wasn't sure if we were still connected.

Her number was still displayed on my phone and the seconds were ticking by on the screen. "Leigh!"

The phone crackled again. "I'm outside the Court House." More crackles. "Lost my car keys." Interference again. "Don't understand..."

Even with the distortion, her voice sounded panicked.

"Leigh! Stay there," I screamed into the phone. "I'm coming." I snapped the phone closed and grabbed my purse and Mama's car keys from the hooks by the door.

The wind slammed the door shut behind me and knocked me off the steps to the ground. I hung my bag around my neck and crawled over to Mama's Cadillac, Snickers beside me.

The traffic on the Dixie Highway was bumper to wind-shaken bumper, heading north and inland. Debris from the parking lots was flying through the air, catching on cars, billboards, bushes. The palm trees were bent almost double and branches from oak trees were breaking under the pressure. Police in orange rain ponchos flying straight out behind them were trying to direct the cars, but the vehicles were creeping along. One of the officers waved at me.

"You're going the wrong way. The bridge south is closed. You gotta take the inland route to the Interstate," he shouted against the wind.

"Thanks," I shouted back. "I'll turn around up there in the parking lot."

He nodded and I kept driving, struggling to hold the car steady in the wind.

I didn't see Leigh's car when I approached Court House Square. The dignified building delivered a hollow-eye stare, the beautiful leaded windows covered with four by eight sheets of plywood. No lights shone between cracks in the boards. The county jail had been evacuated earlier that day, Jack had told me. There were only a few cars in the parking lot between the Municipal Building and the Court House. The streets were abandoned except for those still attempting to leave. I drove around the Square looking for Leigh's car and finally found it parked straddling a set of yellow striped lines behind the Court House. Mama's Cadillac bounced over the curb and skidded half-way to the back entrance of the building.

"Leigh!" I jumped out of the car and ran to the building, Snickers on my heel. He hugged the ground as he ran, but I was worried he would get blown away. I beat on the doors but no one came. The west side of the building was sheltered from the wind, but I could still hear the thunder rumbling, each rumble seeming louder than the next. I stepped out into the storm to work my way around the building, trying every door and window, but they all were secured. Snickers made a quick check of the wind-tossed foundation planting, which assured me that Leigh wasn't hiding under an azalea bush.

The only place I hadn't checked was the tabby storage building.

I froze at the idea of going over there; the only-too-familiar fullness in my chest started, the rising bile burning in my throat. Memories flashing through my head.

It's your fault she's missing, the voices said. *She's only here because of you.* They said. *She's going to die, too. She's missing now, just like Beth Ann.*

I swallowed against the knot in my throat, tucked my head against the sheeting rain and ran toward the old building. The ground was slick from the rain and the fallen leaves. I fell twice. Each time Snickers nuzzled at my face and hands, licking me, encouraging me to continue.

Debris and fallen tree limbs blocked entry to the building. Struggling against the wind, I tried to drag the branches away from the doorway. I don't know why I thought she could hear me, or I could hear her, but I continued to call to Leigh. The dog seemed to sense my anxiety and barked at the door.

Once the entrance had been cleared, I had to battle the winds to get the door open. We slipped inside just as the gale force slammed the door shut with such a bang it rattled everything inside.

It was quieter in the building. The tabby walls were solid and secure. They had stood against almost two hundred years of hurricanes, but the wind whistling through the tiny cracks around the windows, the rattling as acorns pelted the tin roof, the dragging of branches as they were ripped from the trees melded into a cacophony of sound.

"Leigh?" I called. "Leigh, are you in here?" I grasped for the pull-string to the lightbulb that hung from the ceiling and yanked on it. Nothing happened. The room remained dark. I crouched in the middle of the room, holding the dog, listening for sounds.

Snickers whined, then jumped from my arms and ran to a corner of the room. He started to dig through the trash, his powerful shoulders helping him burrow through the mound.

"What is it, Snickers? What have you found?" I crawled over to the dog and pulled off some of the larger pieces of garbage. "Leigh! Oh my God, Leigh! Good boy, Snickers!"

Leigh was still, her eyes closed. Snickers barked, then licked her face, then sat back, pleased at his discovery.

I leaned over and felt her face, listened for breathing. I touched cloth. Leigh had been gagged. After loosening the material, I felt for her hands and untied the cords binding them.

"Leigh! Leigh, honey!"

A flash of lightning illuminated the room for a brief second, long enough for me to see the egg-sized lump on the side of her head—long enough to see the blood staining her hair, running down her face.

"Leigh!" I held her close to me and rocked her like a child. "Leigh, honey, it's time to wake up. Leigh!"

Her breathing came in regular intervals. My own hands shaky, I felt her wrists for a pulse. I couldn't see my watch to time it, but I was comforted to know that her heart was beating. It was erratic and weak, but still there. I couldn't see if she had any other injuries, but she whimpered when I moved her left arm.

Snickers continued to work his way around the walls, sniffing and giving the occasional yip. He scratched at the door to the inner room and gave several short barks.

"Come here, Snickers," I said.

He came and lay beside me. I rocked Leigh and talked to her and sang to her throughout the night and through the storm. And I remembered that night forty years ago, and what happened, piece by piece as if it were a three act play.

CHAPTER THIRTY-FOUR
Liberty, Georgia September 1964

Come on. It's going to start raining," I said tugging on Ebon's arm. When he didn't walk faster, I looked up and saw him wincing. "I'm sorry. Does it still hurt?"

He just grunted like my brothers when they don't want to answer a question.

Daddy took his medical bag and went back to Mr. LaCroix's farm after he took Mama and me back to Liberty. I wanted to go with him, but he wouldn't let me. Mama took me in the house and talked to Trulee, and they cried and hugged each other. Daddy sewed up the cuts on the men and gave them medicine. I know because he let me help him take out the stitches last Monday. Ebon's eye and lip weren't as puffy as they had been, but he still walked sort of stiff-legged. I slowed down and stopped pulling on his arm.

We were late getting to the Liberty Oak. The clock in the Court House tower chimed eight when we were still two blocks away.

"Beth Ann's going to be worried," I said.

Ebon grunted again. "She been late last two times, girl. She can wait."

We stopped just before the corner, where we could wait for Beth Ann without anyone seeing us. She wasn't there. Ebon was right. She was late. I kept looking for her when the flashes of lightning brightened the sky or when the headlights of the old cars circling the square bounced across the grounds. Those cars and trucks cruised around the Square. I would see one turn onto a side road, then a few minutes later, come back down another one to the Court House. They were looking for someone.

The rain came in cold sheets, drenching us. Thunder boomed overhead drowning out the sounds of the cruising cars, the men calling to each other and the clock striking nine.

"She's really late this time," I said through my chattering teeth. "Do you think maybe she's up in the Liberty Oak hiding from the cars?"

"Don't know where she is, but you got to get to your church and I got to get back."

"Maybe she's hurt somewhere. I'm going to go look and see if she's up the tree." I started out for the Square, but Ebon grabbed my arm.

"You cain't go over there. 'Member what she said last week, about bad men? Who the hell you think drivin' them cars?"

"They won't hurt me. I'm Brittan Lee Hayworth. I'm just a little girl. But you better stay here." Shrugging off his grasp, I dodged across the street and over to the Liberty Oak. "Beth Ann? Beth Ann? You up there?" I climbed up the lower limb of the tree. "Beth Ann?"

"She ain't here." Ebon had followed me across the street.

"No." I jumped down to the ground. "I don't know what to do. I've got to find my Daddy. He'll know what to do. You better get back over to your church. Go on now."

"I cain't just go off and leave you," Ebon said.

"You have to, 'cause I'm going to go over the Court House and call Daddy on the payphone. I have three dimes I was going to use for a cold Co-cola. But you can't be here. It's all right. Daddy will come. Now go."

Still protesting, Ebon turned to leave but the spotlight beam of a car pinned him in place.

"You, boy, what are you doing out heah?"

I recognized Deputy Ungler in his patrol car and ran over.

"He's with me. We're trying to find Beth Ann Hamilton. She's 'sposed to meet us here but she didn't. Deputy Ungler, I need to call my Daddy."

The deputy opened his car door, and stepped out, sliding his big stick through a loop in his belt and reaching for his shotgun. "Now, what are you doing out here with this boy?" He said.

"I told you. He's taking me to church, but we have to find Beth Ann. She's supposed to be here, but she isn't," I said. "Please go call my Daddy."

The deputy looked at me, then at Ebon and he spit on him. I must have gasped because he turned to me. "Little missy, I want to know just what the hell you're doing with this nigra boy."

"Deputy, I done told you three times. Please call my Daddy. He's Doctor Marshall Hayworth," I started to cry.

"Jesse, Merle, get over here." The deputy raised his voice over the wind. "Look what we got here. A nigra boy out with a white girl, and another white girl missing. What did you do with her, boy? You take that girl, boy? Take them over there behind that building," he gestured. "I've got to call in a missing child report."

The two men grabbed Ebon and started to drag him. He struggled against them, but each one of those white men probably weighed twice what Ebon did. I ran behind them, hitting them and trying to stop them but I couldn't.

"Let him go! He didn't do anything!" I punctuated my words with fists on their backs, but it had no more effect than a horse tail swatting at a fly.

Jesse didn't even slow down when he backhanded me across the face, knocking me down. I felt the warm blood from my split lip mix with the rain on my face. I scrambled up from the muddy ground, ran after the man and tackled him like my brothers taught me, grabbing around his knees from behind. It threw him off balance and he lost his grip on Ebon. "Run, Ebon, run. Get away!"

Ebon struggled, but Merle turned and hit him in the stomach. With a sick sound, Ebon doubled over and fell to his knees. Merle kicked him in his face, his ribs, his back. I heard the wet smack when his workboots split open Ebon's cheek. "Friggin' nigra. Teach you to run away from a white man." He kept kicking Ebon, until Ebon didn't struggle anymore. He and Jesse grabbed Ebon's arms and dragged him the rest of the way to the tabby shed behind the Liberty Oak.

"Hey, look what we got us here," Merle said to some other men who were waiting behind the shed. "Got us a genuine kidnapper. Tried to get two little girls, one of them is still missing. We're gonna have to make him talk."

"He didn't do anything," I sobbed. "Let him go. I'm gonna tell my Daddy."

"Does your daddy know you been with nigras?" one of the men asked. "Who is your daddy, anyway."

I sniffed. "My daddy is Marshall Hayworth. He won't let you hurt on Ebon anymore. We got to find Beth Ann; she's missing." I looked around at the men and screamed. Four men, shrouded in white robes were standing there holding ropes and pieces of two-by-fours. "What do you want?"

"Your daddy is the one gonna put nigras in the school my kids go to," one of the hooded men said as he hoisted his rope. "Ain't gonna happen. Let's go string him up."

Ebon moaned from his curled position on the muddy ground, and was immediately kicked by first one man, then another.

"Stop it. Don't do that!" I ran over and threw myself on top of Ebon. The next kick caught me in my side.

"Shit!" An arm reached down and yanked me by my braid to pull me off of Ebon, but I clung tighter, his blood smearing on my dress.

"Somebody's coming. Lock them up in that shed."

Somebody yanked my braid even harder, snatching my head back and twisting my neck. He pulled me over and slung me against the shed. Two men grabbed Ebon by his feet and dragged him through the mud to the door.. They pulled him through the outer room and into the old jail. "Hey, we need to shackle him?" someone asked.

"Nah, he ain't going nowhere." One of the other men closed the inside door and slipped a padlock in place.

Merle dragged me inside by my braid and threw me against the tabby wall. "Little snot."

I felt my sides crack when I hit. It hurt almost as much as when they kicked me. I thought about Ebon getting kicked over and over again and I stifled my crying. I had to be strong for him. I couldn't breathe through my nose. It hurt where Jesse hit me, and it was bleeding still. I curled into a little ball and tried to see what all was in there. A little bit of light came in through the only window when lightning flashed in the sky. I crawled over to the door and pounded on it with my fists until they hurt but no one came. I saw a Co-cola crate and dragged it under the window so I could see out. I saw Uncle

Frank walk up to them men. I thought he had come to save me, but he didn't. I heard him say to the men 'You got the wrong child,' and they said to him 'Bet ol' Doc Marsh might just be willing to make a bargain, he finds out we got his little girl.' Uncle Frank told them they were crazy, but he didn't come let me out. It started to rain even harder and it was almost black outside. The thunder was so loud it made the roof of the shed rattle. I crawled between the door where I could try to hear the men, and the window where I could try to see them.

Daddy ran up through the rain to where Uncle Frank was standing under the Liberty Oak. I went to the door and beat on it again, but no one came. Daddy must not have heard me. I went to the window and saw Uncle Frank point across the street to an old building. He kept waving his arms and pointing to that building, I don't know why. Dr. Stevens and Dr. Wensley and the Sheriff joined Daddy under the tree. They all talked but I couldn't hear them. I beat on the window with my fists so hard I broke the glass, but nobody heard it. Blood ran down my hands. I yelled and yelled until I didn't have any voice left, but no one heard me. I saw Dr. Stevens and the Sheriff head over to the Court House, and Daddy started across the street to the building Uncle Frank had pointed to. Dr. Wensley followed him. I waited to see them again but only Dr. Wensley came back.

The wind got even worse, and I could see the trees bending over. The rain fell sideways and beat into the sides of the shed. I stopped feeling sorry for myself when I remembered Ebon. After crawling to the inside door, I tapped on the wood.

"Ebon? Ebon? Can you hear me?" I heard moans from the inside room.

"Ebon? I'm sorry, Ebon." The moaning was a little bit

louder and I could hear something moving. I hope it was Ebon.

"Ebon? Are you alive in there?" I couldn't be afraid. Daddy always said that storms were majestic and nothing to be scared of. When great-grandmama died, Daddy said that death was nothing to be afraid of, but I was. I was afraid that Ebon was dead and it was my fault and I would go to Hell. I was afraid that Beth Ann was mad at me.

"Girl?" The voice was strained, hoarse. "Girl? You there?"

My insides heaved. "Ebon? I'm here. Are you all right?"

He groaned. "They 'bout killed me ag'in."

"We got to get you out of here," I said through my tears. "They will kill you if they beat you up again. We got to get you out."

"Ain't no way out. Door's locked and the window don't open." His voice was ragged, but a little bit stronger.

"I'm sorry I got you into this, Ebon."

"Little girl, you didn't get me into this. I got me into this. Been in worse." He didn't finish the sentence.

I sat curled in the dark, listening to the wind whip through the trees and the rain thundering on the tin roof. The occasional flash of lightning reflected in the pieces of broken glass from the window. The window. "Ebon," I said. "I know how to get you out." I explained the fraternity prank to him.

"Girl, I ain't got that kind of strength left," he said.

"You have to. They're gonna kill you when they come back after the hurricane. You have to get out now." I heard noises from the room, and I waited and listened.

"Girl, I did it. I got the window out." He sounded proud, triumphant. "I'm coming 'round to get you out."

"You can't," I said. "They locked the door. You got to get

out of here before the hurricane gets over and they come back. They'll kill you if they find you out."

I found my second best Sunday handkerchief in my pocket with the three dimes I had to buy a Co-cola, and Jack's emergency number in Dorchester. I tied them all together and slipped them under the door to Ebon. "Be sure and put the window back. Good-bye, Ebon. Good luck." I stifled a sob.

"I'll come back," he promised.

He was gone and I was left alone in the dark. Thunder shook the building. Manacles hanging by their rusted chains rattled against the tabby walls. I wondered if the ghosts Jack told me about, the slaves who died two hundred years before, were here. Rain blew in through the broken window drenching my clothes. I crawled back to the inner door, shivering from the dampness. Spider webs appeared in the flashes of lightning, and I could feel where I had brushed against them, spiders crawling across my arms and face. Branches from the Liberty Oak shrieked across the tin roof of the shed. I curled up into a ball, nursing my hurt side.

"I'm not afraid," I said. "I'm not afraid. Daddy will be here soon. I'm not afraid." But my tears continued to mix with the blood from my face.

CHAPTER THIRTY-FIVE
Liberty, Georgia, August 2005

My cell phone didn't work. I had tested it every hour for the past eight hours. All the towers were out due to the storm, but the illumination from the screen allowed me to check Leigh's head wound. I used Andy's handkerchief, still in my purse waiting to be washed as a bandage.

I wanted to use my emergency bottle of water to clean off her face, but I knew that I might need it later. One of the granola bars went to reward Snickers.

I tried to think of who might know where we were, but it didn't matter. Like that night forty years earlier, it wasn't safe to be out. In all actuality, the old tabby shed was one of the safest places to be. Daddy had told me how sturdy tabby was and that the shed, like the big Court House, was built on the highest point of the town, so we would be safe from storm surges. It had protected me through one storm, and I wasn't afraid of the ghosts in the old jail. I was afraid of someone alive outside.

Snickers stood up and made his rounds of the walls, again pawing and barking at the inner door.

"What's the matter, baby?" I said. "Some old squirrel holed up in there?"

The dog looked at me as if he understood.

"Oh no, do you need to go out?"

I couldn't let him out. The wind was still blowing at storm level. Several loud crashes shook the building as some of the massive branches broke off from Liberty Oak and landed on the tin roof. The limbs muffled the pounding rain, but the thunder still resonated and rattled the sheets of tin.

I tried to shift positions, but I must have moved Leigh's arm, because she started to moan.

"Leigh! Leigh, honey."

Her eyelids fluttered, then opened. Her eyes were unfocused, then came together as she looked at my face. "Aunt B!" She tried to reach up to me, but moaned. "My arm. My head. What happened? Where am I?" She looked around. "We're in that little building behind the Court House. What? The hurricane?"

"Honey, someone hit you. You've got a great big knot. Mama would say that someone hit you up side of the head with a slipper spoon." I gave her a weak smile. "And I think your arm is hurt. If you can sit up by yourself, I'll look at it."

She nodded her head, and I helped her sit up. The light from the windows combined with the illumination from my cell phone was strong enough to see that her left arm just below her elbow was swollen and crooked.

"Let me see if I can find anything to splint this," I said, and holding the phone up like a torch, I crawled over and dug through the trash. "This might work." I pulled two slats from a Coke crate. I crawled back over. "Let's see if I remember my Girl Scout first aid class."

The strips of cotton from Leigh's gag served as a makeshift sling, and the relief showed in her eyes.

"I've got some Ibuprofen in my bag," I told her, "but I don't think you're supposed to take pain meds when there's been a head injury."

"Pass them over," she said. "I'm awake and I'm alert, so to speak." She leaned her head back against the wall and closed her eyes, then blinked them open again. "I promise. I'm not passing out." She gulped down four of the caplets with a swallow of water. "Aunt B, why do you think he would do this? What makes somebody act like this? He kept saying that I know, that I know and he should have killed me before I told everyone else."

"Who knows what makes people do what they do? I should have been more alert after the phone call," I said. "I didn't think he would be fool enough to drive into a storm. Unless he's been here the whole time. What kind of car does he drive? Is it a black truck?"

"What phone call? Aunt B, what are you talking about?"

"David Bradford. After he called at the party last night. I talked to your brother and he..."

"What does David have to do with this?" Leigh asked.

"He beat you up!" I said. "I saw the bruises on your arms and your thigh."

"That." Her tone was flat. "He's grabbed at me before, but not like this. These were from three weeks ago. He swung at me, but it didn't connect. This time I popped him one in the nose and left. He kicked at me as I walked out. David may be a bullying idiot, but he didn't do this. He's too weak and too afraid of his image."

"Why didn't you tell me? Or your father?" I asked.

Leigh shifted her position. "Jax suspected. But it is embarrassing. I'm supposed to be smart and independent, but I let myself get trapped into thinking he would change. How can I help other women when I couldn't help myself."

My leg was cramping, and I shifted positions so I could rub my calf. "Well, if this wasn't David, who did it? And why?"

The inner door creaked and Leigh's head jerked up. "He did. Aunt B, look out!"

I jumped up and turned as Bruce Wensley lurched out of the jail room, brandishing a broken ax handle. It crashed down into the wall by my head, sending bits of plaster flying. He raised his weapon again, but before he could use it, I was on my feet. Inwardly thanking my brothers for years spent watching football practice, I made a diving tackle to his mid-section. The distance was too short to have a solid impact, but I did knock him back into the jail room. We rolled around in the piles of trash, flailing about in the old planting flats and empty fertilizer and grass seed bags. Wensley was on top on me, pinning me down with his left arm and pounding at my face. I could hear Snickers snarling and snapping at Wensley's legs.

"Stupid bitch. I should have just come back and killed you forty years ago."

Turning my head to avoid his putrid breath in my face, I coughed and tried to catch my breath. I could feel my left eye swelling and taste the blood in my mouth. "Why? Why? What did I do?" I asked.

"Always into everybody's business," he panted. "You just had to be in the thick of everything, everywhere. Telling people what to do, what to look for. My daddy was right about you. Why couldn't you have just stayed up north?"

My right knee made a solid impact between his legs.

He screamed and released the pressure on my chest. I pushed him off me, and he rolled over onto his side, curled in a fetal position. I scrambled to my feet and made it out the door when he reached out and grabbed my ankle, pulling me down to the floor.

"Let go of me," I jerked my leg free. I tried to crawl out the door, my fingernails unable to make a good purchase in the dirt floor. I kicked behind me, making solid contact with his chest.

"Bitch. Couldn't leave things be," he gasped, grabbing at me again.

We both rolled onto the floor, this time I ended up on top. He reached out and grabbed my throat with both hands, but I had his throat in mine. Forty-five years of piano does indeed give a woman incredible upper body strength. I choked him until he was gasping and then was still.

I looked at him and with shaking hands wiped the blood off of my face.

Leigh had pushed herself back to the far wall. "Is he dead?" she asked.

"I don't know. I don't want to get close enough to find out."

"You have to tie him up," she said. "If he wakes up, he'll try to kill you again."

Nodding weakly, I looked for the cords that had bound Leigh's hands. I found them and cautiously approached Wensley. He was breathing but didn't move when I took his hands and tied them together.

"Can he get away?" Leigh said.

"I learned how to tie knots from my brothers. One time I practiced on your father and wouldn't let him go until he paid me twenty cents," I said. "Bruce Wensley isn't going anywhere."

"Aunt B, why did he want to kill you?" she asked.

"Because he thought I knew he killed my father."

CHAPTER THIRTY-SIX
Liberty, Georgia, August 2005

H e killed Granddaddy Marsh?" Leigh said. "Why? When did you know?"

"I didn't know for sure until he attacked us here," I said. "But I spent tonight just thinking about it all. He was the one who followed Daddy into the building across the way, and he was the one who came out yelling that lightning had hit and the building was on fire. But there hadn't been any lightning about then, it was during a calm."

"Why did he do it?"

"I'm not really sure, but I bet women or money or both were involved," I said. "Something Trulee and Mama both said about him and women. And once, that summer, I heard him talking about needing money, because Miss Zora, her medical expenses were so high. But Four told me that Miss Zora had money from her family. Money! Root of all evil, especially for those who need it."

"Money? Why would Dr. Wensley need money?" Leigh said.

"Well, I never would have thought it, because he lived high on the hog, but I remembered Daddy saying something about Dr. Wensley never contributing his share to the annual barbecue. He heard me tell Zeller to talk to Auntabelle. Mama wanted the partners to buy out Daddy's share of the practice, back when Daddy died. There was some quiet scandal about the money not being there. Auntabelle had taken some for Uncle Frank, but there was more missing than she could account for. I told Zeller to have a CPA do an audit of the office bookkeeping and of all the staff at the time; I bet he can trace the missing money back to Bruce. Poor Miss Zora." I pointed to Leigh. "Trulee always said *Poor Miss Zora*. I thought it was because of the polio."

"What about the women?"

"Did you see the way Desiree was following him around like a dog in...well, like a dog? All the women love him, everyone loves him. I always thought he was so dedicated to Miss Zora, but once, when I was little, I remember the ladies snickering on about him. I think he was a player?"

"Aunt B!" Leigh started to laugh, but grimaced at the movement. "Aunt B, I can't believe you even know that word." She paused. "Listen."

The rain had slowed to a light drizzle, and the wind no longer stirred the tree limbs on the tin roof.

"Can we get out?" she asked.

I flipped my cell phone open, but there was no dial tone. Snickers whined at the main door.

"Yeah, I bet you need to go out," I said. "If I had just paid attention to you earlier." I went to the door and tried to open it, but it wouldn't budge. I braced my shoulders against the door but could only get it to open a few inches. "Too many branches blocking the door."

"Does anyone know where we are?" Leigh said.

"Probably not," I said. "But at least we have water and granola bars this time. Hey, where's your purse with the gun? We could use it about now."

"Couldn't find it," she said. "Then I lost my car keys when he was chasing me."

"Your cell phone?" I asked, then realized that if my phone didn't work, hers wouldn't work either.

"Dropped it outside. I'm sorry, Aunt B," she almost cried, her jaw trembling.

"Honey, it's going to be fine. We're going to get out of here. We have to. I left Mama's car behind the Court House. With the door open. With the engine running."

Leigh smiled through her tears.

We both turned when we heard a groan from the corner.

Snickers took a guard position, growling at our trussed prisoner.

"Besides, watch this. I have a magic trick up my sleeve." I took the Coca-cola crate out from under the window and carried it into the jail. Placing it under the window there, I climbed up and put my hands on each side of the window frame.

Leigh and the dog crawled over to see what I was doing.

I took a deep breath and lifted the frame one quarter inch and pushed it out. And lifted and pushed. And repeated it until the window fell out of the opening onto the ground below.

"How did you do that?" she said.

"Long story," I said as I climbed through the narrow opening and toppled to the ground.

I sat on the little brick wall separating C4-154 from the remaining plots in Liberty Cemetery. The workers had done a nice job with the re-interment. There were fresh flowers on the marble slab. I like to think that Daddy was at rest with everything now. I laid my head on Zeller's shoulder.

"I'm sorry the other man wasn't your brother," I said. "I mean, at least…"

"I know what you mean," he said. "It was a beautiful funeral. That old sanctuary was filled up to the slave balcony."

I nodded as I wiped away the tears that escaped. "And when Tansie had the Children's Choir sing *I'll Fly Away,* I just about lost it. That was our favorite song."

"So I've heard," he teased me as he handed me his handkerchief. "Don't women ever carry these for themselves?"

"And the doves," I said. "Wasn't it beautiful when the doves were released outside and they flew away?"

"It was beautiful," he agreed.

"Will they bring charges against Bruce Wensley or Cheryl Hamilton?"

"Everything is just circumstantial against Mrs. Hamilton," he said. "I don't think the prosecutor is going to push it. But I don't think that marriage is going to make it to the golden anniversary."

I nodded. "He looked miserable at the funeral. What about Bruce Wensley?"

"Oh, him they're going to prosecute. Murder One on your father and the John Doe- we'll put his DNA and forensic records in our files; Murder Two for Miss Zora, abandoning her in the hurricane. Did I tell you all of her jewelry was missing? Assault with intent on you and Leigh. Plus they are looking up every possible racially motivated charge they can think of. His father was quite the racist. Some of the things we found up in that little meeting room. Dr. Wensley allowed everyone to believe that Ebon Johnson was to blame for Beth Ann and your father," Zeller shook his head. "He incited the riots. Typical sociopath, really only interested in what benefited him. Your Aunt Annabelle was a big help, you know, proving that he had been embezzling from the medical practice." He nuzzled my neck. "You need to talk to her. She didn't know her husband was going to kidnap you. As soon as she discovered what he did, she turned him in." He played with one of the curls at the back of my neck.

I made an unladylike snort. I wasn't sure I was ready to forgive her. "And Desiree?"

"You women and Desiree," he said. "None of you seem to appreciate her hidden talents."

I looked at him, one eyebrow raised in a question.

"They're looking for her," he added quickly.

"What about you?" I asked. "Where are you off to now? More cases? Still looking for Tony?"

He nodded, then looked at me. "It, uh, it would be nice to have a place in Liberty to come visit. Maybe if I'm between cases, you might like some company when you go to Africa?"

"That would be nice," I said, feeling a little glow inside. "When do you have to leave?"

"Tomorrow. I talked to Jack and Trulee's brother, Gus. Fascinating old man. Full of stories of Dr. King and that era.

I'm going to backtrack to the last place they think Tony took Ebon. Maybe if I can find Ebon, he can tell me something about where Tony was going next."

"Oxford, Mississippi," said a deep voice from behind me.

Zeller stood up. "Oxford, Mississippi? How do you know that? Brittan Lee, I don't think you ever had the opportunity to meet the Special Agent in Charge of this investigation."

My eyes blurred with tears again as I heard the deep voice. It was older, but still the same. I stood up and looked at the familiar face.

"Hello, Ebon. Welcome home."

45014249R00178

Made in the USA
San Bernardino, CA
29 January 2017